PERFECT HALVES

BOOK ONE

DOUBLE-EDGED

&

EYES IN THE DARK

ROWENA DAWN

SCARLET LEAF

2018

ISBN: 978-1-988827-56-8

PUBLISHED BY SCARLET LEAF

Toronto, Canada

DOUBLE – EDGED

Book One

DEDICATION:

*To all the people out there who are
trying to find their soul mates.
Keep safe and keep true!*

CHAPTER ONE

Present day – July 19th ...

The young woman was sitting in a cushy armchair in the lobby, a magazine open on her lap. She pretended being lost in a story she was reading.

Her huge blue slouch-hat was designed to cover half her face and matched the short summer dress, showing off her long, tanned and shapely legs.

A pair of big, black sun-glasses completed the ensemble. She looked like Audrey Hepburn in *Charade*. Hidden behind the black lenses, her eyes carefully watched the people coming to the front desk and speaking to the receptionist.

She had already arranged with the much younger man at the front desk to signal her when the person she was interested in would come. He was supposed to raise his hand, as if he'd said *'just one moment, please'*. Then, he was supposed to turn away for a couple of seconds and check something on the monitor.

Since her watch began, two couples had already passed by the front desk and talked to the clerk. They'd just taken their keys and left immediately, so she didn't bother with them anymore.

Finally, after a few more minutes of impatient waiting, a tall, dark man came to the reception area and addressed the clerk. The clerk nodded and raised his hand, the sign they'd pre-arranged. He checked his computer screen for a couple of seconds, nodded again and then, took a bag from behind the counter and handed it to the man.

He took the bag with a nod and, turned around. His eyes brushed expertly over the people in the lobby. He gave the impression he was just mildly curious, yet she noticed he analyzed everyone carefully. She watched him furtively so she wouldn't expose herself.

She imagined her appearance didn't impress him. After he'd looked her over, from head to toe, taking his time when he swept over her legs, he turned around and went toward the elevators. Probably, he didn't think she posed any kind of danger and he didn't worry about her.

Again, her senses perceived nothing clear about him and that annoyed her much more than before. She realized she had stumbled onto the first person in the world she couldn't read at all. That frustrated and infuriated her to no end.

She'd believed she'd be able to sneak a peek into his mind once she'd be in his presence. It made sense she wouldn't encounter any barriers when she was near. Apparently, she'd been wrong. The man always remained completely opaque to her vision.

When he disappeared from her sight, she stood up with lazy and fluid moves. She laid the magazine on the table next to her armchair, as if she'd had all the time in the world. She smoothened her skirt with long and light strokes, and then, her eyes swept over the hotel lounge, furnished with taste and comfort in mind.

With lazy strides, she walked to the front desk. The clerk beamed at her, warmly. He hurried forward to do her bidding as if the other person at the front desk hadn't mattered at all.

She noticed his rush to serve her and believed the huge tip she'd given him earlier determined his behavior. Yet, something else lay behind the young man's grin. He'd enjoyed their game and even imagined all sorts of thrilling scenarios in his head.

His age, but also her appearance had fueled his imagination. Her hat and big sunglasses, as well as the vague clandestine air of the entire affair she'd involved him in, had made him feel like James Bond or someone similar.

"I'll be leaving this afternoon, I think. I won't be waiting until morning. Of course, I'll pay for tonight, though, no worries," she said to the young receptionist, with an apologetic smile when she realized he'd been hoping that something more would happen and the adventure wouldn't end there.

Yet, she'd been interested in only one scene, and that had already ended, although the result disappointed.

"We're very sorry you're leaving, ma'am. Didn't you like your suite?" the young man inquired, and his worry wiped the smile off his lips.

"Oh, yes, I did, don't worry," she reassured him with a wave of her hand and a bright smile. "But, you see, I've already rented a house on the beach for a few days and I've been thinking I should take advantage of it right now, you know?" she beamed brightly at the clerk again. "There's the sea and a pool just for me... Would you mind preparing the bill before I get back downstairs with my luggage?"

"No, of course, not. Your bill will be ready, ma'am," the man reassured her and rushed to the computer to prepare it.

CHAPTER TWO

Always present day – July 19th ...

The young woman left the lobby with her usual lazy stride and headed to the row of shiny elevators, lining the wall on top of a three-step staircase. She pressed the button to call one and waited, playing with her scarf and admiring the geometric motif of the carpet in the hall.

She was deep in her thoughts and failed to notice the dark-haired man behind the column, although the fine hair on her neck stood straight up warning her of danger.

The man watched her unwaveringly, a frown between his eyebrows.

She didn't know he'd heard her conversation with the clerk and in a way, she didn't care. She'd already decided to move on and now, she was anxious to leave everything behind.

She went to her suite and in less than ten minutes, she returned downstairs. She hadn't bothered to unpack upon her arrival that morning and she didn't have much to do to gather her things.

She paid the bill, leaving another sizeable tip for the front desk clerk, who had helped her a lot and asked the valet to bring her rented car to the front of the hotel.

She'd rented a small convertible, nothing fancy, something just to get around. The valet had already lowered the top of the car and that little thoughtful gesture brought a smile on her lips. She felt her vacation had finally started.

The valet put her only suitcase in the trunk and the bag with her laptop in the back seat of the car. He bowed slightly when she gave him a folded banknote, together with a big smile.

Once seated in the car, she turned the key in the ignition first and then she turned on her navigation system, inputting the address of the house she had rented on the shore.

Now, she felt secure enough so she took her hat off and shook her head. Her hair fell all over her shoulders in thick, curly honey-coloured waves and the afternoon sunrays reflected a few shades of red here and there.

Relief set her free. She knew things would get back to normal now and she wouldn't face any more restlessness or unanswered questions. Life as she knew it and loved was back. She had control in her hands and knew beforehand where she stood with the people around her. Happiness for her meant no more uncertainty to drive her crazy and fill her sleepless nights with anxiety.

She drove her car slowly along the hotel driveway and turned onto the road toward the beach. She failed to notice a black SUV, a few cars behind, pulling out and following her. But then, she didn't think to look for something like that.

She drove steadily in her usual prudent manner. She wasn't in a rush. The house would be available to her whenever she got there.

She was on vacation after all. She'd completed the business she had to take care of and, now, there was only the sun, the ocean and her. She would lie on the beach in the morning and swim in the pool in the evening.

She'd already planned to keep far from the world and any kind of stress. She needed peace and solitude for a change.

She admitted it had been somewhat interesting to taste those uneasy feelings although they stressed her at times. They'd brought some spicy restlessness and she didn't regret she'd felt a little different for a while. It had been somewhat… educational.

Yet, it was nice to be herself again and find her old routine. She welcomed a future when she didn't have to find an explanation for things that weren't meant to be explained.

The vacation house she'd rented wasn't very far from the hotel. It took her only fifteen minutes to arrive at her destination.

She drove in front of the bungalow erected right on the edge of the beach and she stopped her car to admire the little house and the surrounding area for a few moments. She liked it. That was going to be her oasis of peace for the following ten days. The view, as well as the sound and smell of the ocean, made her stop regretting she'd left Montreal and taken a few days off.

After a few minutes, she drove her little convertible under the shelter improvised for parking a car and turned off the engine. She got out of the car and put up the top. She'd paid for insurance but she still didn't want to have problems when she would return the vehicle.

The woman breathed greedily the salty air of the sea. The breeze tousled her hair and she grinned. A brief jolt of pleasure swept over her body. It'd been a while since she took a vacation for more than a couple of days.

She took her suitcase out of the trunk and opened the back door to pick up her laptop. She strolled up the paved road to the house and looked for the keys under the flower pot on the right of the door where the broker had told her to look. She went inside, closing the door behind her.

The interior was everything she'd been promised and more than she'd expected. She never trusted the photos displayed next to rentals and she'd thought the broker was just talking the house up to make her lease it.

Yet, the house was vivid and cozy at the same time. The furniture in the living room appeared light and comfortable. She left her laptop on the top of the little coffee table and went to have a look at the bedroom.

She needed to climb a flight of stairs to get there but the room pleased her. The sunlight warmed the yellow of the walls and the brick-coloured cover of the bed.

She knew she could find her peace of mind in there. She'd already connected with the house and now, she felt as if she'd always been a part of it.

She left the suitcase on the floor next to the bed. She didn't bother to change out of the designer dress she was wearing. She went out on the patio facing the sea at the back of the house. She wanted to enjoy the rest of the afternoon.

She poured a glass of wine on her way out and picked up her cell phone because she knew he would call. He would always call and she didn't see him breaking his habit just then.

On the patio, she found a few wicker armchairs and an oval table for six. A big colourful umbrella loomed over them. She left her glass on the table and turned to look at the beach.

On the sand, beyond the patio, two deck chairs waited for her on the edge of the pool if she wanted to sunbathe. Just a little farther, maybe a two–minute stroll, she could enjoy the waves of the sea.

She left her cell phone on the table as well and sat in one of the armchairs. She stretched her legs onto another chair and relaxed. The last few days' tension seeped out of her body slowly.

She closed her eyes for a few seconds and let her mind wander.

She didn't want to think of anything but disperse the impressions of that day. She wanted them behind in the past where they belonged. She'd already fulfilled her purpose.

She had scarcely had the time to decompress for a couple of minutes that the phone rang. She glanced reluctantly at the display and, as always, it showed *'private number'*. She scowled and her scowl made her look much younger than her years, almost like a spirited teenager.

Experiencing a perverse streak, the woman let the phone ring a few times and only then she answered.

"Hello!"

"Kate, is it you, sweetheart?" the very well known male voice came over the line.

"Yes, it's me, of course," she said trying to cover a growl in her throat.

That was a *stupid* question. *Who else could answer my phone?* It had never happened before.

Besides, in moments like that she simply loathed that word *'sweetheart'*. She was distressed because she couldn't discern sincerity or insincerity in his words. That drove her crazy.

She didn't understand why he was the only person she couldn't read. It was maddening not to know what he was thinking and what his intentions were.

"Thank you, my love, I got it. You are fantastic," he continued and the tone of his voice woke the dormant butterflies in her belly.

His voice was low and hoarse, and made her picture a cowboy holding a glass of whiskey in one hand and a cigar in the other. Probably a reminiscence of her childhood days when she loved to watch westerns. Goosebumps covered her arms whenever she heard his voice, and she resented herself because her IQ dropped to two digits. She'd thought herself smarter than that.

'*Of course, I am,*' she thought, '*fantastically stupid, maybe,*' but she replied something completely different, "Then everything is alright, yes?"

"Yes, my love," he answered and paused for a few seconds. "You sound so close now. I usually can't hear you so well," he said with wonder in his voice.

"Probably, you've got a good line," she replied flippantly and her lips arched in a derisive smile.

Of course, he could hear her better. They were both in the same town, for Christ's sake, but she wasn't about to tell him that. She hadn't gone through all that trouble to reveal such information now.

"Now everything will be all right," he continued in a firm voice. "I'll finish everything here and come to you."

"Don't hurry on my account," she replied without thinking, and then she closed her eyes tight in frustration.

Kate was afraid he would understand what she meant and she wanted a clean break up. She didn't want to drag that so-called relationship any longer.

"What do you mean?" he asked in the same hard voice he used whenever he got angry.

His voice had a lower pitch now and Kate perceived that hint of authority, which she loathed deeply.

Kate didn't like his attitude. He probably thought she would respond to his demanding voice and behave accordingly. That reaction was innate to him and he couldn't censor his words, and yet, she still abhorred it.

"I mean I might have to leave the country for a while, Ryan. Family problems, you know," she said just in passing. "Of course, my phone won't work outside the country as I don't have roaming. I'll call you when I can, all right?" she said in a conciliatory voice.

She didn't feel conciliatory right then but she wanted to end the conversation and cut all ties to him.

Ryan didn't answer anything for a while and silence grew menacing.

"Are you still there?" she asked after almost a minute.

"Yes, I am. I'm here, Kate. And when I say here, that means here," his reply came heatedly.

Not a second later, heavy footsteps sounded on the veranda surrounding the house. Kate glanced there and saw Ryan coming to her. An ugly scowl tugged at the corner of his lips. He turned off his phone. The expression on his face didn't announce anything good.

CHAPTER THREE

Three months earlier – April 15th ....

"Come on, Kate, you must try it. You never have time to go anywhere or to meet someone. That shop of yours is taking up all your time. This is your chance," Ellie tried her best to coerce Kate. She was staring Kate down with her big puppy eyes.

Kate smiled. She couldn't find fault with poor, sweet Ellie. She was always trying to find happiness for everyone else even though her own was questionable. Kate knew Ellie didn't have anyone special in her life.

"I don't know, Ellie," Kate replied with a shrug. Indecision tightened her lips. "You know, there are all sorts of loony people out there," she continued with a large wave of her hand. "And besides, I don't think it's really safe to meet someone on the Internet. I've heard so many stories about everything that could go wrong," Kate explained to Ellie.

Kate didn't truly believe that it was safer outside in the real world than it was to connect with someone on the Internet. There were enough crazy people everywhere, in the streets, shops and bars. She'd read enough minds to know what ugly thoughts crossed people's minds.

"Okay, Kate, maybe you're right," Ellie agreed with her for a moment. "But we both know that you're smart enough to read into things. You have that special touch with people and you'll know if something's wrong. Of course, you won't go meet a guy if he doesn't seem all right," Ellie tried to reassure her. She picked up her tea cup and sipped some of the hot tisane Kate had prepared for her just a few minutes earlier.

"Yes, Ellie, but a guy might seem all right and he might not be, you know that," Kate insisted just to rile Ellie a little. She didn't like anyone mingling in her life. "The bad ones are like that," she said with a wide wave of her hand. "And of course, I'm one of the good girls and that's exactly why I'll choose the worst of them," she joked but Ellie took her at face value.

"Don't be so negative," Ellie replied slapping her arm. "Come on, Katie, let's make a couple of nice salads, as you promised, and then you'll open your computer."

"What's the relation between salads and my computer, Ellie?" Kate simulated misunderstanding just to tease Ellie.

Ellie rolled her eyes and scowled at Kate, "You know what I mean, don't play games with me. We're going to eat and prepare a profile for you at the same time. I know the best dating site."

"Have you tried it?" Kate threw over her shoulder on her way to the kitchen.

"Me? No," Ellie mused and followed her.

"Then how do you know it is the best?" Kate glanced back at her.

"One of my colleagues used it," Ellie explained with large gestures. "And she got married, a little while ago. She said it was the chance of a lifetime," she made sure to add.

"I see, Ellie... Have you thought that she might have been one of the few lucky ones?" Kate asked, reluctantly opening the laptop she'd left on the kitchen counter earlier when she got home. "The statistics are not very encouraging," she continued.

She'd learned that throwing statistics in a conversation always won points. No one bothered to verify her statements and she came up ahead.

Ellie dismissed her reply with a quick wave of her hand and went to gather the ingredients to prepare the salads.

Kate looked after her, not wanting to give in so easy, "You know I'm right, Ellie. Tell me, would you do it, if you were in my place?" she insisted.

"Me? No, of course, not! And you know why? I'm sure you do. It's because I'm not good at reading between the lines. I take everything at face value and that always gets me into trouble. You know it," Ellie explained, reminding to Kate about her bad choices from the past. "But you're not like me, Kate. You're smart and you know people so you do have what it takes for such a thing."

Kate smiled. She couldn't do anything else but smile. Ellie had always put her on a pedestal, and sometimes she felt ashamed because of that. That was one of the reasons she never could refuse Ellie.

"Okay, I imagine I can handle this," she shrugged. "I am pretty sure no one can trace me and find out who I am..." she thought aloud. "Maybe just the town if they know how to use my IP address, I think..." A frown appeared between her eyebrows. "Anyway, I'll not answer back to any wacko out there. I won't give any pertinent information about me..." Kate continued pensively. "Okay, Ellie, now, we'll finally see if I'm smart enough to deal with something like that," Kate concluded and Ellie jumped up and down with glee.

As a matter of fact, Kate had a strange feeling about that whole dating thing. She felt as if something had touched her. It was like a sign that something with deep consequences was about to happen and she didn't like it at all.

Ellie laughed at her concerns and, after they made the salads cheerfully, they went back to the computer.

"Look, this is the site I was telling you about," Ellie showed Kate. "You see, Kate, they have so many questions. You can't get it wrong. You will find just the right guy, I'm telling you," Ellie beamed at Kate.

"Yes, they have questions, but with predefined answers. Look at this here. Do you think any of this is me? What else can I choose?" Kate asked frustrated.

"Yep, you're right," Ellie conceded. "It's a little too rigid."

"And imagine the guys have the same problem. Most of these answers don't apply to me so I suppose any guy filling in this form will find himself in the same situation. Even if he doesn't want to lie, he will. He doesn't have a choice if he wants to continue with the form," Kate said, always frustrated.

"Just choose something close enough. There must be something that might work for you," Ellie insisted. She didn't want Kate give up.

"Yes, I can do that, if I want to create a new me from scratch, there is. But I think that I must choose something. They don't let you move on otherwise," Kate scowled.

They needed about two hours to answer all the questions in the questionnaire. Both were exhausted and only Ellie experienced something like a triumph.

"Now, you have to choose a picture. Choose the best one you have, of course," Ellie thought to specify.

"I don't think so," Kate replied, shaking her head. "I have to choose the worst I have. If someone likes me in that photo, then he's a keeper," she grinned maliciously at Ellie.

"You've always had a very strange sense of humor, Kate," Ellie shook her head astounded. "God, everybody puts the best they have out there. No one will try to attract a possible match with the worst mug shot possible. It's like using your passport photo, Kate, for God's sake," she exploded.

"Maybe," Kate replied indifferent to Ellie's words. "But I like to do things my way, and you know that well, Ellie girl. So, I know exactly which photo should go on my profile. I had one taken last year, immediately after those two weeks when I had the worst flu in the city. In fact, I needed it for my passport, if I remember correctly. I was thinking of going to Mexico on a vacation and then I gave up..." she said pensively. "Yes, I think that's the best photo we should try," she said confidently and started browsing the folders on her computer to find the photo in question. She didn't pay any attention to Ellie who was rolling her eyes in disbelief.

"It's like you don't even want to try," she cried out.

"Au contraire, ma petite! This is me trying," Kate said with determination. "You'll see it's for the best."

Ellie made a few attempts to make Kate change her mind, however nothing swayed Kate from her decision. Ellie should have known better than wasting her breath. Kate was stubborn like a mule when she chose so.

The photo she chose showed a pale Kate. She seemed to have cleaned her face very well – so well that there was no colour left in her cheeks. Only her eyes were standing out, green like the sea, a heritage from her departed mother. Her hair looked unhealthy, flat and dull. At least, she had it dressed in a bun, even though it resembled to a bun her grandmother would have created five or six decades earlier.

Up the photo went onto the profile. Kate didn't budge, of course.

"Now you must wait," Ellie advised her as if she'd had a lot of knowledge about online dating. "You might receive some matches tomorrow but I wouldn't count on that. Why did you choose to be matched with guys from all over the world? I really don't understand. You should have chosen just Montreal, Kate. How would you meet a guy from Australia, for instance?"

"You were talking about the chance of a lifetime, remember? If it's to meet my soul mate," Kate replied playfully, "then, I must consider he might be somewhere at the other end of the world, don't you think? What are the chances to meet him right here, in the city? I'd have met him already," Kate pointed out.

Ellie seemed to have her doubts but she didn't want to contradict Kate. Kate was the clever one between the two of them. She was the one who could feel the pulse in any problem and astonishingly, she could say exactly what a person was capable of, even if everything Ellie knew about that individual pointed in a different direction.

Ellie had never been able to find an explanation to all of that, but she'd learned since the first year of school spent in Kate's company not to ever question her reasoning. Kate always knew better. It was a mystery about the how but Ellie had stopped considering that mystery a long time ago.

CHAPTER FOUR

The following day – April 16th ...

Kate turned off the alarm and, with sleepy eyes, checked the notifications on the phone. When she saw several messages in a row, all of them coming from the dating site, she woke up thoroughly. She hadn't expected someone would contact her so soon.

Kate put the phone aside and decided to go through her morning ritual first. She went to the bathroom to take a shower and brush her teeth before checking the messages again.

After she finished with her morning routine, she prepared her breakfast and carried it to the breakfast nook facing the garden.

She ate while scrolling through the messages she'd received. Almost all of them came from the same person, a guy named Ryan, and that surprised her.

She'd got messages from four other guys, and they read only '*hi, how are you?*' Well, that was a way to start a conversation, she supposed, but she'd expected at least a brief introduction or something…

Kate shrugged and forgot about them. She didn't feel like wasting her time with something so generic. Those guys could have written to anybody after all.

She spooned some cereals and decided to read the messages from Ryan.

Message one: *I've just seen your photo. I simply love your eyes. I'd like to meet you.*

She scowled at the phone. Now she thought better. At least, that '*Hi, how are you?*' was inoffensive enough.

This guy, Ryan, took out the artillery from the beginning.

Message two, which had come half an hour after the first one, read: *'When I saw your photo, I literally felt a strong pull in my heart. Please, get in touch with me.'*

She read the message again with wide eyes and said aloud, "Huh! Not so gullible, sorry."

Message three (after another half hour): *'I really think you're the one and I can't wait to meet you. Please, reply!'*

Now, she shook her head in bewilderment and murmured, "This guy is something else." Kate was dumbfounded. She couldn't believe someone could come up with such lame lines.

Message four (another half hour later): *'I do hope you haven't seen any of my messages yet and that's the only reason you haven't answered to me. I know we could have something great going on between us. We are the real deal, sweetheart, believe me.'*

She sipped her coffee and rolled her eyes in disbelief. The guy had taken out the big guns.

Message five (after another thirty minutes – one thing was clear; the guy was precise like clockwork): *'I'm still waiting. I know we two would be good together, sweetie. Just write back.'*

She shrugged dismissively and said aloud again, "Yeah, really?"

Message six (always after thirty minutes – at least he was consistent in timing his messages), *'Still waiting here. I'm here, with my computer open waiting for your reply. Please, answer. From what I read, you are indeed my soul mate.'*

This time she burst into laughter, "Really? Come on, really? This guy is unbelievable."

Shaking her head, Kate returned to her breakfast. She was in no hurry to reply to the messages piling up in her inbox.

She was thrilled a bit, she admitted it. Yet, she also felt uneasy.

There was a specific vibe to those messages. Either the guy was desperate or he was a stalker.

Anyway, she had to go to work and didn't have time to analyze those possibilities. Kate was her own boss but she was both a conscious employee and a very strict employer. She didn't like it when her employees were late and she was always careful to be on time herself.

She cleaned her breakfast dishes and left the house to go to her shop. She didn't bother with writing an answer to any of the messages she'd received.

CHAPTER FIVE

One month earlier - June 10th ...

"I'm really sorry, sweetheart," Ryan said in a hoarse voice. "I know I said I'd come and meet you and you know I did buy the plane tickets... I sent you the confirmation email, remember? But you see, now, I do have to go on a business trip in Asia... It's not like I want to do it but...," he let the sentence in suspense.

"Interesting, Ryan. You've never mentioned a business trip before," Kate replied, cutting his explanations short. She wanted to get to the heart of the matter and wasn't willing to let him make a fool out of her.

"Come on, don't be like that," he snapped at her. "You know I have business all around the globe, I've told you so. It's not like I'm sitting on my ass all day doing nothing," he raised his voice annoyed with her curt tone. "I haven't planned any trip, that's true, but, Kate, look, things happen, and I really have to take this trip. You must understand. I'll come and meet you after I come back. You know you can trust me, baby." Ryan tried to cajole her and lowered his husky voice.

"Really? How come?" she replied with sarcasm. "How do I know that?"

"You're saying you don't trust me?" he replied in a mean voice.

"I'm saying I don't even know you, Ryan," Kate said, matching his voice. "Let's face the truth. You don't know me and I don't know you," she pointed out in a businesslike manner.

"A... a... after all these m... m... months...," he stammered, "We've...

we've talked on the phone, we... we've even chatted a few times a day... I told you everything there is to know about me.... didn't I? How can you say you don't know me? Are you bullshitting me, Kate? Are you? It's not like I'm sitting on my hands here just waiting for things to happen," he snapped, and his voice showed his anger had escalated. He was practically growling by the end of his tirade.

Ryan's sarcasm was dripping all over her skin and a creepy feeling overwhelmed her. Kate was becoming uncomfortable with the conversation and she decided to end it. After all, it wasn't like her to take abuse of any kind from anyone. She preferred to fight.

"Perfect," she replied keeping a cool and distant tone, "take care of your business trip, Ryan. Sayonara!"

She turned off the phone, having time only to hear a shouted *'What the ...'* but she didn't stop to listen to what he wanted to say. She didn't care about it anymore.

Kate was a bit bewildered, though. She'd been unwisely and unwillingly swept into that strange long-distance relationship, in a matter of a few months. There were times when she believed Ryan had put a spell on her but she knew it wasn't possible.

From the beginning, she'd been uncomfortable with the way they eased into talking about everything and nothing at the same time. It didn't seem natural.

Truth be told, Kate was an outgoing person and usually, she got along with people just fine. She had to be a people person or she couldn't have created and nurtured the shop she had and the clientele she'd acquired.

Yet, in her personal relationships, she'd always kept a certain distance. She wouldn't just open the gate to her inner thoughts and feelings to everyone. Maybe it was because she could read people's minds and was often horrified of what she read in most men's minds.

She'd met a few sweet men, but they'd been too sweet for her taste and too willing to do anything to be liked. Maybe it was true women only said they wanted good guys and yet, in the end, they were attracted to the bad boys.

Kate needed a man who proved to be her equal in everything. She didn't want someone she had to coddle infinitely. She didn't feel like being on her toes all the time and taking care not to hurt their feelings.

No matter how patient she was, Kate didn't see herself as a woman ready to cater to a man's every wish or need. After all, she wanted to be the one pampered, and for that, she needed someone strong and dependable. She was looking for someone able to stand on their own two feet and protect her if necessary, a man who'd provide the care and love she desired.

After she subscribed to the dating site, Kate received messages from five men. After a couple of weeks of conversation through both the website and on the phone, she finally met four of them.

Even while talking to them over the phone, she read their mind. It wasn't difficult. Her mental abilities had honed during the last few years and now she was capable to perceive certain thoughts even at a distance.

The thoughts of two of them had been creepy, although loud and clear. They talked about weird fetishes and obsessions, and that made her want to keep her distance. They were harmless, but they weren't for her. She hardly managed a couple of hours during an evening in their company.

One had been beyond creepy, though. What she read in his mind had disturbed her. She found out he'd already met two other women he'd contacted on two different dating sites and both women had met untimely and horrible deaths at his hands.

Kate had made an anonymous call to the police, and given them a few details about the women's deaths. She'd given them the killer's name and description and left it at that. She was confident police could take it from there.

She didn't want to get involved with the police again. She'd done it once, a few years back, when she was much younger and naïve.

At that time, Kate believed she could use her gift to save the world. She scowled whenever she remembered her idealistic enthusiasm at the time. That experience put a stop to any other thoughts about saving the planet.

Kate couldn't forget how the police officers treated her. They believed she was either a freak or a fraud, and, for a time, they couldn't make up their mind about her. They even insinuated she must have been involved with the killer to know all those ghastly details.

That bitter experience made her reluctant to let anyone know about her gift. Not even people close to her, like Ellie, knew about her special talents.

The other two men from the dating site were harmless. They couldn't hurt a fly. Yet, they weren't for her either. They needed someone stronger to manage their life and accept them as they were. They wanted a woman to mother them and she didn't feel maternal enough to embrace that role.

Kate looked for someone stronger herself. She wanted to meet someone she could rely on and who would make her feel as part of a team. She dreamed of a man who would love her, the woman, and not for playing the role of a grown-up boy's mother.

She needed companionship, but she wouldn't settle just for that. Kate longed for everything supposed to happen in an adult relationship: romance, love, physical connection and trust.

The sixth man who contacted her was Ryan. In the beginning, Ryan insinuated himself in her life with messages sent every thirty minutes for twenty-four hours. When she finally gave in and answered back, he continued with witty chat on the Internet.

The man proved knowledgeable in various areas and was a very pleasant conversationalist. She enjoyed their talks. He showed cultural polish and seemed down to earth. Some times, his attitude revealed his dark side, showing the bad boy beneath the polish. That attracted Kate like a magnet.

In less than a week, they exchanged phone numbers, which she regretted when he began calling her day and night, even though she told him, several times, she would prefer sleeping around two a.m. Time didn't seem important to him. He lived somewhere outside the normal time.

Ryan sent her a few photos and in all of them, he wore big hats or caps. She had only a glimpse of his face or his hair. Asked to describe him, she could only say that he was a dark-haired man, because she'd seen the shadow of a dark beard and a lock of dark hair.

He kept promising to take a new photo and send it to her but, of course, he didn't. Something always interfered and he couldn't do it.

Ryan said he lived in Chicago and gave her a Chicago phone number. Kate called that number twice and got an answering machine every time. She never tried again. She just knew no one would answer and the thought bothered her.

Besides, Ryan kept putting off his coming to Montreal to meet her. He would always say he was in the middle of a big contract and his construction company had promised the client a deadline. He explained his reputation, his most important asset, was on the line and he couldn't afford to lose it.

Kate believed Ryan's story about the contract was a lie too, but not because she could read his mind. Kate couldn't even glimpse into his thoughts.

Ryan was the first man who had succeeded in keeping her away from his private thoughts. Whenever she tried to pry, she had the impression he was frowning and pushing her probing waves away. He couldn't know about her attempts to read his thoughts. Yet, his mind felt something was wrong and kept pushing her away.

When they talked on the phone, she sensed something was not quite right but she couldn't put her finger on why or what.

Kate couldn't explain other things either and they worried her. For instance, she'd expect his calls impatiently. She'd find herself longing to hear his raspy voice and his throaty laughter. He was like a poison that seeped into her blood and she couldn't live without.

Ryan's voice made her feel good, at least most of the time. Sometimes, his voice made her tense, yet she was looking forward to those tense moments as well, and that didn't make a lick of sense.

Kate was torn in two directions. On one hand, she needed to stay in contact with him. It was vital to her well-being, although she couldn't say why. On the other hand, she didn't want to hear another word from Ryan and wanted him to stop calling her. His charming ways and sweet words, which would turn into sarcasm in the blink of an eye, overwhelmed her. He would soak her with his arctic condescendence and she felt like decking him.

Kate grew restless during the last few weeks and now she questioned her own wishes. She felt trapped in a maze and couldn't find her way out.

***

Ryan kept calling and leaving voicemails throughout the day. He implored her to pick up the phone and talk to him. He apologized in writing. He sent several emails to excuse his outburst.

He explained that he was just very tired and stressed out because he'd had too many projects in development but he didn't intend to snap at her. It had been just a knee-jerk reaction. His fervent wish was to meet her and because he couldn't do it right then was driving him crazy.

Kate ignored everything until later in the evening. She was tired herself and didn't feel like dealing with him and his moods. Only after nine in the evening, she finally answered to one of his repetitive calls.

"Oh, my love, I didn't mean to upset you," Ryan spoke fast. He seemed afraid she'd change her mind and hang up. "I know it's not your fault everything went awry, but, please, understand I'm just very tired and upset because I can't do what I actually want to do... That's all."

"Meaning?" Kate asked in a calm voice.

She'd decided to keep cool like a cucumber so he couldn't manipulate her emotions anymore. For a few moments, only his shallow breathing filled the line. She was almost sure he would end the discussion there but he proved her wrong.

"I mean I just want to see you so much and I can't wait to be with you. Do you realize how good we'd be together? I can't wait to have a chance to let my fingers wander all over your skin…"

"Don't tell me you're thinking of phone sex right now??!!" she cut him off in awe.

That was something new. He'd tried a lot of things but not sex talk.

"What do you mean by *'now'*?" Ryan asked with impatience. "I've been dreaming of you for so many days… Of course, I'd love to enjoy you…"

"I'm not a cake…" she interrupted him in a cold voice only to be interrupted at her turn.

"Come on, Kate. Don't tell me you're not thinking of making love to me? I wouldn't have thought you'd be a prude," he snapped at her.

She grinned. He'd forgotten about speaking in a sweet voice and his sarcasm showed once more.

"Of course, I'm not a prude. But I don't know," she said in a flat voice to show him the subject was unimportant.

"Kate!" he bit out and she could hear him gnash his teeth.

"Ryan!" she replied, imitating his tone.

Ryan burst into laughter and said, "You're so good for me, Kate. Baby, you truly are the one. And you do know it." he finished with triumph in his voice.

His laughter felt like fingers touching her spine softly, tracing every ending of her nerves, and she unwillingly shivered. He didn't say anything in explicit words, yet he was touching her erotically right then and her body wondered how the real deal would feel.

Something felt wrong, though. A weird sensation churned her stomach and that always warned her something bad would happen or things weren't what they seemed.

Ryan didn't verbally abuse her, even though sometimes his voice made her feel that way. He would push until he got what he wanted.

Most of the time, their strange relationship seemed great, even though it was long-distance but, now and then, Kate felt like a pawn in a chess game and she resented it deeply. She prided herself with the control she had over her life and actions, and she loathed Ryan's manipulation.

"Still there, baby?" Ryan's voice reached her. His words pulled her back from her woolgathering.

"Yes, still here, but I do have something to do right now and unfortunately I can't stay on the phone any longer. Have a nice trip, Ryan, talk to you later," her words tumbled one after the other. She wanted to break the connection between the two of them.

"Is this your way of punishing me?" Ryan inquired, displeasure ringing in his voice.

"No, no, it isn't. It's just that I do have to go. We'll talk later, anyway, won't we?" she tried to appease him, and then, she felt like slapping herself silly.

"Yeah, we will," Ryan said implacably and his words made her shiver.

Kate turned off the phone and shrugged nonchalantly. She was a fatalist at heart. She knew she could only alter her journey, not her destiny. What she wouldn't do was to alter who she was.

CHAPTER SIX

Three days earlier, a few hours after midnight – July 16th …

"You know I wouldn't ask you to give me money if I'd had another solution," Ryan practically growled over the phone. "I've never asked you for anything before and I'll give it back to you. I'm a man of my word, Kate," he said through his tight teeth.

"You can growl, Ryan, if it makes you feel better, I really don't care. I don't mix love, as you call it, with money," Kate replied with detachment.

She was determined not to yield to any shady requests. She'd already done her research on the Internet and knew about the scams going around.

Ryan's modus operandi fell in that vein.

Now everything made sense: the phone calls at all hours of the day and night just to wear her out; his excuses for not being able to come and meet her face to face.... And now the request for nine thousand dollars...

He called her at five a.m., probably to get her while she was asleep and unable to make safe decisions. *As if I'd be so weak,* she scoffed.

Discovering the truth was heartbreaking, but then she'd never expected something would come out of their weird relationship. Lessons were learnt all the time and some of them were painful. She could live with that.

"It's not like that," Ryan squeezed through his teeth. He did make serious efforts not to explode. "I just have a problem right now. I've told you they froze my account in the

States. I'll get back and solve this issue in a couple of weeks. You'll have your money back, with interest, I promise," he tried again.

"I'm not a bank, Ryan. I can't lend you so much money," she said in the same businesslike voice.

"I've asked for a measly couple of thousand not tens of thousands, Kate. I'm sure you can afford it. Of course, if you want to help me out. It's not like you're a pauper, for God's sake! I know you're not." He took a deep breath and continued in a calmer voice, "Kate, I do think we have a truly good relationship. We're going to be together forever, and build something lasting. Am I wrong?" Ryan inquired in a tired voice.

"Now, it's my turn to ask you why you condition the existence of our relationship to my giving you the money," she asked calmly.

"I'm not doing that, Kate, and you know it," he bit down. "You know what? I don't get it. How can you be such a cold fish when I tell you I have a serious problem and only you can help me? I wouldn't have called so early, but I didn't have a choice. Your money is what I need to solve this issue now and leave from this God forsaken country. I'll finally come to you, baby. We'll be together, as we've always wanted, Kate," he tried a different approach to convince her.

"Maybe it's because I don't believe you when you say there's a problem, Ryan. It seems too convenient," Kate replied in the same cold voice.

"So, you finally admit you don't trust me," he practically bellowed.

"If the shoe fits...," she said softly.

"So, all this time... all this time I've shown you what's in my heart, what I'm feeling and thinking and .... And you've just fooled me ...," Ryan started to say but was interrupted.

"Not really. I've just been myself. I haven't lied to you, not even once. I haven't gone on saying you were my soul mate and we'd be together forever and ever..."

"So, you're saying I've lied to you," he hissed through his clenched teeth.

He'll definitely ground his teeth to powder, Kate thought.

"Well, it seems so, yes," Kate admitted without remorse.

"Why? Just because I asked for your help now?" Ryan asked caustically. "I'm good enough to be led around but not good enough to help, huh!" he said bitterly.

"Ryan, you didn't just demand my help, if you remember. You ordered. You didn't ask for it. And anyway, usually people at least meet first, for a couple of times. They talk face to face before going into things like asking for money. No one is doing something like that with good intentions, to be honest," Kate bit out.

"I've had no choice! No choice! That's all! Do you understand me? No choice! If I'd had one, I wouldn't have asked you for the fucking money now, would I?" Ryan replied crossly, spitting every word.

"I don't have a reason to believe there's even a problem," Kate repeated before Ryan rudely interrupted her.

"You're the first woman in my life who's played havoc with my blood pressure, Kate, and that since the beginning. There's always something with you. I've never allowed any woman to do that to me. It's something with you, you know?" Ryan said meanly.

"Since the beginning, you say?" Kate replied softly.

"Yes, since the beginning. You've heard correctly. You've always had to analyze everything I was saying, to doubt everything...."

"I think I've had good reasons." Kate interrupted him again. "You just come out of nowhere, declaring your undying love for me. Come on! You haven't even met me. You just read one stupid questionnaire on that site and you fell in love head over heels. Maybe that works with other women, but I'm not so naïve, Ryan. I don't buy into this. You should have been more original than that," Kate replied cattily.

"Then why have you continued to talk to me if you believed I was a fraud? What was the point?" Ryan asked in a tired and somehow defeated voice.

She didn't expect it from him. He wasn't the man to admit defeat. His stubbornness wouldn't allow him to surrender.

"Curiosity, maybe?" she confessed.

"Curiosity!!!" Ryan shouted in disbelief. "I bared my heart and mind to you and now you come and say you were just curious?"

"Yelling at me won't help with your *'problem'*, Ryan," Kate replied sarcastically. "It will simply make me finish this stupid conversation, which shouldn't have taken place to begin with." Kate's tone was flat to make him understand she didn't care what he chose.

"Stupid conversation, huh?" Ryan murmured. "So, I call and tell you I need your help to defend my freedom and you take it like a stupid conversation. Now, the question is who's been playing who for the last few months, Kate? It hasn't been me, for sure," he concluded.

"Not me, Ryan," she argued. "I've always been myself. I've never professed my undying love. I've never said those worn out *'I love you'* words, people throw left and right," Kate replied flatly.

"But you know I've loved you all this time...," Ryan tried to say but she didn't give him time to finish.

"I know?" Kate inquired. "How could I know, Ryan?"

"Because I've told you so!" Ryan bellowed with exasperation.

She moved the phone away from her ear and stared at it. The man sounded like a howling wolf. He'd probably lost what little patience he'd ever had. In fairness, he didn't seem to have much of that in stock.

She waited a few seconds, and then she returned the phone to her ear and said, "You told me so. Yes, anybody can say that. It's not difficult to say those three tiny words."

"You're such a piece of work, Kate. I can't believe I fell for such a cold-hearted bitch...," Ryan squeezed in before Kate angrily interrupted him.

"Now, you've done it. See you around," she snapped and disconnected the call.

She shook her head in disbelief. The man had the gumption to ask a lot of money, because no matter what he said nine thousand, even Canadian dollars, meant a lot. On top of that, he dared to shout at her at the same time.

She felt she'd fallen in a parallel universe. In the real world, such things never happened or at least not to her.

Kate decided to forget about him and threw the cell phone back in her bag with a nervous gesture. She left her bag in the living-room, far from her bedroom.

On her way back to bed, she heard the phone ringing again but she didn't care to verify whether it was Ryan or not. *As if there's a doubt,* she shrugged. No one else would call her at that hour.

Kate had a lot of things planned for the next morning and she didn't want to waste what was left of her night on that so-called relationship. She needed to write it off and move on with her life.

Yet, back in her cozy bed, Kate's thoughts swarmed around that surreal conversation. She hadn't been able to read Ryan's mind, which was a given already. Yet, his panic was palpable. Ryan had appeared ridden with anxiety, anger and disbelief when she refused to give him the money.

Kate couldn't believe Ryan considered their relationship real, yet she sensed it in him and that made no sense to her. Kate's conclusion leaned toward him being a scammer. Still, a scammer wouldn't show panic or pain and she'd felt both. Her mind reading abilities didn't work with him but her empathy did. Now, she was thoroughly confused with the wide range of emotions coming from Ryan.

Wary, Kate tried to put the conversation with Ryan aside. She made efforts to quiet her mind and fall asleep but, after an hour, she gave up.

The feeling something bad would happen to Ryan and she'd be the instrument of his misfortune bothered her. She hated herself for allowing his words influence her.

Kate got out of bed and went to the kitchen where she turned on the coffee maker. While waiting for the coffee to brew, she watched out of the window. Her garden basked in the light of the moon, and beaconed her outside. Before leaving the kitchen, she saw the book she was reading lying on the corner of her kitchen table and picked it up.

The night air was warm indeed, and the flower scents soothed her. Her house wasn't very far from the heavy traffic streets, yet only the buzz of insects reached Kate's ears. Somewhere in a distance, an owl hooted and made her smile.

Kate opened her book to read. The book had interested her very much, but now, she couldn't focus on the words. She gave up and sipped her coffee, letting her mind wander to everything and nothing in particular.

CHAPTER SEVEN

Always three days earlier minus a few hours – July 16

After spending a couple of hours in the garden, Kate returned inside for a shower. She had to get ready for work and needed to hurry if she didn't want to be late.

Kate was resigned to being a little sluggish that day. She hadn't slept enough, and her mind had kept chasing ideas, without reaching a conclusion, and that upset her. As she needed to compensate for her lack of sleep, she drank more coffee.

Kate turned the shower on and the warm water stroked her skin. It felt heavenly and she forgot about getting on with her day. Only when the water turned to ice, did she turn the shower off.

Curiosity was one of her faults, so, before leaving the house, she checked her phone. As expected, the display showed several voicemails and at least seventeen missed calls. Ryan had turned into a busy bee during the hours she procrastinated. He'd been calling and texting her like crazy.

Kate shrugged. She left without returning any of his calls or listening to any of the voicemails. Later, during the day, she would have enough time to see what he wanted or what else he was saying to get what he wanted.

***

The morning dragged on and the hours seemed longer. Time slowed down and moved at a snail's pace.

Kate longed for her bed. She visualised herself getting between cool sheets and closing her eyes in sheer bliss. After playing that game a few times, she decided to leave the shop and go home if she did't get better by two p.m.

She sent a few 'sweet' thoughts in Ryan's direction. She had to thank him for ruining her night's sleep and, subsequently, her day at work.

After muttering a few choice words with a specific address, she continued checking the inventory. She needed to restock soon or she would disappoint a few of her loyal customers.

"Kate, do you know your phone has been ringing for hours?" Alice's exasperated voice came from behind her and Kate winced.

She turned to Alice and looked at her confused. She didn't understand what Alice was saying.

Alice was her most reliable employee and a good friend, as well. She'd been working for Kate from the beginning, when the little shop, which she named '*Just Magic*', opened its doors before a very curious and cautious clientele.

Alice was not only reliable, but had very good people skills. She knew how to create the atmosphere of magic their customers expected when they crossed the threshold into her shop.

Alice had the gift to frame every sentence in such a way that people truly bought into the magical aura of the shop. Yet, she never said anything directly related to magic or witchcraft.

People needed to believe in magic and that axiom put the idea of such a shop in Kate's mind. Kate knew most of the people coming into her '*magic*' shop came to buy into the illusion of an enchanted world. She made a good profit from that, although it wasn't her only goal. She knew their strong belief in those illusions helped them put up with severe and demanding aspects of their life.

The young shop owner didn't deceive anyone. She just sold her products. What the clients chose to think about those products and what powers they attached to them was their business and not hers.

She sold potpourris, amulets, hand-made soaps and shampoos, hand-creams and flower arrangements. She couldn't be blamed because people thought that the items found in her store had mystical powers and would bring love or prosperity into their lives.

Some of the customers looked at her sideways, sizing her up, as if they'd expected her to sprout wings. Some people believed she was a witch because of the herbal and floral arrangements, but also because of the collection of artifacts she displayed in a case near the cashier.

She also displayed some glass fairies and dragons, created by a young artist who lived near Montreal. People were in awe before them and a lot of customers came from afar just to buy them.

Kate contemplated busily the slices of life crossing her little shop when she realized Alice was still looking at her, waiting for an answer. She couldn't remember what Alice had asked.

"Oh, I'm sorry, Alice, just woolgathering. My brain is in a fog this morning," Kate apologized and rubbed her eyes.

"Not a problem, Kate," Alice waved her concern away. "Is there something I could do for you? It's not like you to be so out of sorts," Alice replied with concern.

Alice knew her boss well. Kate was the epitome of energy and good cheer and she'd never looked so exhausted.

"No, no problems, don't worry," Kate patted Alice's arm. "I just had a bad night and didn't get enough sleep, Alice, that's all. Now, I'm dragging my feet and I'm not capable of anything," she shook her head morosely. "I think I should just call it a day and go home. I don't think I'll be able to get anything done today. Would you be all right if I left?" Kate inquired with apprehension.

She knew afternoons and evenings usually brought more people into the store and sometimes it was crowded in there. Normally, two people were necessary to attend the customers.

"Don't worry, Kate. I've got everything under control and remember, Jeanne is supposed to come at four. We're covered," Alice reassured her and patted her arm.

"Yes, I forgot about that," Kate admitted with worry in her voice.

She never thought she'd ever forget her employees' schedule. She was a businesswoman after all.

She shook her head again to clear it up and said to Alice, "I'll have to come back in the evening, though, to close the shop. You finish at six."

"I can stay till nine, if it's all right with you, and close the shop myself," Alice offered kindly.

Staying over was no trouble at all. Alice knew Kate paid fairly and she needed the money. Life seemed to become more and more expensive every day.

"Would you? Would you stay until closing time? I trust you can close the shop and make the deposit at the bank," Kate jumped at the opportunity.

"Of course, I can, Kate. I haven't made any plans for tonight, no problem. I can close the shop. I'll also make the bank deposit, no worries," she waved her hand with reassurance.

"Great! Then, I'll just go home to bed. I need to sleep a couple of hours at least, I think, and get back to my normal self. Tomorrow, I'll be fine, you'll see. That's all I need, a little sleep, and I'll be perfect," Kate rumbled.

"Don't worry about anything and just go home and rest," Alice slid her arm over Kate's shoulders and directed her toward the office in the back. "I'll close and make the bank deposit and I'll see you tomorrow when I come at ten, all right?"

"Thank you, Alice, you're a lifesaver," Kate replied enthusiastically.

"Dramatic much?" Alice said bursting into laughter, and patted Kate's shoulder playfully.

"You don't even know, Alice. I do appreciate your help today, you know that," she said and headed toward her office to gather her things.

"By the way, I think you should take a vacation, Kate," Alice shouted after her in a serious voice.

Kate turned and looked at her. Alice looked serious.

"You're exhausted, Kate. I've been working for you for four years now, I think, and I've never known you to go anywhere for more than a weekend. You can't go on like this, you know. You do need a longer break to rest and relax, Kate. Your body needs some decompression, to recharge batteries. I don't think one weekend here and there counts. You can't burn the candle at both ends. I'd book a vacation if I were you, Kate. It's no big deal for me to take care of things here while you're away. We can work out the schedule for the shop just fine," Alice explained and watched her expectantly.

Alice didn't think only about her financial situation. She was also concerned about her boss and friend. Kate had worked hard for years and although she was young and healthy, human body had limits.

"I'll think about it…" Kate replied. "I know, you're right," Kate said quickly and put up her hand when she noticed that Alice wanted to interject. "I promise to think about it and take a vacation soon, you'll see."

"All right, boss. It's your call," Alice said and turned to leave.

"Oh, God, you know I hate to hear that boss thing," Kate retorted with dismay.

"Just joking, Kate," Alice glanced back at her and laughed joyfully. Her laughter brought a smile on Kate's lips as well.

CHAPTER EIGHT

A little over two days earlier… July 17th

Kate arrived at home after a grueling drive. She parked her car and went inside the house. She took her shoes off as soon as she closed the front door behind her. She needed to feel free and was tired to bones.

She threw her bag onto the coffee table and turned around to go into the kitchen. After a few steps, she hesitated. She went back and took her cell phone out of her bag and checked the missed calls. There were about fifteen more.

Ryan had made call after call and left a voicemail every single time.

Kate wondered why he wouldn't give up. She would have.

Kate threw the phone back on the table and went to the kitchen where she poured herself a tall glass of orange juice. She drank it slowly, right there, leaning on the counter. After she enjoyed the last drop, she decided to go through voicemails and delete them.

Kate listened to the first two voicemails. An angry Ryan shouted to pick up the damn phone and listen to him. She shrugged and deleted the messages. His tone was far too abusive for a guy who wanted a favor from her.

She didn't bother to listen to the following four. She imagined that they would be on the same line, as Ryan left them very close to the first two. Ryan hadn't had the time to calm down.

She listened to the beginning of the fifth. Now, a sweet Ryan tried to cajole her to call him back. He said he hoped things hadn't changed between them and they still had something to share together. His tone was warm and charming, probably because he realized she wouldn't answer positively to his bellowing. The guy was trying to worm his way back into her heart.

Of course, after a few more sweet and cajoling voicemails, he lost his patience again, *'Answer the damn phone, Kate!'*

Kate shrugged again and then, she told herself she'd been doing that often lately. It was already ingrained in her being. She shrugged once more and then, decisively, she erased all the voicemails and text messages he'd sent. She had enough and didn't want to hear his voice anymore.

She turned the phone off and left it on the table in the dining-room. With long strides, she went to the bedroom, where she yanked her clothes off and got between the cool sheets, exactly as she'd imagined earlier. Soon enough, she fell into a fitful sleep and slept for about three hours.

Kate had a lot of dreams and their protagonist was Ryan. She saw him in all sorts of bad situations, each one worse than the one before. A few times, she dreamed he lay on a dirty floor, blood all over him, and his chest unmoving. One dream flew into another and then another. It was like a ball rolling down the hill and she couldn't stop any of it.

After a fretful sleep, Kate woke up foggy, restless and more out of sorts than before. She rubbed her eyes and hesitantly got out of bed and went to have a shower. She felt clammy all over and she wrinkled her nose when she smelled the sweat coating her skin.

***

Kate prepared a light repast, taking her time with insignificant details. She crowded a plate with the two halves of a grilled cheese sandwich and the quarters of an orange she'd peeled carefully.

Afterwards, she went out onto the deck. First, she'd reluctantly made a detour to pick up the phone left on the table in the dining room.

Kate ate her sandwich, yet she kept looking at her phone sideways, as if it had grown horns. She didn't want to touch it. On one hand, she wanted to will the phone to ring but, on the other, she dreaded it.

She'd never been so uncertain of something in her entire life and that annoyed her. She loathed herself for being so hesitant.

Kate understood the troublesome dreams played a major role in how she was feeling. Her analytical mind told her she should take a step back to prudently reconsider everything from a fresh perspective. Even so, she couldn't get over the bothering thought that her decision would have a major effect upon Ryan's life, and in ways she couldn't even fathom.

Kate allowed herself to fall prey to Ryan's game and she hated herself for that. She was almost sure he tried to scam her. She was a rational woman and even if she worried after having all those dreams, she couldn't just discard her common sense.

The beep of the phone startled her. She checked and sure enough, another text message from Ryan had come.

She hadn't checked the others yet but she decided to skip them and go directly to that one. It read, '*Please, sweetheart, understand, I wouldn't ask this from you if I'd had another choice. I need you to help me now. I need your help. There's no one else I can turn to. I promise you can trust me!*'

After she read the message, Kate snorted inelegantly, something she'd tried to outgrow for a long time. As a child, her mother would always remind her that girls shouldn't behave that way. That was another habit too engrained in her personality to change it now. She put the phone back on the tray, and she returned to her cumbersome thoughts.

Kate knew she still needed to decide and she didn't want to let Ryan sway her just because of the anxiety over her dreams, which made her feel somewhat guilty.

Normally, she wouldn't discount her dreams. She knew her dreams had a way of telling her something important. However, she believed she needed a clear head not just intuition to make her decision.

Kate knew where she stood financially. As a businesswoman, she was very careful with her finances. She reckoned the amount Ryan asked wouldn't beggar her if he turned out to be a scammer. She'd make the money back in a matter of days.

Financial means notwithstanding, two facts concerned and disconcerted her. First, everything sounded too much like the scams she'd read about on the Internet. More than anything, Kate hated to be taken for a sucker. She reviled it when people looked at her and took her for an easy mark because of her youth. Besides, the amount Ryan requested was just under the ten thousand mark, just good to go unnoticed by authorities. She'd have felt more assured, if he had asked ten or eleven thousand.

The second thing, in complete contradiction with the first one, was her deep concern for Ryan. She was almost convinced he was in trouble. Even discounting her dreams, he did seem desperate and on the edge.

She assumed a scammer would have already given up. He'd mark her name under the losses header and move on, looking for an easier mark. That made her believe Ryan didn't run a scam, but he was in an extremely bad situation, and she should try to help him, particularly because she had the means to do it.

Now, if she thought better, in the great scheme of things, she'd never risked anything. She'd never risked either money or her heart.

Kate didn't consider the opening of the shop a real risk. When she opened it, she knew she'd still have her livelihood, even if everything went awry and her business went under. The shop was just a dream come true. Something she loved. Besides, she planned it carefully and made lots of market studies before launching it.

Her parents left her very well off when they died in a car accident almost ten years ago. Kate had wisely invested the money in various funds along the years. She hadn't been greedy and had chosen the safest funds. They might not have brought her a big return per year, but they were secure. Her caution hadn't been in vain. The dive the market had taken a few years before didn't even make a noticeable dent in her funds. She imagined she could play a little risky for once.

Suddenly, Kate realized she did want to give Ryan the money. That shocked her, although she suspected she'd nurtured that idea in her subconscious all the time.

Kate knew her decision was absolutely crazy. She considered it as a smart investment, though. She would find out Ryan's true story and she would feel better knowing she'd done her best to help him if he needed help.

Kate liked being honest with herself. She admitted she'd come to have feelings for him, although she wasn't sure he deserved either her help or her feelings. The admission stunned Kate. She'd never thought she'd develop feelings for a man she'd never seen.

She felt attracted to him or, more accurately, to his voice and his laughter. She liked talking and arguing with him all the time. Almost everything was an argument with Ryan, and a very vocal one.

Both enjoyed those loud conversations. It felt good when they arrived at the same conclusion after a passionate battle of wits.

Kate liked it when Ryan lost his patience and he did, every single time. His patience was in a very short supply although he made efforts to keep his cool as much as possible. Whenever he lost his calm, he'd start speaking through gritted teeth or growling like a wolf.

That amused Kate. His growling sounded primitive, and, somehow, aroused her. It sounded close to a mating ritual and even though she'd been reluctant to admit it to him, she did think of him in that light a time or two. His voice wreaked havoc on her system and made her skin tingle. She didn't like her response to such stimulus. She'd always prided herself with her cold and detached reasoning.

Anyway, Kate resolved to give him the money, and she felt at peace. She made the decision with open eyes. She was prepared not to see any of the money back. She just wanted to make sure she'd done the right thing and could live with herself without regrets and unanswered questions.

Once the decision made, she picked up the phone and replied to Ryan's last message. She didn't bother to read his previous message but wrote, *'Okay, I'll give you the money. How do you propose we do this?'*

In a few seconds, the phone rang and the display showed private number. Only Ryan called her with private number. *The man must have been waiting with the phone in his hand,* she mused.

"Hello, Ryan. I see you've got my message," she greeted him in clipped words. She wanted him to understand everything was just business from that moment on.

"Baby, I've just known you wouldn't let me down. I knew you couldn't give up on me any more than I could give up on you," Ryan almost shouted, his words tumbling one onto another. His joy was evident in every syllable.

"It's not necessary to try so hard, Ryan. I've already said I'd give you the money," Kate replied dismissively.

"What are you saying, Kate? You're saying I'm lying or what?" Ryan shouted back, his tone rising toward the end of the last sentence.

"I'm just saying you've got yourself a deal and it's not necessary to try to charm me anymore," Kate replied unaffected by his outburst.

"So, we're still at the scamming phase, I see," Ryan said bitterly.

Kate discerned a certain resignation in his voice but she resolved she'd already given in by offering him the money, so she wouldn't give in more than that.

She steeled her heart against the pain evident in his words and went back to the problem in question. "How do you want to do it?" she repeated, as if everything had been only business for her.

"All right, you win for the moment," Ryan said with tired resignation. "You win because I need your help and it's not worth having a fight right now. But you won't always win, Kate. You'll see I haven't tried to scam you and you'll be sorry for thinking so low of me," he replied with sadness.

"All right, then. Till then, though, how do you want to do it?" she stubbornly said once more. She didn't want to let him get to her again.

"You could send it by Western Union. I'll give you the name of a guy I know here…"

"No. I won't send the money to a guy I've never heard of, Ryan, and most definitely I won't send such a big amount through Western Union," she cut him off decisively.

"But I can't use a bank account for a transfer. That's not an option, Kate. There's no other way but Western Union," he explained.

"Yes, there is. Tell me the name of the hotel where you're staying and I'll have someone deliver the money at the front desk in forty-eight or seventy-two hours, maximum." Kate replied, always businesslike.

Ryan didn't reply for a few moments. She could hear his breathing and the static on the line but that was all. Kate waited patiently, though. The ball was in his court now and she waited for him to make up his mind. Anyway, she would stick with her solution.

"Are you sure that's how you want to do it?" Ryan asked hesitantly.

That's something new, she mused. She'd never heard him hesitate, in any circumstance.

"Yes," she replied.

"All right, then," he said wearily. "We'll do it your way."

'*Like you had a choice*,' she thought derisively but kept her mouth shut.

After a few moments of silence, she asked him again, "So, to what hotel should I send the messenger?"

"The Majestic," he said, his voice as businesslike as hers now.

Ryan seemed to have finally understood she wanted to keep things like that, just a deal between two parties, no feelings involved in the transaction, nothing.

"All right, then. I'll let you know when to go and get your money. It might take a little over forty-eight hours but no more than seventy-two, if I arrange everything in due time," she specified, making sure she had a reserve of time on her side.

"I've survived until now, I'll survive three more days, I think," he said. "You can't imagine how much I appreciate...," he started to express his gratitude but she didn't give him the chance.

"Yeah, I know," she interrupted him. "I'll go now because I have to arrange a few things. I'll send you a message on the phone when you're supposed to go and get your money."

"Thank you, baby, you can't imagine..."

"All right, I understand already," she interrupted him again, in an angry voice. "I have to go, bye."

"But...," Ryan started but stopped when he realized she'd already disconnected the call and he spoke to the static.

He looked at his phone gnashing his teeth and then threw it furiously on the bed nearby.

"Will she do it?" Adam asked him tentatively, afraid to raise his ire.

Ryan turned to him, his hands braced on his hips. He bowed his head and closed his eyes, his stance speaking of defeat. He didn't say anything for a few moments. Then, he looked at Adam and answered, "Yeah, she'll do it."

He turned around thinking of going out when Adam spoke again, "You think you blew it, don't you?"

Ryan stopped with his hand on the knob and then nodded. He replied quietly, "Well, it seems that way. By now, she's sure I'm a scammer."

"But then why would she give you the money?" Adam wondered.

"The hell if I know, Adam... The hell, if I know.... Would you be all right if I go out for about an hour?" Ryan asked, his hand always on the knob. He couldn't wait to get out of the room.

"No worries, pal. I'll be fine, no problem. Go out, you've been cooped in here for the last two days and I think you're about to go nuts," Adam replied and laughed, although his laughter seemed forced.

"I'm getting there," Ryan said and left the small room.

The room had smothered him for the last few hours and he needed a breath of fresh air. He also needed to think about Kate and her sudden change of heart, which he didn't understand. He'd hoped to persuade her, that was true, but he'd been sure he'd need much more time to do it.

CHAPTER NINE

Two days earlier - July 17th

Kate was serving a client, a woman dressed in a very theatrical getup, when the little bell over the door chimed. She looked at the door to see Alice, who came into the shop swinging her bag on a finger.

Kate glanced at her watch. It was almost ten. She smiled at Alice and continued to show the amber jewelry to the woman with the flowing kaftan, asking herself, and not for the first time, who wore a kaftan in the middle of summer.

Kate wished the woman had decided already so she could go in the back and talk to Alice. Now that she'd made her choice, she was anxious to move on with her plan.

Finally, the client decided on a set sporting a necklace, a bracelet and earrings. Relieved, Kate rang the charge on the woman's credit card and showed her out the door. After the woman disappeared in the crowd, Kate turned the sign on the door to let any potential clients know she would be back in ten minutes and went in the back to talk to Alice.

"Oh, hi, Kate. Has the client left?" Alice turned to Kate, all the while doctoring a cup of coffee with cream and sugar.

"Yes, Alice, she did. I just wanted to talk to you for a few minutes before you go on the floor," Kate said, waving Alice to a seat in front of her office desk.

"Yes, of course. Is everything all right?" Alice asked and sat down.

She took care to smoothen her skirt over her legs and Kate smiled.

Alice had her idiosyncrasies but she liked her for that.

"Oh, yes, don't worry, Alice. Everything's fine. Do you remember we spoke about me taking a vacation?" Kate started, tentatively.

"Yes, of course, I remember just fine. I still think it would do you good to leave Montreal for a while. And I mean for more than three or four days. Have you thought about it?" Alice asked and tasted her coffee to see if it was the way she liked it.

"Well, yes," Kate replied.

She decided not to tell Alice all the story. She disliked skirting around the truth but she thought it was better if Alice didn't know what she planned.

"You see... I seem to have a chance to leave for about three weeks... I'd be going to Malaysia with some friends for a vacation...," Kate said.

She didn't look directly at Alice. She knew she wasn't very good at lying. Her face betrayed her all the time.

"That's great, Kate," Alice rejoiced hearing her plan.

"Well, yes, it is, but I should be leaving tonight at around eleven o'clock, I'm afraid. I know it's quite sudden and that gives you very short notice about the change in your schedule..."

"Don't worry about that, Kate, just go," Alice waved her concerns away. "I'll work a split shift, so I could open the shop in the morning and close it in the evening, and Jeanne can work the hours in between. She's off school, with it being summer, and just yesterday she told me she could use some more hours right now. You know young girls and summer time...," she winked. "So, it's just perfect, you see. It works just fine if she can work eight hours a day, you know? Of course, our shift will overlap somewhere in the middle, but I think it'll be fine… So, you see, you can leave anytime. You should even go home and get ready now. Everything is covered here, I promise you," Alice said.

"So, you wouldn't mind," Kate surmised. She was amused with Alice's enthusiasm.

"No, of course not, just the opposite. I've been thinking about this for a while now. You need a longer vacation. You deserve it, girl, and you know it. You've been working your ass off for a long time and you haven't taken care of you at all. I'll take care of things here, so, just go," Alice said smiling, and she jumped up, ready to show Kate out the door.

Kate burst into laughter and said, "All right, I'm going, I'm going. No need to throw me out of the door." Then, in a serious voice, she explained, "You're the boss for the next three weeks, Alice. I'll prepare the checks for your pays, including the eight hours per day for Jeanne. You will get a raise and a bonus because you'll be working more, okay? You'll have to receive the orders and pay for them … I'll leave the checks for that as well. Of course, you'll have to give Jeanne her paycheck. All those checks will be in this drawer here," Kate showed Alice the right top drawer of her desk.

"I wouldn't say '*no*' to more money, Kate, you know me," Alice laughed and stood up.

She took her coffee cup with her and went into the shop to turn the sign on the door back to open.

***

Kate wrote the checks for the three pays she would be missing and verified the stock once more to make sure she had all the orders put in. She also verified the checks for the suppliers' payments. Alice needed only to pick up a check and pay a supplier.

After she finished organizing everything, she reserved a return ticket for her flight to Malaysia at eleven that evening, and because the plane landed at around ten in the morning, she booked one night at the same hotel where she was supposed to leave the money.

She didn't imagine Ryan would guess she was the messenger. She wanted to have a glimpse of him at least. After all, the man had bothered her for several months already and she couldn't just write those months off.

In the spur of the moment, she also made a reservation and paid for a vacation house on the beach. If she had to fly all that way to Malaysia, and it was a very long way, indeed, at least she could enjoy three weeks in the sun.

Kate spent about twelve thousand dollars, and when she

totalled all the expenses, she sighed. She comforted herself with the thought she was compensating for the six years when she hadn't gone anywhere.

She checked everything again to be sure that things were in order and when everything checked out, she went into the shop and called Alice to come into her crammed office and go over the papers with her.

Jeanne had already started her shift and Kate knew she could take care of the customers for a while. Meanwhile, Kate had to make sure Alice was trained in everything there was to be known about managing the shop for the following three weeks.

***

When she was confident Alice understood everything and could look after the business during her three-week vacation, Kate left the shop and went to the bank to withdraw ten thousand dollars from her bank account. She was a careful person, who planned for all contingencies, so, she also checked whether she could use her debit card and credit card abroad or if she had to rely on traveller's checks.

After her brief stop at the bank, where everything went smoothly and the news was quite reassuring, she went to *The Bay* to buy a small bag for Ryan's nine thousand dollars. She carefully chose a bag any man would carry without objection.

Kate thought about her wardrobe and sighed. She had to spend more money now. She needed a few clothes for her summer experience, somewhat different from her everyday getup.

After she gave it a bit of thought, she decided she had to add something that would help her to be unrecognizable. She wanted to get a look at Ryan when he would come to take the money but she didn't want him to recognize her.

She completed the ensemble with a chic hat. The wide brim and some huge sunglasses covered almost half of her face. Kate didn't recognize herself when she looked in the mirror.

She added a few books to the things she intended to take with her. If she were to spend three weeks alone on the beach, she needed something to read.

When she finished shopping, Kate stopped by her telephone provider's store and arranged for roaming. She also verified whether she could access the Internet on her tablet while away.

CHAPTER TEN

A day and a half earlier at around 11 pm – July 17th

Five minutes after eleven p.m., the plane took off for Turkey, the first leg of her flight. On board, Kate wondered for the tenth time what the hell she'd been thinking to fly halfway around the world in the spur of the moment. It was a very long flight even with the layover in Istanbul.

Kate had already sent a message to Ryan to let him know he could find the money at the front desk of the hotel at four in the afternoon the following day. She'd reserved enough time to get from the airport to the hotel and to rest for a while.

She'd also cautiously banked some time in case of any delays during her trip.

Kate read Ryan's enthusiastic reply but she didn't answer the phone when he called. She refused to have any contact with him for the next twenty-four hours.

The flight attendant came with dinner on a tray after the plane reached cruising altitude and Kate dubiously eyed her plate. It didn't seem very appetizing and as she had already eaten before leaving home, she left the tray aside and went to sleep.

She would be in Istanbul after nine hours and forty minutes. That was enough time for a good night's sleep.

***

Kate woke up an hour before landing. The flight attendants had already started to serve breakfast and, this time, she accepted the tray, and asked for some coffee. She ate her pastries, lazily listening to the chatter around her.

She'd been lucky. The seat next to her had remained unoccupied and no one disturbed her. She'd even used both seats to sleep and felt somewhat refreshed.

Kate drank her coffee and peered through the window. She tried not to think about the second leg of the trip and especially, not about the moment when her eyes would finally lie on Ryan.

She had two hours and fifty-five minutes to kill in Istanbul and another eleven hours to get to Kuala Lumpur. She had enough time to ponder upon what was to come. For the moment, she chose to let her mind wander.

***

Kate deplaned in Istanbul and went to the passport control point. A polite officer directed her to the Primeclass Lounge, one floor below the Food Court, after the control point.

When she entered the lounge, she found herself immersed in a world she hadn't ever imagined. For a young woman who'd spent her life between studies and work, and who hadn't left Montreal in over a decade, the lounge looked like a different world.

Kate spent an hour and a half tasting the delicacies displayed and taking it all in. The cultural differences seemed overwhelming at times but she imbibed herself in all that novelty with a passion.

When the time to embark came, she regretted to leave the lounge. The novelty helped her forget about what waited for her at the end of the flight.

Kate dreaded the flight to Malaysia. The flight took almost

eleven hours and only thinking of that she felt exhausted.

Kate congratulated herself she'd asked Ryan to come and take the money in the afternoon. That way, she could rest and refresh. She could also arrange everything with the clerk at the front desk.

She hoped the receptionist would be open to her plan. Otherwise she didn't know how she would recognize Ryan when he came to take the money.

Of course, if he would be the one coming to take the money. Her research showed that entire networks operated out there. The person coming to get the money could be anyone.

The thought of Ryan being part of a scam operation distressed her. She almost hated herself for letting him worm his way into her heart. She half suspected everything was just part of a very well strategized operation and she was just a mark.

Well, in the end, everyone had to make some big mistakes in their life, and she hadn't made any before. Probably, it was her turn

She could live with that. She would probably think about it now and then and feel ashamed she'd fallen for it, but at least she'd tried her luck.

Once on the plane, she waited for takeoff, and then, she curled in her chair and slept some more. She was lucky again. No one occupied the seat next to hers.

She didn't care about dinner and let the flight attendant know she shouldn't bother with her food. She requested not to be disturbed and, once she closed her eyes, she was fast asleep.

***

The morning sun woke Kate. She was confused about her whereabouts.

She blinked a few times and then she remembered where she was and why.

She looked around. Most people were still sleeping. Quietly, she went to the lavatory to clean herself as much as possible. When she came back, the cabin attendants had already started to serve breakfast and a tray had been left in front of her seat.

After she started to eat, the flight attendant came and offered her coffee or tea. Kate felt exhausted despite the long hours of sleep and needed some coffee to start up her day.

The trip took a toll on her. She felt the strain of the journey and she still had another two hours and a half before landing. When she thought of the forty-five-minute drive from the airport to the Majestic hotel, she sighed.

Her reflection in the lavatory mirror had dismayed Kate. She looked pale and had dark circles around her eyes.

She promised herself never to travel for almost twenty-four uninterrupted hours. It was pure madness.

Kate hoped the four hours she had before Ryan came would be enough for her to feel somewhat refreshed and, more importantly, to look better and not like death warmed over.

Kate sipped her coffee broodingly, looking at the clouds below, and as she was prone to do, she played different scenarios in her mind.

She had some control over the evolution of things and that satisfied her. She had determined how the *'business'* should be concluded. She refused to call that stage in her relationship with Ryan otherwise. She was determined to avoid being swept into a melodrama.

Kate felt bitter. She believed it was natural to feel regret, although she'd never counted on anything real coming out of the story with Ryan.

Yet, she'd felt close to Ryan. The man always perceived the funny side of things and she'd been attracted to his acerb wit and varied knowledge. They would talk about books and films and even philosophy.

Ryan had proved complicated and well read. She hadn't thought a scammer would be so versed in the art of conversation.

More than that, she'd been attracted to him, the man, and she hadn't even met him yet. That simply boggled her mind. She couldn't understand how she could react so strongly to a man she'd never seen.

Kate reckoned she'd have liked a true relationship with Ryan. She'd enjoyed even their sparring and laughter over menial things.

Now, she feared she'd built that relationship entirely in her imagination. She also dreaded she'd never find something like that again in real life. Probably, a few years down the road, she would settle for less and she hated that thought.

The captain's voice interrupted her reflections, prompting the passengers to fasten their seatbelts. The procedures for landing had started and Kate was anxious to see what the next few hours would bring. The thought of laying eyes on Ryan was terrifying and exhilarating at the same time.

With new determination, she deplaned and, after passing through the passport control point, she went to the car rental office to pick up the keys for the car she'd booked from Montreal.

After signing the papers for a small convertible, she began her forty-five-minute drive toward the Majestic and possibly, toward Ryan.

Kate didn't even take the time to admire the surrounding landscape.

She knew she would have all the time in the world during the following three weeks. She'd enjoy the atmosphere and life in Malaysia then. For the moment, she was a woman on a mission.

***

At the hotel, after taking her only luggage bag from the back seat, Kate handed the car keys to the valet. She smiled at the doorman and, going inside, she made a beeline to the front desk, manned by a young smiling man.

CHAPTER ELEVEN

Back to present day – July 19ᵗʰ

The man didn't answer anything for a while and the silence grew menacing.

"Are you still there?" she asked when the silence began to weigh heavily on her.

"Yes, I am. I'm here, Kate. And when I say here, that means *here*," his reply came heatedly.

Not a second later, heavy footsteps sounded on the veranda surrounding the house. Startled, Kate looked there and saw him.

He came into view with a scowl tugging at the corner of his lips. He turned off his phone, staring her

126

down. The expression on his face didn't promise anything good.

Kate's legs fell off the other chair with a resonant clank and she froze in place. She even forgot to turn off her phone. By rote, she managed to let it fall on the table in a slow move.

Her eyes turned into two, wide, frozen, green pools of shimmering water. She stared at him.

The man towered over her in an extremely foreboding manner. He looked like he was ready to pounce on her any second now.

Kate was aware of only one thing. She had one very huge pissed-off male looming over her. Any coherent thought vanished. His figure was the focal point.

At the sight of his threatening stance, her throat constricted and she had to make serious efforts just to breathe.

'Oh, God, the man's so big!' From a distance, at the hotel, he hadn't seemed so tall or so well-built. Now,

Kate realized he had to be about six feet four at least.

Sometime in his past, he'd probably played football for a few years, given his massive muscles. His shirt couldn't even begin to hide them.

He'd clenched his fists so tight that his knuckles turned white. He was tense. The coiled muscles in his arms played under his skin. He looked like he was trying hard to keep his temper in check.

Ryan's dark eyes shone with pure thundering fury and his mouth was drawn in a tight line, making the rest of his face seem rigid and unforgiving. At least, he was trying not to shout or strangle her, although he seemed like he wanted to.

One moment she was sitting and staring stunned at him, a little afraid of his brutal display of force. The next, he reached for her and pulled her up like a rag doll. He shook her so violently that her teeth clattered.

"You stupid, stupid, little girl," Ryan practically growled the words through his teeth, as if it he couldn't unclench his mouth and speak normally.

Witnessing such intense and hot fury, Kate thought that was the end for her. Certainly, she'd be lying dead right there, in a second. She knew she couldn't fight his obvious brutal force.

What followed bewildered her even more. After a few tense moments, during which he continued to shake her so badly that she could feel her bones rattle, he suddenly pulled her close and pressed her to him, holding her in a smothering bear hug. That gesture confused her more.

He buried his face in her hair and inhaled her scent greedily. He looked like a man trying to draw in his next breath with everything he got.

Once her body touched his, Kate felt he was shaking. Nothing made sense to her anymore. She'd probably fallen through the looking glass into a parallel world.

Kate's ears caught his unintelligible whispers. He was whispering something to her, feverishly, but his face was buried in her hair, and she couldn't understand any of the words. Besides, she was still stunned by his reactions and had difficulties in processing anything. She'd expected something else when he'd showed up so mad with her.

Altogether, everything seemed exceedingly unreal. For an instant, she thought she was experiencing all those weird things because of the long flight, which had fried her brain connections.

Kate wasn't aware Ryan followed her to the house from the hotel. Subsequently, his presence on her deck had turned her brains to mush.

His presences there wasn't part of her plan and she feared she'd lost total control of the situation. The only words in her mind were interjections like '*wow*' and '*oh, my God!*' She couldn't articulate any coherent phrases.

Kate tried to pull herself together. She needed to form some coherent ideas.

Her reasoning power had disappeared the moment she saw Ryan from up close. He was much more than she'd imagined.

His physique astounded her. Kate had never been the type of woman to sigh or faint over big muscles and a broad chest. She'd preferred the intellectual type.

Now, the reality proved she'd been lying to herself. Ryan's body had basically robbed her mind of any rational thought. She felt a bit ashamed of such a girly reaction. She hadn't ever reacted that way. Not even when she was a teenager.

Kate had never expected to see a man so entranced by holding her. He couldn't form any comprehensible sentences. Oddness notwithstanding, his reaction delighted Kate once she became aware she had such power over him.

That time around she was positive he couldn't just play a part to mislead her. He couldn't be such a good actor.

"Ryan," she managed to mumble. Her face was still buried in his chest. Every breath brought the smell of his slightly sweaty skin and played havoc with her senses.

Ryan didn't answer, as if he hadn't heard her. The man held her tight against his body with his left arm, all the while trailing the contour of her face with the callous fingers of his other hand. His raspy touch left a pleasantly burning sensation in its wake and made her experience that strange tingling in her lower belly once again.

His lips brushed the ridges of her ear and the featherlike touch prompted her to shiver slightly. Now, that strange tingling was present everywhere, all over her body and inside her body. It brought a myriad of unknown but painfully pleasant sensations to life. All of them exploded inside her and made her blood sing.

"Ryan," she said more forcefully.

Kate needed to get back to normal and get out of that trance of senses. This time, she met with some success in her attempt to bring him back to reality.

"What?" Ryan mumbled slightly annoyed for being interrupted.

He didn't stop though. He continued to trace the contour of her cheekbone with his fingers and his slightly open and wet lips followed closely.

Kate laughed softly at his annoyance, and that surprised her. After a few seconds, she remembered what she wanted and said, "I do think that we should talk first, Ryan, don't you?"

Kate's voice hesitated. She didn't know for sure whether she wanted that sweet torture to end.

For the first time in her lifetime, she believed talking was overrated. Allowing her body to experience something so electrifying couldn't be wrong.

"What's there to talk about?" Ryan asked gruffly, pulling slightly away and looking straight into her eyes with annoyance. "You're here, although we both know you shouldn't be...," he frowned, but continued, "I'm here... and I need you, baby, really, really bad, and right now. No more postponing, no more waiting...I can't wait anymore. I've been thinking of this too much and..."

"We've just met, Ryan," Kate interrupted him in a dry voice.

She tried to be logical and help him see reason at the same time, although it wasn't easy for her to be rational when her skin was burning.

"But we know each other well enough, Kate. Come on. We've known each other long enough, don't you think? We've talked and argued for so many hours that… No, no more talking or arguing would bring us closer than this, Kate… Don't you see I'm right, baby? Please, think, or better don't think," he almost implored her and then brushed a lock of her hair aside to get to the curve of her cheek, which he cradled tenderly in his palm.

He tilted his head forward, his eyes intently on hers, ready to notice the slightest glimmer and reaction. He brushed her lips with his lightly, enticing her to accept the inevitable and give in.

Kate stared at him for a few seconds. Then, she had to reckon she wasn't able to refuse his request. She couldn't say '*no*' to him. And besides, if she wanted to be completely truthful with herself, she had to admit she didn't have any intention to refuse his advances. Her entire body already vibrated in tune with his. Now, she longed for far more than his light touches.

They didn't truly know each other, if she wanted to be technical. Yet, that could have been true even if they'd met constantly and had all those conversations face to face.

Kate still didn't know who he was. She had no idea whether he was a scammer or not, but she didn't want to think about that anymore and, more specifically, not when he held her in his arms as if she'd been something very precious to him.

She was there and he was there and that was all that mattered. She wasn't a risk taker, but that was one of those moments in life when it seemed like it was worth jumping into the unknown with open eyes.

Staring straight into his eyes, to gauge his reactions, Kate reached out and touched his chest timidly. She tried to find her bearings in making love to him. She had limited experience and she'd never taken the initiative before. Kate needed to find her rhythm. After stroking his chest with featherlike touches, her hands slid down his torso slowly, stroked his midriff with by now shaky hands, and then stole behind his back.

His pupils were getting more dilated and intense, and she surmised he enjoyed her touches probably as much as she enjoyed having her hands on him. She melted into him. She aligned her torso to his so she could feel much more of his body.

Her moist lips found his collarbone and she left a trail of wet kisses on his feverish, dark skin, tasting his musky and manly flavor. She traced a swirling path from one side to the other of his collarbone with the tip of her tongue and relished in the salty taste his skin left on her tongue. At the same time, her fingers burrowed into the hard muscles of his back, massaging lightly at first. Then she alternated light touches with deep ones. His muscles flexed and shivered under her playful fingers and a short victorious laughter flew off her lips.

The sound of her laughter surprised Ryan and he arched his left eyebrow. Kate was also astonished how much she liked feeling his body without any restrictions and playing it like a violin.

Ryan's eyes, even half-lidded, were still keenly focused on her. The suspense and his expectations had dried his lips and he licked his upper lip briefly. He inhaled sharply when she reached up and the tip of her tongue licked the hollow at the base of his neck in a whorl.

"Enough teasing, baby," he grumbled.

His voice was tense and hoarse. He whisked her up into his arms and made her cry out in surprise. She threw her arms around his neck for support, afraid that he would drop her any moment now.

Watching Kate's face intently, he started toward the house with big and hurried steps. She felt he was in a rush to find her bedroom immediately and start feasting on her. That image made her both blush and shiver, which prompted Ryan to grin like a wolf and his innate primitive streak became more vivid in his eyes. It promised a lot more was about to come. For a moment, Kate was afraid the intensity of what would follow might consume her.

Kate had never believed she would enjoy being carried away like that or she would be pleased to have fueled such raw masculinity in a man. As a rule, she'd run away from that type of man. Prudence didn't go hand in hand with raw emotions.

Kate enjoyed deeply Ryan's arrogance and his intense demonstration of sheer physical power.

Instinctively, Ryan chose the correct path to her bedroom and carried her inside the room after only a few huge strides. There, he let her slide slowly along his body until her feet touched the floor.

He loved how she felt against him and how his skin burnt at the direct contact with the woman's body. He didn't let her go. He kept her close for a few more seconds, his eyes searching hers as deep as possible. He wanted to make sure she was on the same page with him and wanted the intimacy they shared as much as he did.

Once he was assured he didn't misunderstand her, he pushed himself to arm's length and allowed his eyes to roam freely all over her body, from head to toes. An appreciative and hungry grin appeared on his lips and assured her he was pleased with everything he saw.

The man reached behind her and found the zipper of her dress. Excruciatingly slowly, and the anticipation almost killed her, he lowered it and followed the progress with his eyes. The dress came loose around Kate's breasts and now he could relish in a little more than a hint of her bosom. The rosy skin beaconed to him and he didn't bother to fight his desire. Ryan carefully traced the contour of one breast, directly on her skin, with one of his fingers.

Kate's eyes didn't leave him. He focused intensely on what his finger was doing. His eyes never strayed from the path his callous finger was following, as if the texture of her skin had fascinated him.

Her body captivated his eyes. His rough skin left goose bumps on her body in its wake. When she slightly trembled, Ryan suddenly looked up and noticed her pupils had widened and her lips had parted, inviting him to taste them.

Ryan had already decided not to refuse her or himself anything, so he leaned forward, licked his lips nervously, and then touched them to hers. He caught her light exhale in his mouth, and answered back with a deep growl of his own.

That profound rumble reminded Kate of ancient times. That was how her fancy nature had imagined the warriors of the past, raw and ravenous.

Ryan brushed his lips to hers a couple of times. He tested them, trying to learn their texture and shape. Only afterwards, his tongue dove into her mouth, and tasted her. He teased Kate mercilessly. His tongue danced slowly over hers, mating with her.

By now, he had already closed his fingers over one of her breasts and pressed the little bud with the centre of his palm. He liked how it felt when the little peak bumped into his hand. He stroked it with his knuckles and then squeezed it gently between two fingers at first, and then more strongly. When he rolled her nipple between his fingers, Kate inhaled sharply and her arms stole around his neck, looking for support. That made him wallow in his power. Knowing she needed an anchor because her legs shook, made him feel close to invincible. At the same time, he inhaled her scent and allowed the taste of her tongue explode onto his, which brought him almost to the brink.

Ryan loved the way she responded to his mating ritual. Her answer was unconscious. She allowed her tongue blend with his and matched her moves to his.

Kate's fingers knotted in his hair. She didn't care if he hurt or not. Ryan didn't care either. He just wanted to make her experience so many sensations at the same time, so they would wreak havoc on her brain and body.

Ryan suddenly pulled back again and glanced with proud at her swollen lips. He had done that to her.

The man grinned mischievously at her, as if he had plans for something more. Then, he drew her toward him again. Their bodies bumped one into the other, and Ryan took her mouth in a mind-numbing kiss. He then stroked her lips with his tongue and nipped at her lower lip sharply, which made her cry out and pull his hair in response.

He merely chuckled. It was that throaty laughter of his that made her always shiver.

Then, he turned his attention back to feasting on her mouth and tried to become one with her. His skilled tongue played on hers, stroking and teasing, brushing slowly on her teeth and her lips at times.

Ryan pulled back only when his body screamed for air and he

exploded with too much need for air. His blood roared in his ears, covering even the sound of the waves coming through the window Kate had left open earlier.

"I love your dress, baby," he said through clenched teeth, "It suits you... But let's get rid of it, okay? I need to touch you everywhere," Ryan fervently whispered to her. His patience was frizzled, hanging on a thread.

Kate was so dizzy she couldn't make sense of his words. She glanced at him confused and that made him laugh again, pleased with himself.

"The dress, baby. Let's take it off," Ryan repeated louder.

To make her move, he decided to lead through example. He reached back and pulled his shirt over his head, throwing it somewhere in the room.

When she saw him taking his clothes off, Kate finally understood what he wanted from her and she pushed the straps of her summer dress off her shoulders. She let the dress pool at her feet. The texture of the cotton sliding over her feverish body cooled her skin.

The woman needed that respite from the fuzzy world in which Ryan had pushed her with his lips and fingers.

Kate stood in front of him clad in her skimpy panties and her bra. When she noticed the hungry look in his eyes and the way his eyes roamed over her body thoroughly, she blushed violently. Ryan seemed to memorize everything.

The man didn't miss the blush spread all over her face and neck, and beamed in response. He took his shoes off and told her, "Few women know how to blush properly after puberty. I love it on you, Kate."

She wanted to reply something witty but, surprisingly, her mind didn't hold a thought. She shrugged. She'd never been good at sexual banter anyway. She'd become aware flirting wasn't part of her genetic makeup long before her teenage period ended and she'd accepted her shortcomings without complaints.

"You'd like me to take off the rest, wouldn't you?" Ryan inquired naughtily.

He'd already thrown his shoes away and unzipped his jeans. His eyes fixed on Kate, he took his jeans off together with his underwear and Kate's wide eyes stared at him. Her reaction brought another satisfied grin on Ryan's lips. All her responses flattered Ryan and made him more confident in his skills.

After a few seconds, Kate shook her head and reached back to unhook her bra, but Ryan stopped her.

"No, babe, allow me. I'd love to unwrap you. You're my gift right now."

Reticently, her arms fell aside and he reached behind her, his eyes always on hers. He unhooked her bra and pulled the straps down, freeing her breasts. Throwing the bra on the floor carelessly, Ryan closed his palms over the two mounds and massaged them lightly, growling possessively again. That growl and his touches were enough to make her blood boil again.

When his palms closed on her, Kate staggered and grasped his arms to find her balance. Her nails dug into his skin but she didn't care about his pain.

He lowered his head and brought her left breast to his mouth. His tongue licked the underside of her breast, tasting the salty skin, breathing her in. At the same time, he slid his fingers all over her right breast and rejoiced when he felt her shaking under his touch. When his fingers finally reached the tightened nipple, his mouth closed simultaneously on the other one. His tongue swirled around it and made it harder, just perfect for him to suck on.

Kate cried out. Too many sensations, all of them extremely intense, shot through her. Tension surged in every fiber of her body. Her preservation sense demanded she pulled back, but his arm stole behind her and held her fast in place.

Ryan didn't leave any room for her to move, and all the while he continued to feast on her hungrily. He licked her nipple, molding it with his tongue and then, suddenly, he sharply nipped at it with his teeth. Kate exhaled shakily. Ryan sucked the little bud, until he felt the tension exploding in her body and she dissolved in a sea of sensations. Ryan didn't stop until Kate began to shake and whimper in his arms.

He glanced at her face. Her eyes were closed and her lips, wearing the mark of her own teeth, had parted in a mute shout. That urged him to reach up to her full mouth. He followed her suit and bit her lower lip sharply, making her cry out again.

Kate tilted toward him blindly. She needed support and she rested her head onto his shoulder in complete abandon.

Ryan nudged her head up with his thumb and, to her surprise, the man maliciously bit her lower lip once more. That prompted her to cling onto his shoulders with shaking fingers.

Feeling her tremble, he took the time to assuage her tormented reddened lip with wet and soft touches before sucking it into his mouth. He growled when he filled himself with her texture, taste and smell. He sucked on the plump lip, something he'd been craving since he saw her photo.

Nothing else existed for him. Ryan didn't perceive the murmur of the sea or the smell of salt lingering in the air. He was just breathing and feeling Kate and that was it for him.

After something that felt like a small eternity, his lips started their journey away from her mouth, and stroked her jaw, tracing the shape of her cheekbone. Then, he kissed one eyelid and then the other.

His featherlike touches descended then on the other side of Kate's face. Ryan licked the whorl of her ear lazily, and then, he sank his teeth in her earlobe softly. Kate gasped and her fingers burrowed into his shoulders, her nails leaving marks behind. He continued to pepper little kisses on her neck here and there, until he reached the point where her neck melted into her shoulder blade and, there, he sucked strongly, alternating the suckling with elusive licking and bites, savouring all the while the passionate sounds coming from Kate's lips.

Kate had lost any lucid thought and her brain knew only one thing. She needed Ryan and she needed him right then. She'd had enough foreplay. She felt like she would have died if he hadn't furthered their lovemaking faster. Kate was set on fire. She burnt everywhere.

Ryan read her thoughts in her eyes. He grinned at her and shook his head. He wanted her to understand he was the one in control of their lovemaking and she had to respect his timetable.

Then, he slightly bent and his fingers delved into her panties. He pulled them excruciatingly slowly down her legs, and his knuckles stroked the length of each leg all the way down, leaving a trail of goosebumps in their wake.

Once he removed her panties and thrown them away, Ryan kneeled before her and pulled her to him, to bury his mouth in her belly button, where he allowed his tongue to play and tease while his fingers burrowed in her hips. He knew he was marking her and she would show bruises on her hips the following day.

At the thought he was marking her, he became much more territorial and possessive, as if some latent Neanderthal genes had taken control of his mind. He couldn't look beyond the feeling that she belonged to him at visceral level.

He continued to stroke her body with his mouth in his way downward. The soft skin stretched on her hipbone, as well as her spicy smell, fascinated him.

Ryan's senses were raw and his body screamed for completion. He needed to bury himself inside her and forget about everything else.

Ryan stood up and kissed her briefly, almost perfunctorily, and then, he lifted her into his arms and laid her down on the bed. He followed and covered her with his body. He tried to stroke the inside of her thighs some more but his hands were shaking violently.

He couldn't wait another moment. More roughly than he'd

wanted to, he delved inside her, filling and stretching her beyond what she'd have thought possible. She cried out at the shock and he hissed through his clenched teeth.

"Did I hurt you, baby?" Ryan asked after a moment, although the effort required a lot from him.

Kate felt too good and he wouldn't have stopped making love to her for nothing in the world.

"No, I was just surprised," Kate replied in a whisper and her right palm stroked the side of his face, reassuring him and encouraging him to continue.

Yet, even through the haze of his pleasure, he noticed tears in her eyes and cringed. "I hurt you, you're crying," he said with dismay.

"Oh, no, no, I'm not crying, Ryan. I was just surprised… pleasantly surprised, actually," she rushed to say, afraid that he would leave her aroused like that. Her body was demanding fulfillment.

"It feels good, doesn't it?" he grinned at her then.

Ryan braced on his elbows and cradled her head in his palms. He kissed her softly with tenderness.

"It does Ryan, but if you don't start to move...," Kate replied in a threatening voice and pushed her pelvis up toward him.

Ryan laughed and arched forcefully into her, making her gasp again. He began making passionate love to her and lavished her lips with wet and demanding kisses. His chest brushed hers every time they came together and both felt electrifying shocks in their nerve endings. He pulled her left leg around his waist and pushed harder inside her, and at the same time, he stroked her thigh with the tips of his fingers. He enjoyed feeling her quivering violently.

Ryan's arousal increased when her shaky fingers caressed his back. The idea of being inside her and being surrounded by her like a tight glove excited him even more.

He'd have liked to kiss her again but realized he couldn't. His mouth had tightened because he tried to last longer.

Her smell intoxicated his senses and he knew he would be done soon. He reached down, stroked her womanhood and buried himself in her deeper. Ryan caressed her body with his at every move, and finally, she uncoiled. The tension inside her was released in a powerful wave of pleasure.

Kate gasped and then, cried out. Her eyes opened wide. They were trained on him, full of astonishment. What she felt was much more than she'd expected.

Only then, satisfied that she'd reached fulfillment, Ryan also let go. He roared into her neck and collapsed on top of her, but immediately turned on his side and took her with him so he wouldn't crush her with his weight. Then he felt wetness on his thigh and looked down in alarm. Stunned, he discovered he'd forgotten something essential.

"I didn't use anything. Damn it! Of course, I didn't. Bloody hell, I didn't have anything to use. Oh, damn it!" he cursed a string, disgusted with himself.

Kate stared at him nonplussed for a few seconds. She didn't understand what had come over him. Then, the truth dawned on her and she replied, "I'm on the pill, no worries there. I'm healthy…"

"So, am I, baby, don't worry about that. I was concerned only about a pregnancy. We've never talked about that and…"

Kate didn't reply. She just shrugged, and laid her head back on his shoulder. She was too exhausted to discuss anything anymore. She needed to sleep.

Ryan looked at the top of her head with indecision. He'd have liked to clear matters with her right then, but he gave up when he saw she wasn't ready for that conversation.

He kissed her hair, and gathered her in his arms, as tightly as possible, and said, "Rest for a few moments, sweetie. Later, we'll have to talk though."

She didn't answer back, as she'd already fallen asleep. The gruelling trip, the anticipation of spying on Ryan, the shock of having him in her vacation house, but most of all, the most intense lovemaking she'd ever experienced, had worn her out.

Ryan looked at her and grinned with pure male satisfaction. After a few seconds, though, he frowned. There were still far too many things that needed an answer. Yet, he had to wait for her to wake up so, he settled her better in his arms, and watched over her sleep.

CHAPTER TWELVE

When she woke up, Kate found herself alone in bed, covered with a silky sheet up to her shoulders. Her body felt strange and when she looked down she saw the traces left by Ryan's beard and his demanding fingers. She wore his prints on her hips and she was shocked to realize she'd allowed a man to mark her.

Kate got out of bed and scowled at her muscles' loud protest. She'd never been so thoroughly loved and used before and her body complained.

She went to the bathroom and looked at herself in the mirror. Her hair looked mussed up. Her swollen and bruised lips reminded her of

Ryan's clever mouth, and she tingled all over again.

She glanced back at the bed she'd shared with Ryan and shook her head. She couldn't believe it. She had jumped into the bed with a man after only a matter of minutes.

In the shower, she let the water soothe her aching body first. She kept thinking of Ryan and the surreal afternoon she'd spent with him. Kate believed he'd already left and sorrow filled her heart.

She'd been assured she would find strict necessities in the fridge and went to grab a bite. She was sad but the vigorous lovemaking had left her famished.

Ryan's presence in the kitchen shocked her. He was making an omelette and talking on the phone at the same time.

"So, Adam's the same not worse," he said and then, as if he'd felt she'd entered the room, he glanced at her.

Kate stopped right on the threshold. She didn't trust either him or herself if she came inside the kitchen.

Ryan smiled at her but his smile didn't reach his eyes, which shone with cold detachment. He continued his phone conversation, as if her arrival didn't matter.

Kate resented his attitude and for a moment, she thought of going back to bed. Her hesitation lasted one second, though. She changed her mind and advanced into the kitchen. That was her vacation house, after all, and she refused to let him take control over the house or her actions.

"Well, Nick, I'll see what's what and depending on what I find out, we might have to move again. Call you back," Ryan said and hung up.

He replaced the phone back into his pocket carefully. Then, he turned to the stove and flipped the omelette.

"So, you're finally up," he observed in a cold voice, without turning to her.

"Yes, I am," Kate answered softly. She didn't know how to react in front of this new Ryan.

She'd got used to the temperamental Ryan and the man in front of her eyes was completely different.

"I was very tired, of course, what, after that long flight and then the wait at the hotel..." she continued and stopped when she realized she was rambling.

"Oh, yeah, the wait at the hotel, indeed," he replied maliciously. "We need to talk about that now, don't we?"

Kate shrugged non-committedly and sat at the table. She knew he would bring the subject up sooner or later when she found him in the kitchen. She didn't care for it but doubted she had a choice.

"I see you're cooking," she said just to fill in the silence. "Is there something in there for me too?"

"Of course, there is," Ryan replied. "I started cooking when I heard you move around the bedroom. I hope you like Spanish omelette. For anything else, we need to make a trip to the shop," he joked lightly.

"I thought of doing that tomorrow. I hoped I would find enough food in there for tonight," Kate replied pointing to the fridge. "I didn't have time to check, you know…" she stopped slightly embarrassed when she remembered what sidetracked her.

Ryan came to the table, leaned over her and asked in a very serious voice, "Any regrets, Kate?"

Kate looked straight into his eyes. To her surprise, he showed concern. She hadn't expected it from him and she tried to probe his mind once more, only to feel him pushing her away. She noticed he frowned and looked at her inquiringly. Yet, he said nothing.

She didn't know how it was possible but he seemed to feel her probing his mind. She'd never encountered that before. It befuddled her.

At the beginning, when she discovered her gift, she'd been scared. Thankfully, her grandma was still alive and she explained she had a gift passed down on females in their family, every generation. She advised Kate not to speak of her talent to anyone. People would try to take advantage of her or consider her a freak or worse.

Kate grew up and learned that people had difficulty in accepting someone who was very different. They considered such individuals a threat. She kept her gift secret and not even her best friend, Ellie, knew about it.

Kate suddenly realized Ryan hadn't said anything and glanced at him. He still waited for her to answer to his question and his inquiring eyes pulled her back to the real world.

"No. No regrets, Ryan. Not now and not in the future. That's something I can promise you," Kate finally replied. "I wanted it and I really enjoyed it, as you very well know. So…," she shrugged.

"That's good, baby, because I'm afraid I can't stop now. One taste of you and I've been hooked. No matter why you're here and the consequences of your arrival, I still need to taste you again," he said and brushed a lock of her hair away from her face and behind her ear.

"What do you mean by '*the consequences of my arrival*'?" Kate inquired with a frown.

"All right, we'll do it right now then," Ryan said, nodding.

He stood up and went to take the omelette off the stove. He divided it onto two plates and set a plate and fork in front of her. He went back to the counter for the tomatoes and cucumbers he'd cut on a cutting board earlier. He put them on a plate which he laid in the middle of the table for both to share. With a wide wave, he invited her to eat.

Ryan spooned some eggs and chewed in silence for a few moments. Then, he asked her, "Who sent you here?"

Kate looked up at him confused, "I beg your pardon?"

"Now, don't play coy with me, baby. Who sent you here?" Ryan repeated in a steely voice and continued to eat, watching her intently.

"I don't get it," Kate said. "Who could send me, Ryan? If I remember correctly, I came here to leave the money for you, as we discussed," she explained in a confused voice.

She began to get angry with him. Her voice was strained and a note higher than usual.

"There must be more to that, Kate," the man replied, shaking his head. "No one makes such a long trip, and spends so much money, just to deliver some cash to someone." Ryan argued, always very calm and cold.

Kate didn't recognize that Ryan. She'd expected fury and recriminations because she hadn't told him she was coming to spy on him. Yet, she hadn't expected his cold assessment and dry tone. Both implied he'd already put their recent closeness behind and she didn't like it.

"Well," Kate said and shrugged, "I wanted to see you. I thought I'd be entitled to do so considering how much time I spent talking to you over the last few months and how much money you had requested from me," she argued. "Besides, I hadn't taken a vacation for a few years now, so I decided to combine the two. So, what's the problem?" she leaned forward and almost shouted the question in his face.

"The problem is I don't know if I can trust you," Ryan replied without emotion.

"That's grand," she shouted, losing her calm.

She threw the fork on the table and, suddenly, stood up in a fury. Her chair fell to the floor with a resonant bang.

"That's indeed grand of you, Ryan! *You* can't trust me!"

Kate threw her hands in the air and walked to the window. She took a few deep breaths to calm down.

Ryan didn't show any concern. He continued eating his food, although he still watched her. She was a riddle he needed to solve. Nothing more.

Kate turned back to him, her eyes sparking with thunder. He understood she was mad like a cat and waited for the blows to come.

"What about how much I can trust you? Huh? What about that, Ryan?"

Kate shouted and, with angry strides, she made her way back to the table. She was livid.

"You insinuated your way into my life. Day and night, night and day, you tried to find and push all my buttons. Then, you ask me for so much money that, of course, I had to trust you. How come? If I had asked you something like that, would you have trusted me, Ryan? Think about it. And now, you have the nerve to come here and say you can't trust me. That's just the cherry on top!" Kate shouted once more and tapped the table with her palm.

She went back to the window again and once more, tried to bring her breath back to normal. Watching the waves of the sea or the flow of a river had always helped her.

After a few moments, feeling calm enough, she turned to him and said, "You know what, Ryan? I want you out of here right now and I want you to stay away from me. Don't you ever dare to talk to me or call me. Do you hear me?" she finished her tirade in a banshee-like roar, forgetting about her earlier decision to remain calm.

Ryan coolly nodded and went on with his eating as if nothing had happened.

"Why the hell are you still here? I told you to leave," Kate bellowed to him again.

His indifferent attitude pushed her to lose her temper much more. She felt like slapping him over the head. Yet, the man didn't care she was spitting mad. He just continued eating his food.

Furious because of his dismissal, she went to him and punched him in his shoulder with her fist as hard as she could.

Ryan grinned at her, grasped her fist, opened it and kissed her palm.

His tongue swirled around her middle finger, and pulled it in his mouth. He began suckling on it and that made her gasp. All the while, he stared into her eyes.

"Wh... what are you doing?" Kate stuttered and tried to pull her hand away.

"Just kissing your hand, Kate," Ryan replied, and smooched her palm again. Afterwards, he allowed her to pull away.

"You're not in your right mind. That's it. Now, it's clear to me," Kate concluded and pulled away from him, afraid that his mind, which she couldn't read, was twisted.

Ryan laughed cheerfully, finished his food and took his plate to the sink. Then, he turned back to her and said seriously, "I'm in my right mind, baby, no worries. But, I'm in a bend and I was afraid you weren't who you said you were. That was all about," he assured her and his eyes looked very serious.

Kate watched him carefully and asked, "Who did you think I was?"

"Well, when you showed up at the hotel, I thought I'd misjudged you and you lured me into a trap," he confessed.

"But... but... you made love to me," she shouted incredulously.

Kate couldn't believe a man who thought a woman had tried to trap him would sleep with that woman in less than an hour.

"Yes, I did. I couldn't have stopped, Kate. I've been thinking of you for far too long... Your being here didn't help my willpower, you know," Ryan replied bitterly and laughed at himself.

Kate gazed at him for a few moments and then went back to the table. She picked up her fork and started eating, trying to pretend everything was normal. She ate in silence, her eyes always glued on him. Ryan's eyes stared at her, as if he'd tried to decide if his assessment was correct.

"I think," Kate spoke evenly this time "you'd better tell me the whole story, Ryan. I think I'd better know what's going on."

He didn't reply for a few moments. He considered her words first, and then, he returned to the table as well. He sat down and nodded.

"Yes, I think I should tell you the entire story. If nobody had sent you here and you just came to see me, I'll have to make sure you'll be okay. That means you need to know what's going on and from this moment on, you must listen to me and do exactly what I'm saying and when I say it," he said with conviction.

"In your dreams, Ryan," Kate replied haughtily. "I don't take orders from anyone and…"

"You'll take them from me," he interrupted her in an implacable voice. "Your life depends on that,

Kate, and you have to get that through your thick skull, do you hear me?"

"More drama?" she mocked him to mask her fear.

"Drama, you say," the man shouted at her. "You, stupid little girl! This is no drama. This is reality, do you understand, Kate? If I must hog-tie you, I'll do it, but you'll listen to me," he repeated and his fist hit the table top with a resonant bang.

Her eyes grew wider when she heard his menacing tone. Her hand shook and she put the fork back on the plate with a loud clank.

"I don't understand why you'd want to scare me like this," Kate said in a small voice.

Despite her early misfortune of losing her parents early in her life, she'd never been in a dangerous situation. Kate was a prudent woman and she'd always avoided the wrong crowd of people. She didn't believe in having an adventure just for the adventure's sake.

"I'm sorry, baby, but it's necessary. I wouldn't do it, but you're in danger now because of your association with me. I've never thought you'd be but then, I didn't know you'd come here yourself, fucking hell. So now, you'll do what you're told, am I clear?" Ryan's voice boomed at the end.

"No, not clear, at all," Kate replied belligerently this time, pushing her chin up in the air. "Either you explain what's what and why or I'll do as I please, and damn your male ego."

"My male ego!!!??" Ryan shouted with disbelief. He grabbed her arm and shook her. "You think my ego's the matter, Kate?"

"Manhandling me will not make me cooperate, Ryan," she replied as furious as him. His fingers dug into her arm and his tone didn't sit too well with her.

Ryan stopped shaking her and took a step back. He ran his fingers through his hair in exasperation. He turned away from her and made a few steps while trying to regain his control. He knew it wasn't the right moment to let his temper take the lead in their discussion.

He wasn't proud of the way he'd been handling things with her, especially because he knew he'd hurt her. Yet, he needed to make sure Kate understood what was at stake.

Unfortunately, Ryan had always lacked tactfulness and he needed that now, if he wanted to keep her safe. She was stubborn and wouldn't have listened to him if he'd threatened her.

He faced her again and said, "Have a seat, Kate. I'll tell you everything I can."

"And you'll also tell me how I came into your game, because I'm pretty sure I was just a pawn," she replied spitefully.

He just looked up at her and didn't say anything. After a few moments, he confessed, "Yes, you were… In a way… In the beginning."

Kate didn't have a reply for that, but her eyes threw arrows in his direction. They also revealed her deep hurt. After a couple of seconds, she also sat down, facing him, and waited for him to continue.

"I'll have to start with the beginning, I think, so you can understand my reasons and everything I've done," Ryan said, running his hand through his hair, mussing it up.

Kate nodded and waived her hand, inviting him to continue.

"About half a year ago, one of my best friends, Adam, disappeared here, in Malaysia. In the past, we were a team, a three-man team… We would take impossible missions or missions the government didn't want to touch… They called us when they needed a team of experts to take care of certain… things, let's say. We went together everywhere around the globe, in covert missions, fighting our way in and out of compounds no one could penetrate."

Kate's wide eyes proved her bewilderment. The story captivated her.

A brief smile appeared on his lips and he said, "It was a thrilling period, baby, I admit, but beside the fact we found out what we were made of and of course, made a lot of money in the process, it wasn't a very happy one. Every single day, we had to put our lives on the line and somewhere near the end of our time as a team, things got somehow blurry… We stopped believing in what we were doing… When something like that happens to people like us, it means we lost our focus and could go down at any moment," Ryan said bitterly and his smile turned rueful.

He stopped for a few moments and looked out of the window. In the distance, the sea was glimmering in the sunset, reddish light all over it. It reminded him of Kate's hair and he turned back to her. She waited silently for him to continue.

He inhaled deeply and went on. "Well, the three of us banked the money we made and went our own ways. I know Nick bought a ranch and breeds horses. Adam invested here and there and put the basis of a generous pension plan, and I simply invested half of the money and kept the other half in banks... By now, we could talk about a few millions. Over ten years of very special ops brought us quite a lot of capital...." Ryan paused again and looked away, trying to recollect his thoughts. "Anyway, about half a year ago, the guy who used to direct our missions contacted us for another op. He came to me first... I was the leader and the strategist of the team... Anyway, I flatly turned him down... Don't get me wrong, Kate... I like Mark, or I used to, before all of this happened, but I'd had enough... I thought about starting a business, find me a girl...," Ryan said and grinned at her. "You know, start a family... I'm already thirty-seven, and I'm not getting any younger... I'd like to have children while I can still play football and run around..."

Kate looked at him, checked him up and down, and asked, "Are you really thirty-seven?"

"Actually, I'll be, next month on the 24th," he replied with a smug smile on his lips. He felt proud she found him looking younger.

"Nice, you don't show it. I thought you'd be somewhere near thirty but not over," Kate said giving him another all over.

"Nice to hear it, Kate, but the truth is that I am thirty-seven... That's a fact... I do need to get on with my life... I had about a year after the last mission and I did look around but .... I don't know, women don't seem to be what I hoped for… I had women come onto me when I was working for Mark, and I'd been hoping to find something different… As my luck was… not a chance. It seems I always attract the wrong kind… I started thinking of Internet dating, although I didn't hold too much hope with that either… Anyway, I should get on with the story that brought us both here."

"That would be good," Kate replied and nodded. "I think I have an idea, but I prefer to hear it from you, not to guess."

"Well, as I said, I refused Mark. I told him I was done with all that stuff and he should find someone else. Afterwards, I heard he contacted Nick and Adam, my other two pals, and Nick refused him as well… Adam accepted the mission, though, especially because he was told that the mission was particularly cut for only one person. It wasn't like he had to enter somewhere by force or something like that. He had only to infiltrate a group and report back to Mark. Mark told him not to say a thing to anyone, including to Nick or myself… Secrecy, you know… That son of a bitch didn't even tell Adam we two had already refused the mission," Ryan growled and jumped out of his chair, furious again.

He marched to the window where he stopped. He ran his fingers through his hair one more time.

Kate waited for him to chill out. Her eyes followed his movements through the kitchen. She understood he was feeling powerless. It was obvious he was the type of man who liked control over every situation.

Silence stretched out for a few minutes. Kate watched him flexing his fists. His shoulders tensed. She regretted she couldn't see his face, and especially, his eyes.

Finally, Ryan turned around and looked at her. "In a nutshell, Adam left alone and got into a very bad situation. Someone betrayed him, although we're not sure yet whether the trap was a set up for all of us. When Adam called for our help, and we came, we were expected. We managed to clear Adam out, but he got badly hurt during the fight... We didn't dare to reach out to anyone... I tried taking money out of one of my credit cards and in a matter of a few minutes, people crawled all over the place looking for us... I tried to contact Mark, but I couldn't get through to him... After a thorough analysis, we decided against trying to use our funds or to reach out to someone related to any of us... Somebody is clearly looking for us... Anyway, Nick and I have no one in the world. We couldn't turn to Adam's brother, either."

Ryan stopped, put up his hand to indicate that he would like her to sit where she was, and went to the living-room to check the bar. Sure enough, he found a bottle of scotch and came back triumphantly with it. "We have something to drink. Let's find glasses," he said with a false cheer.

After he left the bottle on the table, he went to the cupboard to look for two glasses.

Kate knew he was just acting right then. He wanted to hide his insecurity and anger but he wasn't very good at that. She also understood he needed to release some of his pent-up fury.

Ryan brought the glasses at the table and poured generous portions of whiskey.

"I don't really drink," Kate said softly.

He only shrugged and, putting one of the glasses in front of her, he said, "Once won't kill you."

"I hadn't thought it would," she murmured and took the glass in her hand. "What are we drinking for?"

Ryan thought for a moment and replied, "Why not for new

beginnings? We've had a new beginning today, haven't we?" he asked winking at her.

"Why not?" Kate murmured again and sipped from her glass.

Ryan watched her drink and then swallowed a mouthful and hissed. "Strong stuff," he said and took the bottle in his hand to check the label again. "Good stuff," he repeated, and replaced the bottle down on the table. He took another mouthful from his glass.

Kate sipped daintily a couple of times and then, her patience at an end, she asked, "Will you continue with the story?"

"Story? Yeah, you could say story, I suppose. It doesn't seem real," Ryan agreed after considering her words for a few seconds.

"I didn't mean it like that..." Kate started to say but he interrupted her with a gesture.

"I didn't say that, baby. I was simply making fun of myself... You know, after over a decade of covert operations, with a ratio of over eighty-five percent success, I found myself here, in a place resembling paradise but which turned out to be a living hell for all of us... We needed help for Adam, medical help. Good medical help, and the kind that doesn't talk but does a good job... Well, that kind of help is expensive. Of course, most of the cash Nick and I came with was gone in less than a week... We had to find a place to lay low, and after the experience with the credit card advance, we had to find another place... Of course, we didn't dare to withdraw money from any of our cards afterwards. Luckily, I still had an untraceable card with me... It held only a few thousand dollars and we knew the money wouldn't last...," Ryan explained with wide gestures and paused.

He drank some more whiskey to gain courage. He knew the hard part was just coming about.

"That's the card I used to open the account on the dating site, by the way," he said glancing at her for a second. "Initially, we thought of renting a yacht with that money, but I was positive they would keep an eye on men leasing yachts and we couldn't pick up a woman and ask her do that for us... Not in a very short period of time. We needed someone to trust and trust needs time to build...," he said and shrugged.

Kate wanted to touch and comfort him. Ryan seemed very deep in his memories, though, and she didn't move. She waited for him to continue.

After another sip of his drink, Ryan continued, "Anyway, we knew we had to find a solution... We needed a solution that didn't involve reaching out to someone who could be traced to us... So, at first, as a joke, just to have a bit of laugh on my expense, the guys mentioned I was thinking of finding the woman I wanted on the Internet and asked why I shouldn't do just that… After I'd found one I liked, I should try to ask her for help, they said… I would have killed two birds with one stone… I'd get the money to get out of here, money we'd return afterwards, of course, because we're not leeches, and I'd also get the girl."

Ryan stood up and went to turn the light on. Kate had been so drawn into his story that she hadn't realized the room was dark. The light of the day was slowly waning.

She blinked a few times and Ryan burst into laughter, "You look like a little owl blinking like that."

"Thank you very much for the comparison," Kate replied not too delighted to have been compared to an owl.

"I like owls, they're cute," Ryan shrugged and defended his choice of words. "You're cute too."

"You've already got the girl, Ryan, so you can turn down the charm," Kate said flatly.

"You think it was just charm, Kate? Do you really think I lied to you and tried to charm you so you'd do what I wanted?" Ryan replied back heatedly.

Kate didn't answer and he got upset.

"You know, if I had merely tried to charm a woman, it wouldn't have taken me so many months. I'd have done it sooner," he replied in a mean voice pointing to her.

"You're saying I'm easy?" she replied quarrelsome.

"No, Kate, I didn't say that. Quite the opposite. I'm saying if I'd only wanted to charm my way into a woman's heart to get the money, I'd have chosen an easy one. I wouldn't have needed four months to gather my courage to ask for the fucking money!" Ryan bellowed, even though he'd begun his tirade in a very calm voice.

He got closer to her and, looking straight into her eyes, asked, "Do you know how difficult these months were, Kate? There were times at the beginning when we didn't even know whether Adam would live or die. We had to make rations so we'd have food for more time. I was literally going crazy not knowing if the mission had just gone wrong or it was a trap for all of us. I strongly believe, though, it was a trap for all of us. Adam said he thought he'd been targeted from the beginning and his cover hadn't lasted twelve hours... You know, Kate, if you hadn't mattered to me, I'd have moved on, found someone else I could have convinced to give me the money sooner. It wasn't only for me, it was for them as well, and I've always been these men's leader, and I have a duty to them, you understand? It wasn't like we intended not to pay you back."

She nodded but kept silent.

"I chose to wait, to know you better, to let you know me… Well, as much as I could let you know… I felt drawn to you from the first moment I saw that picture you put on that site… I thought a woman who had the courage to put such a picture on a dating site was a very smart woman. I analyzed it carefully. I saw it was a passport photo. I was sure you'd be a beauty. What I wanted though wasn't only beauty but also brains. I've always wanted a woman I could talk to not a doll looking good on my arm. Candy arms I can find very easy. I've never had problems with that… So, I stuck with you and even if the guys pushed me either to open the conversation about the money with you or to find someone else, I didn't give up."

"That's… interesting, I'd say." Kate replied hesitantly. Ryan narrowed his eyes and prompted her to say in a rush, "What now?"

"No one followed you here, I made sure of that. Yet, I'm afraid to leave you alone. If anyone has made the connection between the money you brought here and the reason you came, you're in danger and I'll have to keep an eye on you. The problem is I'll have to stick with the guys as well."

"Interesting conundrum, then," Kate replied.

"Not really," Ryan said and shook his head. "I can't take you to our nest. That isn't for you, clearly. We only have a dirty little room. But I can bring the guys here, if you don't mind. We'd lay low for a few days to see if anyone is onto you, and if not, you can rent a small yacht without a crew… I don't know, act like an eccentric woman with a lot of knowledge in boating… We could get out of Malaysia in a few days, and reach Singapore. It's only 197 nautical miles in between. I have a guy there… No one knows about him, I'm damn sure about that… I know he could get papers for the guys and me to fly to Montreal for instance. So, what do you think?"

"Let's say I agree with all that, although for instance I could rent the yacht and you three could sail to Singapore without me," Kate replied.

"If that's what you want, fine with me. It's your choice. But, before I leave, I'll have to make sure first you're already on a plane to Montreal. I wouldn't agree to leave you here, no matter what. Even if I had to drag you to the airport kicking and screaming, I'll do it," Ryan replied sternly.

"Yeah, that would look good, for sure," Kate replied drily. "You'd be arrested before you'd set foot into the airport, Ryan." She noticed he wanted to interject, and she put up her hand to stop him. "All right, we'll see. For the moment, yes, I agree with you. You should bring your guys here. There are two bedrooms, I understand, plus the sofa in the living room. I could take the sofa...," Kate started to arrange things but Ryan cut her arrangements short.

"I don't think we'd both fit on that sofa, Kate, and after this afternoon, I hope you don't think I'd let you sleep away from me, sweetie, do you?" Ryan inquired and stared her down with his intense eyes.

Kate blushed but didn't answer. Ryan grinned at her with satisfaction and continued, "Adam should take the other bedroom and Nick will be just fine on the sofa. He's slept on worse than that. You'll be sleeping in my arms, in the bedroom we shared this afternoon, all right?"

She nodded but kept silent.

"I like this streak of yours, Kate. For a businesswoman, you have quite an old-fashioned streak, and I do love it. Don't you ever change, baby," he leaned and whispered close to her ear.

He brushed his fingers on her cheek and pushed a rebellious lock of hair behind her ear.

Then, he tilted his head over her and kissed her, softly at the beginning and then more forcefully. He parted her lips and sank his teeth into her lower one. He stroked her mouth with his tongue at leisure and made love to her mouth for a few moments. It seemed like an eternity to her.

After he was satisfied, Ryan drew back and whispered again, "I'd enjoy having you in my bed all the time, to do whatever I want, when I want."

"What?" she cried out. Her eyes were wide and reflected her shock. "Define that *whatever you want*, Ryan."

The man merely laughed and patted her cheek tenderly, "Don't worry, Kate, I'm not into kinky stuff," he said and then paused. That made her eyebrows shut up. "All right, not very kinky stuff, maybe just a little kinky stuff..." She stared at him speechless. He needed to reassure her some more, "I'll never do something you wouldn't want, baby, and that's a promise."

Kate didn't say a thing. She still stared at him. Ryan reached out and nudged her head to nod and said, "I hear you, Ryan, and I'm not worried."

His childish behavior reassured Kate and she laughed, "All right, all right, I hear you."

He pulled her up and fastened his hands behind her, "What are you saying about going back to bed, baby?"

Kate looked at him and touched his lips with her fingers, then with her mouth. She drew back and asked him, "But shouldn't you take care of your friends first?"

"Damn, I've already forgot about them. I can't even wrap my head around being so …. Yes, you're right, I must call the guys and ask them to move here," Ryan said and took his phone out of his pocket to make the call.

CHAPTER THIRTEEN

"We'll stop here," Ryan turned to Kate after he stopped the car. "Nick will bring Adam out here, Kate. That means I'll leave you with them for a few minutes, so I could go and pick up the rest of our stuff. When I rented this room, I told them I was a painter and I don't want to raise any suspicions by leaving any kind of stuff inside that room. No self-respected artist would do such a thing," Ryan explained to her.

"But wouldn't your leaving in the dead of the night raise suspicions?" Kate asked him.

Ryan shrugged and explained, "I paid in cash and in advance for a month. I still have two more weeks paid. They'll assume I moved to another location. I already told the guy who rented the room to me that I didn't know how long I'd stay but I wanted the room available to me for another month. No, he won't get any ideas, Kate. He got his money and he didn't seem interested in more than that. Of course, he's never seen the guys and I always took care to park my car somewhere else. This type of car would have raised suspicions," Ryan replied and when he saw she wanted to ask something else, he put up his hand to stop her.

Kate noticed he glanced at the rear-view mirror and saw something. She swallowed her question.

"Stay here," Ryan said and got out of the car.

Kate looked after him. He walked in the direction of two men, coming slowly down the street. When he reached them, they exchanged a few words and he shouldered the man who appeared unsteady on his feet. Ryan with the help of the other man brought their wounded friend to the car.

"Kate, this is Adam and this is Nick," he introduced them to Kate when he reached the car. "Guys, this is Kate."

Kate waved and smiled at them. Both men were tall, almost as tall as Ryan, and both were sturdy. Adam, the hurt one, was almost as dark as Ryan, but Nick was dark blond. All three shared the same steely shine in their eyes. They were cut from the same cloth.

Adam was hurt and very pale, but Nick was the one who drew her eyes. The man was built like a bear. A long scar ran on his left cheek and would have made anyone step back in a confrontation with him.

"So, you're the sweet Kate," Adam said with a noticeable Southern accent and his eyes twinkled despite his pain, which had painted lines on his face.

"You're lucky you're hurt or I'd flatten you," Ryan growled at him. "Get into the car and stop making nice with my girl," he ordered curtly.

Kate thought Ryan was joking but the frown on his face belied her assumption. The truth dawned on her. Ryan was a jealous man. Kate questioned her wisdom about building a relationship with him. Jealous types were dangerous and she'd learned to avoid them.

Ryan helped Adam get into the car, ignoring Adam's grunts. He knew Adam would be embarrassed if people noticed his weakness.

"Nick will stay right here, next to the driver's side until I come back," Ryan said to Kate in an authoritative voice that didn't brooch any comment. "I want you protected at all times and if anything happens, Nick will drive you away."

"Ryan...," Kate started to say but Ryan interrupted her impatiently.

"I know, sweetie, but believe me, it's for the best, all right? Anyway, I'll be back soon and let's hope that everything goes smoothly."

With those parting words, Ryan turned around and vanished into the darkness. She looked after him with scared eyes.

"He'll be back," Nick told her in a gruff voice. He'd noticed she was worried and wanted to make her feel at ease. "He always comes back," he added.

"How do you know?" Kate asked him. His detached assessment hadn't appeased her worries.

Nick merely shrugged and then said, "I just know."

Kate didn't say anything. She decided to seize her chance to learn the truth and she focused first on Adam, determined to read his thoughts. It wasn't too difficult. She didn't feel he resisted like Ryan. She cheered happily in her mind and focused on unlocking Adam's secrets.

She was about to cheer herself again when she realized Ryan had told her the truth, but Adam put a hand to his forehead and grunted.

Kate got scared. Adam felt her intrusion and that wasn't good at all. The man looked up at her and frowned. She tried her best smile but, apparently, her best smile didn't work.

"What the hell is going on?" Adam snapped at her and his outburst attracted Nick's attention.

"What, Adam? What happened?" he asked.

"Something's damn wrong here, bro, believe me. I felt something like tentacles in my mind. Now, I have a terrible headache. She was staring at me at the time so…," Adam said, and left Nick to fill in the blanks.

Both men turned accusingly to her. Their terrible scowls made her cringe.

Kate never thought something like that would happen to her. First, she couldn't read Ryan's thoughts, and now that. She hadn't expected any problems with Adam.

"She's been doing something to me, Nick," Adam bellowed. "I don't know what but she has," he pointed an accusing finger to Kate.

Nick leaned over her and Kate retreated to the car door. His stance frightened her and her heart beat faster.

"What's going on here?" Ryan's voice penetrated her fear and brought a glimmer of hope. "Nick, why the hell are you threatening Kate?" Ryan barked. His expression didn't promise anything good to his mates.

"She's been doing something to me, Ryan," Adam repeated stubbornly. "I know she has. I haven't lost my mind yet. I saw her staring at me and then I felt something pushing into my head and now I have a headache, man," Adam explained upset and confused at the same time. He rubbed his temples to soothe the pain.

Ryan frowned and turned to Kate. He stared at her insistently and waited for her to say something in her defense. Adam's words seemed a bit out there, but Ryan didn't know Adam to be fanciful.

"I haven't done anything, Ryan," Kate said but noticed no one believed her. "I mean I haven't tried to hurt him or anything," she continued and their scowls turned uglier. Things didn't look good for her.

"Then what happened, Kate?" Ryan insisted. "Why is Adam having a headache and why does he feel you're responsible?"

"I don't know," Kate said and waved her hand. "I really don't know, Ryan," she repeated more forcefully when Ryan glared. She thought better and decided to tell him the truth. "Okay, Ryan, I'll tell you something but you'll think I'm a freak," Kate said wretchedly and then, fell silent for a few seconds.

"I'm waiting, Kate. Talk, now," he barked and his voice made her wince. The man was indeed a born leader.

Kate gathered her courage and said softly, barely audible at all, "I can read minds. I couldn't read yours, Ryan, which was a first, but I could read Adam's. Still, no one felt my probing before and no one had a headache afterwards, I promise."

The three men watched her in silence. Her revelation stunned them. They didn't reply and Kate felt dejected.

Then, Nick grumbled, "Well, anything's possible, guys. Do you remember that guy who worked for CIA? The one we had to free from that compound in South America? With those ugly glasses?"

Adam nodded and agreed with him, "Yeah, everything's possible."

Ryan remained skeptical for a few more moments. Then, he remembered that not far before he'd felt like someone was probing into his mind and frowned. "And you say you couldn't read my mind?" he asked Kate.

Kate shook her head. She admitted she'd tried several times, while they were talking over the phone and even when they met face to face but she hadn't been successful.

"You want to say that you can read someone's mind over the phone?" Adam looked at her with doubting eyes.

He believed there were people with certain abilities but he thought there was a limit to what they could do. Reading someone's mind over the phone didn't seem possible.

"Normally, yes," she replied and shrugged as if it had been a common occurrence. "For instance, one of the guys from the dating site was actually a serial killer and I could read his thoughts and delivered him to the police. Anonymously, of course. I don't need that hassle," she explained.

"That's interesting," Nick said pensively. "You know what guys? When we get to Singapore, we should call Mark. She can listen into the call to see what she can read, huh?" he told his friends, his regularly somber face lit with a special light.

Ryan nodded absently. He was still looking intently at Kate. "So, you can't read my mind." he repeated.

"God, man, you have an obsession," Adam remarked disgustedly. "We're talking about serious things here, Ryan. Can you wrap your mind onto something else but your love affair?" he asked sardonically.

"This is bloody serious for me, Adam, so stay out of it," Ryan bit out and turned to her again, "Kate!"

"No, Ryan, I can't read your mind," she finally replied exasperated. "I wouldn't have reacted the way I did when you asked me for the money if I could," she continued with biting irony.

Ryan contemplated her for a few more seconds and nodded satisfied with her answer. Kate made a good point and he was content she wasn't able to read his mind. One question remained though. He didn't understand why she couldn't read his mind but could read Adam's, so he asked her.

Kate shrugged and replied, "I don't know why, Ryan. It's the first time something like that has happened to me. Such abilities don't come with a manual, you know," she ended in a sardonic voice to cover the truth.

She thought she'd found an explanation. Her inability to read him was due to her emotional connection to him. Yet, she didn't want to tell him that.

"All right, then," he accepted. He knew that he couldn't get an answer if there wasn't any. "Pile up, Nick, and let's go," Ryan said and went to the back of the car. He threw everything he was carrying in the trunk and returned.

He hesitated for a moment, his hand on the ignition key, and then, he turned to Kate and asked again, "You really can't read my mind?"

"No, I told you, I can't!" she replied exasperated.

She threw her arms in the air and rolled her eyes. Her patience was wearing thin and she didn't understand why he persisted to ask the same question over and over again.

"That's good, baby, really good," Ryan said, a wide smile on his lips. He leaned over and kissed her lips.

His behavior prompted Adam to snicker and Nick to scowl, yet Ryan didn't care about what any of them thought or did. He started the car and drove back to Kate's house on the beach.

***

"Wow," Adam said when he saw the house and especially, the back of the house. "This is really cool, man! We have a pool and the sea is close. Look at here, the beach is private," he noticed enthusiastically and turned to Kate. He winked at her and said, "You know how to live in style, Kate."

Kate shook her head but beamed at him and replied, laughing, "Not really, Adam. You see, I haven't had a vacation for a long time, so I thought: why not? If I decided to go

211

to Malaysia, why wouldn't I take a memorable vacation? That's why the house is the way it is," she explained.

"Good for you," Adam approved and gave her the high five. Rubbing his hands, he said, "And good for us. Guys, do you mind if I remain here on the deck for a while? I've been cooped up in that stinky little room for a few weeks and I'd really enjoy some fresh air."

"Not a problem, Adam," Ryan replied. "Take your time. I must go and buy some food from somewhere because what we had back there is not enough. All of Kate's reserves are depleted," he explained to his friends and picked up his car keys to leave.

Nick looked at Kate dumbfounded. He shook his head, and then turned after Ryan and asked, "Really? How much could she eat?"

Ryan burst into laughter at the scowl on Kate's lips and replied to Nick, "She didn't have too much to begin with, Nick, and I helped, of course."

"Ah, that explains it," Adam concluded with a grin of his, and lounged on a chaise-long, crossed his arms on his chest and breathed deeply. "God, how I missed this. This is just paradise, guys."

He closed his eyes and settled down, intent on listening to the murmur of the waves and breathing in the salty smell of the sea. In a few moments, Adam dozed off.

Kate, Nick and Ryan looked at him for a few seconds, then, Ryan took Kate's hand in his and pulled her inside the house. Nick followed them but began to feel like the proverbial third wheel when Ryan brushed his lips over Kate's hand.

"Anything to drink here?" Nick asked, looking around to cover his insecurity and embarrassment.

Kate jumped at his voice. She'd forgotten about Nick's presence and Ryan smiled with satisfaction. He knew he was the cause for her being so absent-minded.

"There's some whiskey there, Nick. Kate will show you, won't you Kate?" he turned to her and winked. "It's the good stuff, Nick. Powerful stuff, though, so take care. Anyway, I'll buy some beer if I find some," Ryan said.

"Maybe you can find some soft drinks as well?" Kate asked him. "I'm really not too fond of whiskey or beer," she explained.

"I'll see what I can do," Ryan replied on his way to the door and left, leaving them alone.

Kate remained standing, looking after him pensively. Nick interrupted her thoughts, "So, where's that whiskey, Kate? Adam could use a glass as well...," he said and then added, "If he wakes up, that is."

Kate turned to the kitchen and threw over her shoulder, "Follow me, big guy. I'll prepare the drinks for both of you."

Nick frowned behind her. He didn't understand her but then, he hadn't had too much to do with that type of woman. He'd avoided the wholesome women all his life. He'd considered they didn't worth the trouble, as he hadn't planned to get married and go the whole nine yards. He was satisfied with some fun now and then. His affairs didn't have a long-life span.

He shook his head and followed Kate into the kitchen. She took two glasses out of the cupboard.

"The bottle is there," Kate showed him. "Here's the glasses, Nick. I suppose you'd better pour yourself. You know how much you want to drink, I think. Anyway, better than I do."

Nick took the glasses from her and poured a drink for Adam and a taller one for him. He was about to leave when he turned and told her over the shoulder, "Thanks, Kate.

And don't you dare read my mind," he stared her down.

Kate blushed violently at his parting words. She was trying to do just that and his words made her feel guilty.

Nick stared at her with narrowed eyes and left. Kate decided against going out to join the two men on the deck. Instead, she went to the bedroom, took a shower and went to bed.

***

She'd already fallen asleep when Ryan's strong arms stole around her. Her head fell on his chest. It felt good. She felt protected. Contentedly, she sighed and went back to sleep.

CHAPTER FOURTEEN

"It's been three days already, guys," Adam told them with a frown. "Look, I'm much better. No one's come after us so far, so we're good. I think it's time to go," he continued. "I want to get out of this God forsaken country and the sooner, the better. I've had enough."

He was sick of lying around all the time without anything to do. He needed a change but, most of all, he needed to be on the other side of the ocean. He wanted to go home.

Nick glanced at Ryan to see what he thought about Adam's sudden outburst because he, for one, was worried. He understood Adam's brush with death and the following several weeks, during which Adam had been bedridden, had had a serious impact on their friend.

To Nick's dismay, Ryan didn't show any signs he was aware of what was going on with Adam. He seemed busy watching Kate swimming in the pool. She was skimpily-clad in a blue swimming suit and Ryan's eyes couldn't leave her alone.

When Nick noticed Ryan's chief concern, he rolled his eyes annoyed. He growled, "Come on, man! Snap out of it for now. You've had her for four days already. Not even you can be so smitten," he remarked with disdain.

"What the fucking hell are you talking about?" Ryan turned to Nick furiously, his eyes narrowed to slits. "She's not the entertainment here, Nick," he barked at his friend.

Nick took a step back and put his hands up to show Ryan he didn't mean anything demeaning about Kate.

"Don't you get it?" Ryan continued. "She's the one for me, and you have to respect that, got it?" he punctuated his affirmation by nudging Nick in his chest with his finger.

"How hard the mighty fall," Adam remarked sotto voce and shook his head.

Yet, his words reached Ryan's ears and he turned to him irately, "I don't care what any of you two bulkheads think about me, Adam. It's my business not yours," he concluded and glanced at Kate again. "Anyway, I can't wait to see what you'll do once you found a woman who means the world to you! What you'd do then…"

"That's not me," Adam interrupted him, and shook his head for good measure. "Forget it, Ryan. I'll never lose my mind over any chick. Period. It's not worth it."

Nick nodded in complete agreement.

"She's not a chick, dumbass. That's what neither of you can get through your thick skulls," Ryan replied. He stood up and flexed his fists and that prompted Adam to frown at his fighting stance.

"Oh, oh, oh, guys," Nick tried to calm them down. "No harm done, Ryan. It was just stupid talking, man," he observed and stood up. Nick went to Ryan and put a hand on his shoulder in a friendly manner. "Come on, Ryan, don't forget Adam is still not one hundred percent and it wouldn't be fair…"

"Let him come," Adam snapped and stood up, although his movements were not as fluid as his friends'. He panted in frustration. "I can take him," he specified and copied Ryan's stance.

"Really?" Ryan replied and shoved Adam. That made him fall back in his seat like a puppet. "You can take me, huh," he said derisively. "See? I can wrestle you even with one arm tied behind my back. You've got no chance, man, wake up," he told Adam.

"Guys, guys, guys, this is not the time to do that. Just chill out," Nick intervened, taking a position between them.

"What's going on?" Kate inquired alarmed and all three turned to her guiltily.

They were shocked to see her there. They'd been so caught in their squabble that they hadn't heard her come out of the pool and step on the deck.

She waited for them to answer but no one volunteered an explanation. Adam and Nick looked anywhere else but her and not just out of remorse. They didn't want to further aggravate Ryan's possessiveness.

Their friend was beyond smitten and even though they'd noticed Kate looked good and was funny, they didn't share his attraction and couldn't understand his recent behavior.

"Ryan, I asked you what was going on," she repeated stubbornly and stared Ryan down.

Kate felt undercurrents and was afraid the men had had a fallen out. She would have tried to read Adam and Nick's minds but she didn't want to be exposed doing it once more.

"Nothing, Kate, don't worry," Ryan finally replied and waved his hand. "We were just fooling around... We didn't have anything better to do and we got restless, that's all," he explained to her.

Adam glanced at her first and then at Ryan, and shook his head. He gave up understanding what was going on between the two of them.

"Drop it, man," Nick warned him in a whisper and touched his shoulder "Let's talk about leaving, Ryan. I think it's time, even past time," he observed.

"Oh, that's what bothers you," Kate surmised and her face lit up. She was relieved there wasn't any other reason of contention between them.

No one tried to set her straight.

"I was wondering about leaving as well," Kate said. "I'm a bit antsy and I can't wait to see the second part of the plan unfold," she confessed and glanced from one man to the other.

"Well, I've done some research these day and come out with a company that rents good yachts at reasonable prices," Ryan started explaining and waved the others to sit down. "At about seven thousand, eight thousand tops, we could rent a forty-foot monohull with three cabins, two heads and all the necessary equipment. More important, I think, it's sturdy enough to take us to Singapore," Ryan continued. "Of course, the price is only for the yacht. We'll have to pay separately for fuel and food, and I understand they can provide that too... It would cost a little more, about nine hundred for the fuel at least," he said pensively. "I don't think it would be a good idea to let them know we'd stop in Singapore so we'll have to buy a little more fuel and food... The food will be about five hundred...," he specified and looked at them. He wanted to see what they thought about the costs.

Adam and Nick didn't move a muscle. They had that immobile façade they would show whenever they plotted a mission.

Ryan hadn't expected any kind of serious opposition from them and indeed, at his inquiring expression, they nodded slightly. Having their answer, Ryan turned to Kate to see what she had to say. She merely shrugged. Anyway, she didn't know anything about all that.

Having his answer, Ryan continued, "So we're looking at a total of nine thousand fifty tops," he concluded and again waited for their reactions.

"Okay, that works, I think," Kate replied pensively. "I can put the charge on my credit card, it won't be a problem. There's one thing I'll have to do though," she said. "I'll have to let my bank know beforehand, so they don't decline the payment. Once the bank is warned about the amount I need to pay, I don't see any issues coming from that quarter," Kate assured them.

"You'll get your money back, Kate, don't worry," Nick told her morosely. "We don't take money from people and run away," he assured her. He didn't seem comfortable with taking her money and his face darkened.

"I haven't even thought about that, Nick," Kate waived his concerns away. "I'm not worried about that, period. I was just saying I have to let the bank know so the payment would clear, nothing else."

"I understand that," Nick replied stubbornly. "I've only wanted to make sure you also understand you'll get the money back from us as soon as we're on the other side of the ocean."

"Oh, I'm tired of this money thing, honestly. Why does money always have to come first?" Kate snapped. "Could we talk about something more important, like how we'd plan this? I'm pretty sure it takes a little more than my booking the boat on the Internet," she pointed out.

Nick scowled at her but dropped the subject. He turned to Ryan and waited for his input as he was the strategist in the group and they always counted on his ideas.

"First, Kate must learn a few things about yachting," he explained and glanced at her. "You have to, Kate. You will go and sign the papers for the leasing. You will also have to check the yacht. The three of us have to avoid being seen as much as possible," Ryan said.

Adam and Nick nodded. They knew they shouldn't be seen. The plan could succeed only if no one was the wiser about their whereabouts. Kate nodded as well, although she wasn't very confident she could learn everything about yachting, even in theory only, in a very short time. Then, they waited for Ryan to continue.

"Kate, I think you should tell those people you want to surprise your boyfriend with a cruise for his birthday," he addressed Kate directly and took her hand in his. "Of course, you'll let them know you have basic training and understanding in sailing, but make sure to specify your boyfriend will be the one who's going to man the yacht... I think that would be helpful. They shouldn't get suspicious if, for instance, you can't answer some of their questions or you come through as being too green.

No one of us can ask more from you, Kate," he said and glanced at his friends who approved his statement.

Kate nodded and looked at the other two guys as well. They put their thumbs up to let her know they were confident she could do her part.

Ryan continued, "As we need three cabins, it would be also a good idea if you let it slip you've invited two more couples to join you two for seven days of fun... I don't know," he shrugged, "Just chat like women usually do. Try to make them think you're worry free, and you're thinking only of having fun and being with friends for a few days...Does that work for you?" he asked her.

"Yes, why not? I'm a fast learner so I don't think I'd tip my hand too easy. They won't even guess I don't have any experience with yachting or whatever. I was on a boat before but I've never manned one, of course..." Kate pondered upon Ryan's words a few moments more, and then she said, biting her bottom lip, "No worries about the chatting up. I will imitate Ellie's style of speaking. That girl can't keep a secret if her life depended on that. Everybody knows what's going on in her life and what she's thinking," she explained.

"Ellie?" Adam asked.

"Ah, my best friend," Kate answered when she remembered they didn't know Ellie.

"Focus here, people," Ryan ordered and tapped the table top. "You can gossip later."

His words made both Kate and Adam scowl at him but he didn't care.

"Good. Then, let's go inside, Kate, so you can make the reservation online. At least, we could have that out of the way, and then we'll take it from there, all right?" he asked and glanced at each one of them to see if they agreed. Once he was satisfied they approved, he continued, "I've made the calculations and if we sail at five knots, not more, even if we stop twice for complete rest, it shouldn't take us more than let's say three days, to be generous with time... And, Kate, again, it is not a boat, it's a yacht. Don't you tell the guys from the renting office something like that."

Kate nodded although she didn't enjoy his correction. Boat, yacht, the same thing. Then, she went inside.

Ryan didn't follow immediately. He remained seated and enjoyed the sight of her backside for a few more moments.

"Snap out of it, man. It's already getting beyond embarrassing. We got it. You're crazy about her. But let's go! You'll have enough time for that later," Nick grumbled. "It isn't like you haven't seen it before or that this is the last time you'll ever see it," he pointed out.

Ryan glowered at him but didn't reply. He didn't want to fuel a new discussion. Besides, bruised in his male ego, he wondered if he did come through like being completely wiped out.

He followed Kate into the house. When he reached the bedroom, she was already in the shower and the water was running. After a few seconds, he took off his clothes with impatient gestures and opened the shower door.

"Mind if I join you?" he asked her politely. He intended to get in the shower with her anyway but thought he should ask at least.

Kate wiped the water off her face, looked up at him and smiled. "Why not? I'd love to," she replied and Ryan grinned at her.

He joined her in the shower stall and closed the door behind him. He pulled her to him forcefully. Kate had already learned he liked it that way, and she didn't dislike it either.

Ryan kissed her soundly, feasting on her mouth like a starved man. His hands roamed all over her back and his touch banked small fires under her skin.

***

"Okay, I think I got it. I can answer any questions they might have and I can make a thorough check of the boat," Kate concluded, when she shut down the computer late in the afternoon.

"Not a boat, but a yacht, baby, I've told you already. Men are sensitive about this shit. You know, boys and their toys..." Ryan said, looking up from his laptop and grinning at her.

"Well, whatever," Kate shrugged. "I know the basics and everything's fine. The reservation is made, the charge cleared just fine, so I can go get the boat... sorry, yacht," she corrected herself, "the day after tomorrow, early in the morning. Then we can finally leave Malaysia and turn towards greener pastures," she summarized the situation.

Adam grunted in satisfaction. Their predicament was about to end. He went and took a beer from the fridge to celebrate.

Ryan noticed he moved with much more ease than before. He was grateful his friend had pulled out because, for a moment there, the situation had been touch and go.

When Ryan saw Adam was hit, not by one bullet but three, he hadn't thought Adam would make it through, even with the best medical help their money could buy.

Neither Nick nor Ryan believed Adam would survive his wounds. Considering their living conditions during the last few weeks, they were convinced Adam would have died because of an infection, even if he hadn't died because of his wounds.

Luckily, Adam was a strong and stubborn bastard. Probably, those two basic features helped him stay alive.

"I think you should rest until we get to the yacht, Adam. You need to regain your strength and soon. Only God knows what we might encounter," Ryan bellowed after Adam.

Adam's head popped up from behind the door, "I've rested enough, mother. I need to move. I'm dying inside not doing anything all day," he replied patting his chest.

"You'll have enough time to do whatever you want after you've regained your health," Kate interfered and that gained her a scowl from Adam.

Kate didn't take exception at his scowl, but smiled sweetly at him. She'd already learned he was only bark and no bite, at least with her.

"Kate, no offense, you've been very helpful, and you're very sweet... No need to scowl at me, Ryan, it's not like I'd ever poach on another's man's territory, and you know it," he glanced at Ryan and reproached to him in a steely voice.

By then, Adam had learned how Ryan reacted when it came to Kate. He knew Ryan would have something to say and Adam wanted to smother any kind of squabble before it began.

"Anyway, Kate, sweetheart," he turned back to her "I know what I need better than you."

Ryan snarled at Adam's endearment for Kate, but didn't make any comment. His friends' remarks about him being totally spellbound with Kate nudged at him.

Yet, Kate sensed something and turned to him inquiringly. Instantly, Ryan's expression turned blank. He thought he'd better not open a new can of worms and decided to speak about his concerns with Adam when he had a chance to catch him alone. He wanted to settle that thing once and for all.

He knew Adam didn't have any nefarious intentions, yet Ryan didn't like to hear another man talking to Kate like that. She belonged to him and that was what mattered.

CHAPTER FIFTEEN

Kate had already checked the yacht and signed the papers, and now she waited on the deck, drinking some Coca-Cola and admiring the marina. She was bored out of her mind.

She wondered when the guys would come. She didn't enjoy the solitude and that was something new. She used to like being alone now and then. In her line of work, solitude seemed a blessing sometimes.

She knew the men had to make sure no one waited for them, but she'd already been waiting for three hours and was fed up.

She'd already checked her emails and answered to a few of them. She'd checked her Facebook account and tried to entertain herself with a few amusing videos, but it didn't work. She was tense and worried about Ryan. The slow passing of time was unbearable.

The sun was almost above her head and she silently thanked the person who'd installed an umbrella on the deck. At least she wouldn't get a heatstroke waiting there in the sun.

A sudden rocking movement under her feet prompted her to look up. Ryan finally came aboard with his duffel bag in hand.

He smiled at her when their eyes met. He came closer and touched her cheek tenderly. Then, he leaned over her and kissed her as if he hadn't seen her for days not only a few hours.

After he tasted her to his satisfaction, Ryan whispered to her, "Everything's fine, baby. Adam will follow in about five minutes and Nick will be the last to come aboard. Then, we'll sail away and figure out our future. What do you think?"

Kate nodded and took a moment to return the favor. She kissed him back and stroked his lips with her fingers. She let them linger on his lips for a few more seconds before pulling her hand back.

"Maybe you'd like to join me on the deck after you take your duffel bag downstairs. I chose the largest cabin for us. Oh, you'll find beer in that cooler over there," Kate told him and beamed at him when she saw the light in his eyes.

If the guys hadn't been supposed to come soon and they hadn't been scheduled to sail out in under an hour, Ryan would have taken their light flirtation further.

He always responded to her with passion and that pleased Kate. It wouldn't have been fun if her desire for him had been one-sided. After she'd enjoyed the fine conversationalist Ryan, as well as the hot-headed Ryan, now, she enjoyed the lover.

She wished to be with Ryan in the future. Kate knew they could build something together based on what they'd already shared.

She couldn't wait to put that sordid story way behind them and to start a new life, just the two of them.

She still speculated over their future when she heard heavy footsteps on the deck again. Kate looked up and Adam grinned at her. His hair looked thoroughly mussed.

He'd been stressed out and he'd run his fingers through his hair repeatedly. She discerned tense lines near the corners of his mouth. Kate smiled at him and waved an enthusiastic welcome.

"If you want, you can go below deck and leave your stuff," she pointed to the backpack Adam was carrying. "Then you should come back out here and have a beer," she continued, always smiling warmly at him.

"Will do, boss," he replied and saluted her with friendly mockery.

Her smile widened. Her welcome had already chased part of Adam's tension. He saluted her again and went below deck to leave his stuff.

Ryan's enthusiastic voice talking to Adam reached Kate's ears. She overheard them poking around, as men would do in such circumstances and she smiled amused. She'd never understood those male rituals, but she took them as they were.

Adam and Ryan were still talking and laughing below deck, when Nick climbed onto the deck. His bear-like appearance always startled her, although she'd noticed he was the most level-headed and kindest of the three. Ryan had a serious temper and Adam was fast in giving burning replies.

Nick came to her, tapped her cheek with his fingers and said, "Hello, little sun pie. You know, I think you should remain under the umbrella. Your face is already red like a lobster. Anyway, at least, the sun coloured your hair just fine. Now, you have streaks of red and many other nuances..."

"What the hell do you think you're doing?" Ryan's voice boomed behind him.

Nick turned around, completely unaffected, and stared Ryan down, "You know very well I'm not doing anything, bro. Just having a little chit-chat. Cool off!"

Before Ryan could answer, Nick took his backpack and went below deck, passing by Adam who was looking from him to Ryan and back.

"You know he didn't mean anything," Adam tried to appease Ryan's livid fury. "Nick isn't like that," he pointed out although he supposed Ryan should have known that by then.

"I know," Ryan snapped. "That's why I freaked out. Had it been you..."

"Yeah," Adam laughed merrily, "I'm the horny toad…"

"Ryan…," Kate started hesitantly. "What's the matter? I don't understand any of this."

She had no idea what was wrong. She knew she'd had a light conversation with Nick, and Ryan didn't like it. Ryan's reaction made her feel uncomfortable.

"You liked flirting with him, didn't you?" Ryan accused her with fire in his eyes.

"What?" she gasped and her eyes widen with shock.

"He flirted with you and you flirted back," Ryan accused her flatly.

"Are you mad?" Kate inquired with disbelief. "Nick didn't flirt with me. Why would he? He just noticed the sun burnt my skin. That's not flirting, Ryan. It's just casual conversation," she explained to him as if he'd had only half a brain.

"Damn! The woman doesn't even know when a man flirts with her,"

Ryan shook his head in desperation, and turned his back to her furiously, his hands braced on his hips and his head down.

"He didn't, Ryan," she replied hotly. "And if this is what you think of me, then..."

"Don't go there, Kate," he warned her turning back and pointing to her. "Don't even think about it."

"You're jealous," understanding suddenly loomed on her. "You're just jealous and making a scene," she advanced toward him, angry as a cat.

"And if I am?" he answered back gruffly and his tone made her stop, taken aback.

"I don't know," she threw her hands in the air giving up. "What the hell," she turned her back to him and took a few steps on the deck.

She didn't like that streak of jealousy in Ryan at all. Possessiveness of any kind was unpleasant and she considered it was dangerous in the long run.

She returned to him, and copying his posture, hands on hips and head held high, she said, "Well, actually, Ryan, I do know. I don't like your possessiveness. At all. I'm not an object. I have to have freedom to speak to other people without being afraid you'll drop them if your fancy strikes," she spelled her terms.

"Kate, it's not like that and you know it," Ryan tried to appease her. "Yes, I do consider that you belong to me…"

"I belong!" she yelled. "I belong, you say!"

The men cringed every time she raised her voice. They hadn't heard her shouting before, but she seemed to have good lungs.

Adam whispered to Ryan, "There are people around, bro. Quiet her down or our plan could end before it even started."

Ryan nodded to him imperceptibly and then went toward Kate, holding his hands up conciliatorily. "Baby, you misunderstand. Just listen," he rushed to say when he saw her shaking her head. "Yes, I said that you belonged to me, but that means I belong to you too. We belong together and to each other. That's what I meant. You don't have to go nuts because I didn't say it better. I'm a man, Kate. I don't know any fancy talk. I sometimes speak without really thinking, you know," he explained apologetically and stroked her shoulder to calm her down.

Kate narrowed her eyes at him with suspicion. She sensed he had some agenda but then, she cooled down and said, "All right, Ryan. Let's say I believe you. It's not like I can read your damn mind," she ended the argument angrily and stomped below deck to spend a few moments alone.

Back on the deck, Ryan grinned with satisfaction. He was mostly satisfied because she couldn't read his mind.

The other two men exhaled relieved. The argument had ended and now they could finally sail away.

"Let's have a beer first," Nick proposed, "and then let's get out of here. I can't wait to get to Singapore and be on a plane to the States."

"Canada." Ryan corrected him.

"What the...?" Adam who was leaning over the cooler to grab a beer interjected, but Ryan's gesture stopped him.

"Listen up! Canada's the best choice for two reasons. First, I have to know Kate is back in Montreal where she's safe. Second, I think Canada's a better place to arrange a meeting with Mark, guys. Neutral territory," Ryan explained glancing from one to the other.

Adam started to shake his head in disagreement but then, he thought better and stopped. After another moment, he came to him and tapped him hard on the shoulder, "You're a genius, man! A freaking genius!"

Ryan scowled at him and wanted to give him an acid reply but reconsidered. He didn't care what Adam was saying if he had his cooperation. He turned to Nick and looked at him inquiringly.

"I'm in," Nick nodded and replied in his usual grave voice. "It's a sound plan. Anyway, we do have to keep the girl safe. That comes first. She risked enough coming here blindly, you know. And no, Ryan," he said putting up his hand, "I'm not saying that because I have the hots for her, man," Nick shook his head. "She's your girlfriend and that's all I need to know."

Ryan nodded. He understood where he stood with Nick. Then, he asked Adam to give him a beer from the cooler.

CHAPTER SIXTEEN

"Okay, in an hour tops, we'll dock in Singapore," Nick told Ryan watching the horizon and opening a bottle of beer. "It's good we get there in the evening. We're less likely to be noticed. What do you think?" he asked.

"Yes, I think it's a good timing," Ryan consented. "Adam is much better now and I saw he started exercising yesterday afternoon. I'm just a bit concerned he might exaggerate and reopen one of the wounds, though," Ryan said pensively and bit into a juicy mango.

"I wouldn't worry about him, Ryan," Nick shook his head. "He's fine. He's aware of what he can do or not. He was very careful. I watched him."

"If you say so." Ryan replied but didn't seem convinced.

"Is Kate all right?" Nick asked him. "I haven't seen her since early this morning. It's been a few hours already. She didn't seem to be sea sick but…"

"She's alright, just a bit tired," Ryan waved his concern away and finished off the mango throwing the core into the sea under Nick's disapproving eyes.

Nick had a very special concern for the environment and didn't take lightly anything related to littering even if it was something biodegradable. Yet, he kept his tongue. He knew he'd risk a lengthy tirade from Ryan who didn't share his strict views.

"Tired?" Nick chose to ask. "How come?" he expressed his confusion. "We haven't let her do anything on the deck for the entire trip, man. She only spent some time reading under that umbrella and she swam for about an hour yesterday afternoon when we stopped…"

"Well, there's tired and there's tired," Ryan mused, unwilling to go into too many details. There were matters he didn't like to discuss even with his best friends.

"Ah, that tired," Nick concluded when the truth dawned on him. "You seem a bit insatiable, if I may say so. We heard you with all the insulation on the yacht," he shook his head in concern.

"Why do you care?" Ryan turned towards him with narrowed eyes.

"I don't, why would I? I was just saying. I haven't known you to be like that. You're the type to love them fast and leave them. I don't remember you've ever gone back for seconds," Nick observed, watching Ryan with his impenetrable eyes.

"Well, they weren't Kate, were they?" Ryan barked back.

"Oh, man, don't start with me. I was just wondering what's changed, that's all," Nick replied in a conciliatory voice.

"What don't you understand? It's not quantum physics, after all. She's it," Ryan bit out, exasperated he had to spell everything out. He thought Nick the smartest between his two friends but now he wondered if he should reconsider that assessment.

"It seems so," Nick murmured and went to adjust a sail only to get away from him.

Ryan muttered furiously to himself. He was an easy target for his friends. He lost his temper whenever Kate became the topic of conversation with any of them.

They probably started those discussions because he'd built a certain reputation with women in the past. They couldn't understand the change in him. Ryan also knew he perceived everything as a reproach or had the feeling he was the butt of their jokes.

He knew he needed to stop being so belligerent. He feared his jealous behavior might drive Kate away and that was the last thing he wanted.

"Why are you grumbling, baby?" Kate's voice came from behind him. She wrapped her arms around his shoulders and kissed his cheek.

He turned to her and looked at her seriously, pondering what he should say and decided to go with the truth. "I was just muttering to myself, because I keep making an ass of myself. I'm afraid you'll walk away," he confessed involuntarily and felt like slapping himself over his head. He wanted to be honest with her but even honesty had limits.

"I see," Kate said and, leaning on him, she hugged him tightly. "I won't walk away, Ryan. I know you're mostly bluster," she replied cheerfully.

"What??!" the man shouted incredulously.

She looked up at him and laughed, "Like right now. You shout and grumble and scowl... but, in the end, that's all there is to it and I don't see why I'd walk away. It's not like I'm in any sort of danger when I'm with you, right?" she asked.

"Right," Ryan agreed and turning around, he hugged her, holding her tight to his chest.

"Ouch! That hurts, Ryan. I still want to have intact ribs when I go and grab a cola from the cooler, baby," Kate joked, and her frivolous reply made Ryan lighten up and laugh as well.

He finally let her go and said, "In less than an hour we'll be in Singapore, Kate. You'll have to call the guys with the yacht to return it and then, we need to get on a plane to Montreal."

"There's no direct flight to Montreal, Ryan," she said smartly.

"I know that, smart ass!" he bit back. "I meant we'd take a plane that would help us get to a connection for Montreal later," he explained through gritted teeth.

"I know, Ryan, but I like to make you explode. That's fun. You're such a pretty picture fuming like this." Kate said laughing.

"I told you my blood pressure had never been the same since I met you, didn't I?"

"Yeah, you did," Kate nodded. "But what's a bit of blood pressure between us when we can have so much fun together, hmmm?" she mused coyly.

"Right," he said dryly. "It's only my blood pressure, not yours. It seems you react better than I do... to everything."

She shrugged and smiled mischievously at him. Then, she turned away throwing over her shoulder, "It happens, baby, what can I say?"

He swatted her backside and she jumped up.

"Hey, what are you doing?" she scowled at him.

"Just fooling around, Kate. Come on!"

The woman rubbed the spot he spanked and said, "Next time, fool around by putting less sting into your swat, Ryan, or I might retaliate in kind."

"Like how?" Ryan inquired lifting an eyebrow.

"Well, I can spank you as well," she replied in a dry voice.

"Kate, Kate, Kate," Adam's voice came from behind her. "I didn't know you had such a kinky side, girl," he laughed heartily.

Kate glanced at him and blushed so violently that even the tips of her ears turned red. She tried to salvage the situation, "We were just joking around, Adam."

"Come on, girl. There's no shame in spicing the game a little. Didn't Ryan teach you that?" Adam asked and winked at her.

Seeing she was mortified, Ryan interceded, "Drop it, Adam. Stop embarrassing her."

Kate shook her head and turned to go back below deck, but Ryan took her hand and turned her to him, "Kate, Adam's just joking. And even so, what we do, the two of us, it's our business and you don't have to feel ashamed of anything, you hear me?" he demanded in a very serious voice.

She nodded but still went downstairs to her cabin. She didn't think she could face Adam just then.

"Did you have to make her leave?" Ryan scowled at Adam.

"That wasn't my intention," Adam shook his head. "I didn't know she was so sensitive. I'll be more careful from now on, Ryan. She seems a little old-fashioned, if you ask me."

"I know she is, and that's her charm, you stupid," Ryan replied in a stern voice.

"What's the problem now?" Nick asked from behind Ryan. His voice had a hint of exasperation. "With you two, there's always something. It's like a fucking drama all the time around here," he observed and his tone implied that he didn't like it. He was sick of all their petty squabbles. He longed for the times when something like that didn't happen.

Ryan pushed him away and went after Kate, leaving them on the deck to do whatever they wanted.

CHAPTER SEVENTEEN

"We're approaching Singapore, Ryan. Come out on the deck. We need another pair of hands here," Nick's voice thundered from above deck and made Kate grimace.

"Does he always have to thunder like that? Can't he talk in a normal tone of voice?" she asked Ryan.

Ryan just shrugged and went above deck to help his mates with the approach and anchorage. After about a quarter of an hour, he bellowed down to her, "We're here, Kate. Call the guys to return the yacht and let's move! Now!"

Her voice came as loud as his, "Who made you general, Ryan? Would it be difficult for you to phrase your requests differently? Would it kill you?" she ended her speech with a screech to be sure he heard her.

"My god, the lungs she has on her," Adam exclaimed completely stunned with the volume of her reply. "Anyway, we'll have to get our stuff from under the deck as well, so let's move, general," he said to Ryan and saluted him mockingly.

Ryan frowned at him but then burst into laughter, "She's something else, isn't she?"

"That she is," Nick grumbled and went below deck to take his bag. "We really need to move, guys. We don't know if they found out we'd come this way or …."

"I know," Ryan said quickly to stop Nick from developing an entire lecture. He followed him downstairs to help Kate with their things.

***

"I called the company and a guy will be here in five minutes. It seems they have an office in the marina so everything will be dealt with soon."

"That's good, Kate. The sooner we leave this city, the safer we'll be, you know," Ryan replied and started stuffing things into his duffel bag.

Kate looked incredulously at him for a few moments and then asked in a haughty voice, "Don't you think you should fold those shirts? Before stuffing them in there like there's no tomorrow?"

"No, I don't," he replied flittingly. "Anyway, I'll be travelling for at least the next twenty-four hours and I'll look dishevelled anyway. So, what's the point to trouble myself with packing carefully?" he asked.

Kate shrugged and said, "As you wish. At least I managed to fold these before you came. Put them on top so you have something clean and only slightly wrinkled to put on."

"I like it when you're behaving like a little wife," Ryan said looking at her and grinned.

"Little wife, Ryan? Really?" she snapped and braced her hands on her hips.

"Come on, baby, it wasn't meant like an insult," Ryan tried to explain. "Quite the opposite. It was just my way of saying I'd like it to be true."

Kate froze and the dress she had just folded fell on the floor unnoticed.

She couldn't say or do anything but stare at him.

He cringed and murmured, "No romance in that, I know. Fucking hell! I'm so stupid," he slapped himself over the head.

Coming out of her shock, Kate knelt next to him, took his hand and said softly, "You don't have to try for something romantic, Ryan. I prefer the real you and what you've just said was… Well, it was very sweet. I just hadn't expected it, that's all."

"So, had I been smarter and said it as I should have, would you have said *yes*?"

Kate looked at him intently searching his face to read the truth behind his words. That was another moment when she regretted she couldn't read his mind. Yet, satisfied with what she saw on his face, she nodded, "When you find it in yourself to ask, yes, I will say *yes*. And you don't have to set a scene or anything, Ryan. You just have to be you."

"Does that mean I can ask you anytime? Even right now?" he asked with hope in his voice.

She nodded but kept silent and just watched him intently.

Ryan took her hand, kissed every one of her fingers, and then looked up at her and asked, "Will you marry me as soon as possible, Kate? Spend your life with me, play havoc with my blood pressure and bring me back to earth whenever I go around the bend?"

Her eyes glimmered with unshed tears and she nodded. She didn't know whether her voice would work.

"And will you have kids with me? I'm getting old, baby, and I'd love to be able to enjoy their young years while I don't need a cane or a wheelchair to chase after them."

Kate laughed, nodded again, leaned forward and gently brushed her lips to his, only once. Then she simply kept the connection between their mouths, to feel him close.

They were both so focused one on the other that they didn't even notice Adam and Nick in the doorway. Both men's faces betrayed their shock. They shook their heads in befuddlement. Adam elbowed Nick and signaled him to come out onto the deck and leave them alone.

CHAPTER EIGHTEEN

"Well, that went well," Adam observed as soon as they'd reached the airport and managed to buy tickets with the money Kate had brought to Malaysia for them.

The others nodded, relieved. The second part of their plan had come through.

Ryan had obtained passports from a contact he had in Singapore and now they could travel without problems.

"When should we call Mark?" Adam asked Ryan.

Ryan was their expert in arranging meetings. Ryan looked around and spotted a few isolated chairs in the corner of the lounge. He waived to them to follow him and they piled onto the chairs around him.

"I think we can do it right now, what are you saying?"

Kate nodded and the guys looked at her, and then at Ryan and approved.

"We'll go with the speaker, okay, so Kate could hear him," Nick said. "Maybe she can tell us what's what. That of course, if we can get through and talk to him, because we couldn't call him from Malaysia at all, you remember."

Ryan approved and dialed Mark's direct number.

After three rings, Mark answered, "Talk to me!"

"Mark, Ryan here."

"Where the hell have you been, you bastard? I've been looking for you everywhere. For months! And where are those two mates of yours, Adam and Nick?" Mark's voice boomed over the phone and Ryan adjusted the volume quickly because a few people had already turned their heads around and looked at them.

"We're all here, and you don't need to shout. We hear you just fine. But if you continue to bellow, the people around will hear you too," Ryan stated calmly.

"Okay, okay, I got it. I'm calm now. You've been off the grid for months. I expected a call, something, but nothing came. What the hell should I have thought? I was told Adam's cover was blown," Mark explained his anguish.

"Yes, it was, but it wasn't much of a cover to begin with. They were waiting for him, man, and he hardly got out with his skin intact. Of course, that didn't last either. When Nick and I came to take him out, they chased us down and Adam was shot."

"Don't tell me that Adam's dead. Ryan, don't tell me that," Mark implored.

The three men looked one to the other in shock. They exchanged inquiring looks because they couldn't believe Mark would get sentimental on them. They'd never heard him talk like that before. Apparently, he did feel something for them.

"He's not dead, but he was close to that. Someone wants us dead, Mark. They had left him alone and hadn't tried to kill him until they had all three of us in their sight," Ryan explained.

"That's what I thought," Mark agreed with his assessment. "Something was strange with that covert op, from the beginning," he told him. "The man who made the plans has disappeared and no one can find him, dead or alive. We're still looking into everything. Anyway, where can we meet?" Mark asked.

"Well, I was thinking it would be a good idea to set up a rendezvous on a neutral ground," Ryan replied. "Like, I don't know... Canada," he proposed as if he'd thought of that just then. "I know we could catch a flight to Montreal or Toronto soon. Wait a minute, let me see."

He muted the phone and said to the others, "We'd better not show our hand and tell him we intended to go to Montreal anyway. Let's let him think we're choosing right now, okay?"

His buddies nodded but Kate intervened, "He's telling the truth, Ryan. He hasn't been involved in this business and he's genuinely stressed with the situation and everything that happened to you three," she said, waving her hand. "When you told him about Adam, that he'd been shot, he hurt. He cares about you all," she reiterated, glancing from one to the other.

"That's great, baby. I'm happy he's not the enemy. But someone might monitor his calls and that's why we couldn't call him from Malaysia. So, if someone's listening into this call right now, we don't want to tip our hand and let them know we're interested in Montreal not Toronto. We'll let them think we chose Montreal for convenience. Okay? We don't want to lead them to you, Kate. You're not at fault in this," Ryan told her very seriously.

Kate frowned but before she could say anything, Adam intervened, "Not a bad idea, indeed."

He looked at his mates who nodded their approval circumventing Kate's opinion. Their attitude drove her mad but there was no time to tell them what she thought.

Ryan unmuted the cell phone and said, "Mark, Nick says the first connection we have is for Montreal. We'll meet you there in exactly fifty-six hours from now. We'll call you fifteen minutes before the meeting and let you know where we'll be. I don't really know any of the cities up there and I have to check the ground."

"All right, Ryan. Get back safe. All of you, do you hear me?"

"Loud and clear, boss, loud and clear," he replied.

Ryan turned off the phone and, putting into his pocket, told them, "So, time to roll the dice. We'll see how our luck holds. How long until boarding?" he asked Kate.

"Boarding should begin any minute now. We have a long haul to Istanbul and there we have a layover. I think it's two and a half hours or anyway something around that," she explained.

"Good," Adam approved. "Let's find something to eat. I hate plane food," he said bitterly.

"You'll love the lounge in Istanbul," Kate told him. "The food is really something fantastic. I ate so much when I came to Malaysia that I almost couldn't move," she told them and they grinned.

"Great! That's for me," Adam said and led the way to Burger King, craving a big juicy burger with fries. That was something he hadn't had in a while and he couldn't wait to rejoice in the taste.

CHAPTER NINETEEN

"I think we should rent a car," Nick said, looking around for a rental agency.

"No need," Kate contradicted him. "I have my car parked here in the long-term parking. I think it will fit you all. It's not a girly car, but a big, mean SUV," she continued playfully and the guys started laughing.

"We'd have survived even with a different car, Kate, no worries," Ryan told her and kissed her palm, something he seemed to enjoy doing a lot.

She beamed at him and led them to the parking lot where she'd left her car before taking the plane for Istanbul.

"Ta-da, this is it," she said showing them a sturdy Ford Escape. She was very proud of her car.

"That'll work," Nick said. "Not bad for a girl," he elbowed her and chuckled.

Kate laughed as well and opened the doors and the trunk. They threw their things in the trunk and she started toward the driver side of the car when Ryan stopped her.

"You can call me whatever you want, baby. You can say I'm a damn chauvinist if you want, but I drive. Always."

The woman frowned at him but then, she thought, why not. She was too exhausted to bother herself with driving. She had a GPS in the car, and   Ryan could find her place easily. So, without a peep, she handed him the keys and walked around to the other side.

Her attitude dumbfounded Ryan. He'd expected some vocal opposition and prepared an entire tirade. Now he felt cheated.

"You guys, in the back," Kate told Adam and Nick with authority. "I might give him my car keys, but I won't ride in the back," she put her foot down.

The two men grinned and got inside the car without a comment.

Kate input her address into the GPS and turned to the men in the back of the car, "You'll stay all at my place. I have enough space and we'll get food, Adam, don't worry. There are places where we can find food even at this hour. It is quite early," she said checking the time. "We got here at 5:40 and it took us only forty minutes to get out of the airport. It will take us about another twenty or thirty more minutes to get to my house, so it will probably be around seven when we arrive. We can buy food from Metro," she concluded.

"That's a good idea, baby," Ryan agreed with her, "but we're too tired to cook tonight. We need something already cooked, so we could eat, and go immediately to bed and sleep a bit. We need to be in good shape tomorrow morning."

"We can find prepared food at Metro. They have chicken, sausages, various salads, pizza, cakes, whatever you want," Kate answered exuberantly. "Maybe we should stop there before we get home," she proposed. "I'll show you where when we get close, okay?"

Ryan nodded but didn't seem to pay too much attention to what she was saying. He looked preoccupied with something else and kept checking the rear-view mirror.

"Is there something wrong?" Adam asked him.

He knew how Ryan behaved in certain situations, and his attitude was telling him something was going on.

"I think we have some company, guys," Ryan replied in a cool voice and checked the mirror again. He'd been trained to keep a clear mind in dangerous situations. "Actually, I'm pretty sure. How the hell did they find us?" he wondered and a hint of fury and puzzlement colored his voice.

"Probably the call to Mark," Nick replied. "If they have the means for face recognition, it wouldn't have been hard to find us. Remember, Ryan, that was why you sent those photos to Kate. So they couldn't trace your connection to her," Nick reminded him.

Kate's eyes widened, "I always wondered why you sent those photos. I couldn't see anything. It could have been an alien from out of space, for all I knew. I thought you just didn't want me to know how you looked."

"Well, I had to, sweetie. Now, everyone, take care, I will try to lose them, okay? They're already close and I don't want to risk anything," he said and pushed the pedal to the floor, making the car jump forward.

Kate grasped the arm rest and held on for her life. Her breathing became shallow and fear overwhelmed her. She'd never been in such circumstances and the increased speed of the car was enough to make her tremble.

Ryan was a good driver, though. Even in the evening rush, he controlled the car with easiness, while overtaking car after car and moving from lane to lane, setting off a chorus of horns behind him.

He was good, but the car chasing them got closer and closer. Ryan knew he had to find a way to get off the freeway and find narrow streets where he could lose the tail.

He saw an exit coming up. He'd just cut in front of a car, which of course honked them, and aimed for the exit, when he heard the rear window exploding, followed by vicious swearing coming from his mates in the back seats. He swerved onto the exit and despite the speed limit, continued to drive as fast as possible to keep his advantage.

"Is everyone okay?" he asked, when he felt it was safe enough.

He turned his head for a couple seconds. Adam and Nick were brushing shreds of glass off their clothes. Yet, despite a few cuts, they seemed all right and Ryan breathed with relief.

Then Kate's moan reached his ears and his blood ran cold. The explosion had been in the back of the car and the thought of checking on her had never crossed his mind.

"Baby, are you all right? Sweetheart? Come on, talk to me," he said, turning to her and trying to take her hand.

"Watch the road, damn it," Adam bellowed when the car swerved to the right, ready to get onto the shoulder of the road. "I'll see to her."

"The hell you...," Ryan started shouting back but Kate's frightened voice interrupted him.

"Watch the road, Ryan. I think I'm fine. The bullet only grazed my skin, but it hurts, damn it, and I couldn't stop moaning, all right?" she clarified what had happened.

"Are you sure you're fine, Kate?" Ryan asked, his voice shaking.

"I'll be fine if you keep your eyes on the road, Ryan," she screamed when, due to his inattention, the car moved into the oncoming lane.

Luckily, no cars were coming toward them at that moment. Ryan swung the steering wheel and got back on track. He checked the rearview mirror and saw the other car hadn't made the exit and followed them, which was a blessing.

Still, he couldn't be sure whether they'd taken Kate's plate number or not and that was bad. Apparently, they had the means to find out who she was and come after her.

"Kate, I don't think it's a good idea to go to your house tonight, sweetie," Ryan said in a calm voice not to alarm her beforehand.

"Why not?" she cried. "I want home, Ryan. I want to sleep in my bed tonight," she said stubbornly and her tantrum prompted Adam to roll his eyes.

Nick just watched her as if she'd been a very strange museum exhibit. She had seemed a reasonable woman before that incident.

"Sweetie, if they got the plate off your car, then they know where to find you and, implicitly, all of us," Ryan explained to her patiently, as if he'd been talking to a child.

He considered she was in too much pain and he had to be gentle with her. Ryan was going crazy because he didn't know how bad she was hurt. He wanted to stop the car right there and check her out, but at the same time, he wanted to put as much distance as possible between them and their pursuers. He also tried to decide where they should go so they wouldn't be tracked any further.

Kate looked at him for a few seconds as if she hadn't understood what he was talking about. When comprehension dawned, her face lit up and she said, "No, they can't. I bought this car a week before I left for Malaysia from a guy who went back to his country. I didn't have the time to change the registration or anything. I have only the receipt. No one can track me using the plate of the car and no one can get hurt because that guy took his entire family with him," she explained further. "I understood they'd decided they could do much better back home with what they'd made here than they would have if they'd continued to live in Montreal."

"Are you sure, Kate? Because these guys are ruthless, sweetie, and I don't want you in any kind of danger," Ryan tried to reason with her.

"I'm absolutely positive, Ryan. I even gave those guys a ride to the airport when they left. The car was the last thing they sold."

"I was talking about the registration, Kate," Ryan scowled at her.

"So, you care only about us but not about them," she replied upset.

"I didn't say that. I only asked if you were sure no one can trace the car back to your home," he lost his temper and roared at her.

"Ryan, she's hurt," Nick said calmly. "I don't think yelling at her now is a good tactic."

Kate continued to stare Ryan down belligerently. He merely shook his head and checked the mirror again.

"Okay, we've lost them. So, we're going to your house then," he told her.

She approved nodding and then added, "Of course, we need to buy some food first..."

She didn't manage to finish because Ryan glanced at her in disbelief and asked her, "Are you out of your mind?"

"What now?" she asked with consternation.

There was always something with Ryan and she just couldn't keep up with his moods.

"You're hurt, woman. I need to see how hurt you are and you're thinking of going shopping. Typical female," he finished exasperated.

"What? I'm not talking about going and buying shoes, Ryan. I'm talking about food. It's a strict necessity in any household," she reminded him.

"Out of question," he bit back. "We're going home, look at your wound and decide then."

"Who died and made you the boss?" she asked him heatedly.

Adam coughed discretely and then tapped her on the shoulder softly and said, "He's the boss, Kate. He's always the boss. If he says we're going to your house first, that's what we're doing. Or, if I can suggest something else," he said looking explicitly at Ryan, "either Nick or I, or both, I guess, could go to that Metro thing and buy food and come to Kate's house afterwards. If you tell us where to go, Kate, we can do it. Meantime, you can check her out."

For a few moments, silence reigned in the car. Unable to stand the tension anymore, Kate turned to Ryan and asked sweetly, "Well? Boss? What do you think?"

He narrowed his eyes and looked at her pointedly, and then replied, "All right, Adam. Kate will give you directions to get to that store."

"Wouldn't it be better," Kate inquired always sweetly, something that was already getting under Ryan's skin, "if we drive them to the store, leave them there and I provide the info for them to come to my house? Although," she added turning to Adam "there's some distance to get to my house from the store on foot. It will probably take you about fifteen minutes if not more."

Nick waived his hand to show that the distance was inconsequential for them and she smiled at him despite the pain she was feeling in her left arm. It felt like someone was thrusting a knife into her arm repeatedly and she had to make serious efforts not to moan or cry out in pain. She thought she'd better keep Ryan calm, at least until they got to her house. He seemed easily irascible and she wanted to get home in one piece.

They left the two men at the store and Kate gave them her debit card and PIN number and explained to them how to get to her house from there.

Then, Ryan drove directly to her home, parked the car inside the garage to have it out of sight, and turned to her, "Now, let's go and see how bad you're hurt. It killed me that I had to wait so long before I could see," he confessed and she smiled at him. Her smile was genuine this time.

Kate got out of the car and went straight into the house through a side door, closely followed by Ryan who was carrying all their bags. She showed him to the kitchen where she threw her handbag onto the table and stiffly sat down.

"You can do your worst," she said, stretching her arm toward him.

Ryan saw blood coagulated everywhere and that scared him. He didn't know the exact location of the wound, so he took a kitchen towel and wet it, then came back to clean her arm.

"You want to use my cotton white tea towel to clean the blood on my arm?" she practically roared at him. "Are you out of your mind, Ryan? Do you know I can't take out the blood stains from that? Blood doesn't come out even with bleach," she pointed out.

"Kate, things are just things. This is just a towel. Your arm is more important, I think," Ryan tried to placate her and spoke as calm as possible given the circumstances.

It didn't work. She glowered at him and stood up, "We can clean my arm directly in the sink. We just let the water running over it. There's no need to use my good tea towel," she repeated and went to the sink with determination.

"It's a tea towel, for God's sake. I'll buy you another one, Kate," he said, coming after her.

He couldn't reconcile the woman who generously used so much of her money to help them with the woman who was crying over a blasted towel.

"It won't be the same, Ryan, and you know it. More importantly, I'll know it. Where's the problem if I clean my arm straight under the water jet?" she inquired stubbornly.

"It might hurt a little more," he said, not very certain of that fact, but he had to say something in his defense.

"Huh!" she exclaimed. "It hurts enough now. It can't be worse."

Then she turned on the water, checked the temperature and put her arm under the jet. She yelped suddenly when the water got in contact with her wound.

"I knew you wouldn't listen, Kate. You're too stubborn for your own good, sweetie. Come on, let me clean your arm carefully so we can see what's there," Ryan stroked her cheek and grinned at her, trying to persuade her into doing his bidding.

She looked at him mutinously for a moment, and then she said, "All right, you do it."

Ryan gently took her arm and started washing it, cleaning the blood thoroughly to get to the actual wound. After he wiped all the blood away, he saw the bullet only had grazed her skin. It wasn't very bad but not very good either and his heart cringed. He knew she must have been in serious pain.

"You'll be fine, Kate. Soon, you'll see. We'll need some antibiotic to put on this. I have something in my bag," he said and went to his bag to take out the powdered antibiotic he'd used on Adam. He liberally powdered some over her wound.

He checked her arm carefully again, and pensively said, "I think we'd better cover it with a bandage to be sure it stays clean, all right?"

Kate rolled her eyes, then looked at him and said, "But I need a shower, Ryan, and very, very bad after so many hours spent in planes and airports…"

"Don't worry, baby," Ryan comforted her. "I'll help you shower and I'll take care not to wet the bandage, you'll see. Everything will be just fine."

Kate smiled naughtily at him, knowing what a shower together meant for him but Ryan chuckled at her and said, "Not tonight, baby. You're hurt, I wouldn't do that to you."

"You make it sound like a chore," Kate replied not very satisfied with his answer.

"No, sweetie, it's just that you're hurt and very tired. I'd be a complete asshole to make love to you tonight. I won't make any promises for tomorrow, but tonight, I'll just hold you while you sleep all right? Let's take you out of these clothes and shower you before the guys come back," Ryan said, starting to lift her sleeveless shirt. Then, he allowed her to guide him to the bathroom.

CHAPTER TWENTY

After an uneventful night and a very satisfying breakfast, at least according to Adam, who apparently liked to eat, Ryan contacted Mark and told him about the adventure they'd had the previous evening.

"I have a very clear idea now who the person of interest might be," Mark told Ryan. "I already have my second-best team looking into this. You know you three are my best team, Ryan... Anyway, they should take care of this business today."

"That's great, Mark," Ryan replied. "By the way, those guys are your best team. We're out of the picture, remember?" he pointed out.

Adam and Nick nodded, and Kate simply beamed at him, happy

that he wouldn't be in danger anymore.

"Are you sure, Ryan? Is it because of this fiasco?" Mark inquired, unwilling to let his best men leave.

"You know very well we've already decided not to take any more jobs, Mark. Before this happened. I want to marry, and Adam…"

"You want to marry," Mark interrupted him in a stunned voice. Then, he started laughing. "How the hell will you marry if you don't even have a woman to marry? You're bullshitting me, man."

"Actually, I do have a woman to marry," Ryan replied and smiled at Kate who was holding his hand. "We'll marry by the end of this weekend, if I have something to say in the matter," he said, continuing to watch Kate and see her reaction.

She grinned at him brightly and nodded her consent. It wasn't as if she hadn't thought of that, especially after he asked her to marry him.

She wanted to marry him because she was sure their lives would never get boring. Why, with their constant bickering and making love and interesting conversations…

No, Ryan was the best choice for her. He had the strength and mind she'd have liked in a man and he could surprise her all the time because she couldn't read his mind.

She'd realized that was what she wanted, even though she didn't know it. She wanted a man like him, someone she couldn't read.

Kate knew she'd have doubts sometimes and maybe occasional if not frequent heartaches, yet it seemed much better than the alternative. She'd have been bored to tears by the end of the month with a man she could read like an open book.

"I seem to have a say in the matter, Mark, so I'll be married by the end of the week, man," Ryan announced with more exuberance than anyone had ever seen him display before.

"And I'm not invited, I surmise," Mark said in a dry voice.

Ryan exchanged looks with Kate and when she agreed, he replied to Mark, "Actually, if you're still in Montreal by the end of the week, yes, we'd like to have you here."

"All right, then. Now you're talking," Mark replied with joy. "Now let me finish with those guys and then we'll meet. Give me a call after a couple hours, Ryan. It should be done by then," Mark said in an implacable voice and disconnected the call.

Ryan looked inquiringly at Kate.

"He's telling the truth, Ryan. He's got a lead and is confident he'll have those people under lock and key in less than two hours."

Nick looked from her to Ryan and back again and said, "We could have used her in the past. Imagine how many bad things we might have avoided having such info."

Adam and Ryan chuckled and then, Ryan leaned and kissed Kate.

"Soon, this will be over, love, and we'll get on with our lives, all right?"

She nodded happily and hugged him, not embarrassed in the least to have spectators to her love.

EPILOGUE

Kate married Ryan on Saturday morning, August the 3rd, in her garden, with a few friends in attendance. She invited only Ellie, Alice and Jeanne, and Ryan had his three friends, Adam, Nick and Mark next to him.

Mark kept his word and caught the men who had pursued them. A few years ago, one of his other teams had gone rogue and when one of their first covert operations had been rendered ineffective by Ryan and his men, they swore revenge.

They'd created the most recent undercover mission with the help of another rogue agent. They had hoped Ryan would accept it and they could take him out.

Her wedding day was as beautiful and as sunny as Kate's disposition. Her friends expected Kate to be nervous and a real nightmare, truth be told, because they knew when Kate was nervous she couldn't control her temper. Surprisingly, she was serene and at peace with everything.

She hadn't been dreaming of that day forever and hadn't made plans. She'd never been so girly. But she felt everything was just right and she was happy she'd found the right man to spend the rest of her life with.

Ryan wasn't the most easy-going man on earth, and she was sure they'd have their share of rows and misunderstandings along the years. Yet, she knew he was exactly what she needed.

In opposition to her sunny disposition, Ryan was a real mess, which was also unexpected.

The man who'd gone into dozens of combat situations with a clear mind and a steady hand, was scared out of his mind now, and his panic showed in his tense eyes.

He was afraid Kate wouldn't like the ring he'd bought for her. He'd chosen something simple because he felt it would suit her, but now he had doubts.

He was also afraid she'd change her mind in the last moment and say *no*. That scared him so much he'd barely breathed until he heard her saying '*I do*'.

Then, his tension disappeared and he became the man everyone knew, confident and calm under pressure.

Adam and Nick looked at him, not recognizing the comrade they'd gone into battle with for over a decade. Nick kept shaking his head and Adam even whispered to Nick, "If I ever get like that, you have free hand to shoot me, man. I won't ever fall in love, I swear. Love seems to make the smartest man as dumb as a doorknob."

Nick laughed and told him, "I'll hold you to that, bro. You'll see."

Adam waved his concerns away and his eyes wandered toward the buffet Kate had prepared for guests. He'd eaten just a few hours earlier but now was hungry and needed a refill.

EYES IN THE DARK

Book Two

TO CORINA AND EMIL

PROLOGUE

A thin crowd surrounded the casket and not because of the cold spring rain, which had been pouring for the last twelve hours. Not many people had attended the church service either.

'A funeral in the middle of the week will do that to you,' Diane shook her head with grief. People had jobs and families. She couldn't blame them for their absence.

The pastor's words flew past her ears. She'd never been a religious person and didn't find any comfort in the ritual now, either.

When Diane's eyes had swept over the faces of the few people inside the church just moments before, her heart had tightened. Bad luck had taken away her aunt's chance at having the people she'd known for years at her side on this last day.

The late Martha Elgin had been well known and respected in the county. *'I never even imagined so many people loved her,'* Diane thought and wiped her tears.

The constant string of people, coming to pay their respects during the last three nights of the wake, had impressed Diane MacLean, Martha's only niece.

She only realized the priest had ended the service when people began to move and file before Diane to present their whispered condolences and regrets once again.

Some squeezed her hand with affection while others hugged her, although they'd known her for only a few days. Afterwards, they left the cemetery, huddled under big umbrellas.

They would come to the house later, where Diane, with the help of a catering company, had prepared a last repast in her aunt's honor, scheduled for three in the afternoon.

Soon however, Diane remained alone near the casket, her eyes misty with tears, while two burly young men were waiting impatiently under the canopy of a big oak. They wanted to finish with the burial and find some shelter inside, away from the rain. Their eyes laid squarely on her, willing her to leave already.

Diane whispered her farewell and touched the lid of the black lacquered casket with a shaky hand. She loved her aunt and regretted she hadn't come to visit her for almost three years already. Now, her words fell on deaf ears.

She nodded toward the grave diggers and followed the stone path leading out of the cemetery and to the parking lot. She failed to notice the three men hidden in the shadow of a cluster of trees behind her.

The tallest leaned forward and whispered a few words. Nodding, one of the other two made his way through the trees to the same parking lot.

The man beat Diane to the punch. Comfortably seated in his car, he watched her coming up the trail slowly.

She seemed tired and didn't care about the rain, even though her umbrella didn't shield her very well. The remote look in her eyes betrayed her scattered thoughts.

Diane didn't notice the man in the car. She placed the umbrella in the trunk of her SUV and hurried to the driver's side.

She drove away, oblivious to the other car, which was trailing her closely now. She drove under the speed limit, although she was expected in town. Her aunt's lawyer

had invited her to the reading of the
will.

'I already told him I might be late.
What's the rush after all? The will won't
change.'

CHAPTER 1

The air tumbled in his lungs and he tasted the smell of the earlier rain in the air. The smell of wet leaves, rustled by the wind all over the forest floor, invigorated him.

He watched the woman closely from underneath the shade of the trees where he'd found a good spot to hide.

'It's just a necessity,' he lied to himself. He knew he liked what he saw. His imagination already roamed on paths he knew he should have avoided.

He held still, afraid he would make a noise by stepping on the twigs that littered the floor of the forest and give his position away. He had enough time to make his presence known and didn't want to scare her before the time was right. He'd outlined a plan and never strayed from a well-thought-out plan.

His eyes roved over the woman's body. Her neck arched and reminded him of a deer at a watering hole at dawn, sniffing the air to feel the hunter lurking.

He grinned. *'Yep, sweetheart, you sense me here, but you're not sure. Yet.'*

Fatigue had etched visible lines at the corner of her eyes and around her mouth. He'd been watching her for a few hours now and had seen her working hard as she tried to put the ranch house to rights.

The wind teased him with a faint whiff of green apples and lemon, stirring long-forgotten memories. He bristled and scowled the memories away.

The woman shivered and rubbed her arms. The night air was getting cooler.

Her rich coppery hair hung in a messy ponytail. Wisps of hair framed her face and made her look vulnerable.

Suddenly, the man decided he'd watched his fill. '*Show time,*' he said under his breath and stepped out from his hiding place.

"Hey, you over there!"

She almost jumped a feet up when the rough voice whipped through the air. It came from the left side of the yard where lots of bushes and tall trees darkened the night even more. Her wide eyes turned there and caught the glimpse of a tall shadow moving in the dark and a flash of fear seized her breath.

The man closed the distance between them, a grin in the corner of his mouth. Something close to satisfaction bubbled in his veins.

Her eyes widened even more when his tall and broad shape seemed to engulf the space. The fear in her eyes stirred an unknown emotion deep inside him. He tried to label it, but came out empty.

He ruled out compassion although he couldn't explain why. It wasn't as if he had even remembered how compassion felt like.

For a few tense moments, they stared at each other intensely. Neither one moved.

Fear flickered in her green eyes again. A huge male was striding through her yard as if he'd owned the damn place.

His steely black eyes reflected his innate boldness, laced with a hint of amusement and a feral sliver of unidentified hunger. That hunger troubled her. She didn't care about his amusement or anything else.

They assessed each other like two swordsmen.

'Why the heck didn't I listen to my instincts?' She'd thought herself alone out there at the small ranch house, yet, all evening, she had the feeling that someone was watching her. The

sensation had electrified the fine hair at the nape of her neck but she'd foolishly dismissed it.

The ranch was far from any crowded roads, which was fine with her. She didn't need legions of people around and she didn't miss the noises of a big city.

Since the death of her aunt, a few months before, she'd been thinking of moving out of town and making a life for herself there, in the middle of nowhere. A week ago, she'd finally done it. Now, she doubted she'd made the right decision.

"I've got a gun, right here," she shouted at him. Her voice shook. "And I know how to use it," she continued in a shrilling voice. Fear almost smothered her and she hardly pushed the words out of her mouth.

His brash laughter reached her ears and her blood ran cold. *'He doesn't believe me,'* she thought with a shock and for a fleeting moment, she regretted she hadn't taken those self-defense classes she'd been thinking about back then when she was living in the city. '*Well, too bad. It's too late to cry over spilled milk now. Time to face the music.*'

"Yeah, I bet you do," he hollered back, laughing louder. "Sweetheart," he drawled, and honey dripped off his lips, betraying a specific southern accent, "I'm sure you could darn shoot me if you wanted to. But I doubt you do," he continued and lifted an eyebrow, as if he'd dared her. "I just want help for one night, maybe two, tops," he lied boldly through his teeth.

His fake sweet voice made her fear step aside. Anger took its place and climbed up to her lips at his biting sarcasm.

"Town's in that direction," she replied, pointing to his left. "There, you can find all the help you want, mister," she added in clipped words. "There's nothing here for you," she clarified with a sharp gesture.

"I don't feel like going into town right now," he shrugged. "I'm tired. I've been walking long enough. My car broke down a few miles back down that road, and I need a place to stay. I think I like this one," he said in a flat voice, which brought shivers along her spine.

Then, he came closer and under the spot of light from the veranda.

"How dare you?" she pushed through her tight lips with difficulty. Her hands fisted and her nails bit into her palms.

He was rather tall, a bit too tall for her taste. If he'd been shorter, she might have had a chance to fight him back. He was also much heavier than she was. His build reminded her of a fighter. *'This guy's bad news, Diane,'* she thought.

"Be a good Christian girl," he said sweetly. "You won't let a poor man outside in the night, here, in the forest, to fend for himself alone, cold and hungry, will you now?" he asked her with a charming smile and opened his arms wide, taunting her.

"I certainly would," she replied and braced her hands on her hips.

She wanted him to understand his words wouldn't move her. She wasn't a simpleton. The times when people opened their doors to strangers were long gone. Anyway, she was a city girl. That habit wasn't in her make-up.

He stepped closer and reached the stairs of the veranda, undeterred by her refusal. He braced one arm on the handrail. His smiling eyes assessed her resolve.

His eyes pleaded innocence, yet she could read toughness behind his smile. She knew he was far from what he wanted her to believe.

The man was built like the rangers she'd read about. Over six feet tall, his eyes were on the same level with hers, even though he was at the foot of the stairs. His shoulders were broad enough to carry her away if he felt like it.

'*Oh boy, oh boy,*' she mumbled in her mind. She had to do something and get rid of him.

'*Damn my urge to admire the night. If I'd been inside, at least I'd have had a door between this bear of a man and me… Although I don't think a locked door would make too much of a difference if he wanted in,*' she thought, her eyes taking in the rough maleness before them.

"Come on, missy, don't be a bitch," he tried to cajole her. "I need only one bed for the night," he tried to persuade her, always with that smile, which got on her nerves. "I promise it won't be yours," he added.

She noticed his smile never reached his eyes. The man's eyes were two black arrows trained on her, surveying her every movement. Chips of ice sparkled inside his dark pupils, chilling her to the bone.

His evident sarcasm crawled on her skin and his nonchalant attitude scared her more because she didn't understand his game.

"Are you crazy or what?" she replied with anger in her voice.

"Or what, I think," he softly answered back.

"How could you think I'd let you sleep in my house?" she said furiously.

'It's like she wants to spit on me and be done with me,' he mused. *'Not so easily done, honey. The game's over when I say it's over. Now, be a good girl and give in. I won't bother you... too much.'*

"All right, then your barn, what about that?" he offered a compromise.

'It's not like I can't afford it for the moment. You'll play a different tune tomorrow, honey.'

"You can lock your doors tonight, and tomorrow, we'll talk some more. What are you saying? It seems like a good trade to me," he shrugged again and tapped the cowboy hat, he had in his hand, on his thigh.

She didn't like his words and was afraid to think about what sort of trade he was talking about. *'Yeah, like a locked door would stop you from coming in.'*

However, she knew she was at a disadvantage. If she wanted to end that ludicrous discussion, she had to accept his offer and hope he would keep to the barn.

"Go to the barn and wait for me," she said brusquely. "I'll bring you some blankets so you won't feel the cold of the night. All right?"

He smiled at her again, but this time, he showed her two rows of perfect, big, white teeth. His smile reminded her of a wolf in front of its prey, and she shivered.

Then, he bowed mockingly and turned around to go to the barn erected on one side of the big yard.

She didn't move until a metallic squeak reached her ears, letting her know he'd opened the rusty barn door.

Then, she ran inside and belatedly locked the door behind her. It was pointless, but she needed that blanket of security for a moment.

She hadn't forgotten she had to go back out there with the blankets she'd promised. She had to give him some food as well. She couldn't do otherwise if she wanted to avoid his coming to the house to ask, but she couldn't make her feet move. Her legs shook so badly that she needed to lean on the wall to keep herself standing.

Finally, the fear that he might come back forced her to move and she climbed the stairs to the second floor. With shaking hands, she took two blankets from the linen cupboard in the hallway upstairs.

Then, she raided the kitchen and prepared three large sandwiches. *'Better safe than sorry,'* she thought.

It took her longer than she expected, but then, she kept dropping things. Her fingers shook and she couldn't control them. She took a can of soda out of the fridge and headed to the front door.

Her heart beat faster. She was so scared that she practically jumped out of her skin. Before opening the door, she cautiously moved the flimsy drapes, which covered the side window, and looked out, carefully.

The light in the barn was on, but she couldn't see anything else. '*I hope he's waiting for me there and not here.*'

Her only other choice was to call the sheriff, but by the time he'd have made it there, she could have been fodder for the vultures.

She opened the door and went out into the dark. In a few long strides, she reached the door of the barn and shouted, "Mister, are you in there?"

The door of the barn opened with a screech, and startled, she jumped back a few steps and screamed.

"Did I startle you?" he asked, mildly interested. His tone showed he didn't care one way or another.

"What do you think?" she scowled at him. "Here are your blankets," she said angrily and shoved the blankets to him.

Then, she turned back, forgetting about the food she still held in her hand. In the corner of her eye, she caught a glimpse of his right brow going up sardonically. She realized he was pointedly eying the sandwiches in her hand and she had the impulse to throw everything to him.

She controlled herself and handed him the food. Afterwards, she turned around again to leave the barn without a word.

"Good night to you too," he said sarcastically, and burst into a hearty laughter. It sounded crazy to her ears.

He knew her imagination had run wild and that was why she behaved like a scared doe.

She mumbled a few choice words she wasn't supposed to know. The words reached the man's ears and his mirth became louder. He was pleased both with the situation and her colorful vocabulary.

She didn't stop. She left the barn in a hurry, but she couldn't help but notice the man's musky scent and something like butterflies fluttered in her stomach. She refused to dwell on that strange sensation and focused on her fury.

She almost ran back to the house. She wanted to put as much distance as possible between her and the giant residing in her barn for the night. She locked the door behind her and breathed with relief when she heard the lock clicking into place.

She gave up on drinking her usual cup of tea before going to bed and went directly upstairs to her bedroom on shaky legs.

She changed into her pajamas although it took her a while. Her fingers shook so hard that she barely could button her blouse.

An owl hooted into the night and the sound filled her with anxiety. It sounded like an omen. She hesitantly went to bed, bothered by bleak thoughts. The feeling that something was about to happen kept her awake for a long time.

CHAPTER 2

The dawn was just coloring the horizon when the man came out of the barn, rubbing his eyes. His mood had soured the night before and never recovered. He admitted that sleeping in a barn hadn't been the best choice for him, and his eyes thundered with ire.

Nature called and he visited the cluster of trees at the back of the yard. *'She wouldn't be too happy if I went inside to look for the bathroom.'*

Coming back, he ruffled his hair with impatient fingers and looked around. His eyes fell on the old well in the yard first, but then he saw that a new water pump had been installed in its proximity.

He stretched at first, to appease the ache in his shoulders, and then, he took off his shirt. Modesty was alien to him. He didn't care if his hostess watched him.

No one had ever described him as being shy, and he knew he had the body to offer a good show for free to the woman in the house.

'After all, it's nothing but fair game to pay her back for making me sleep in the barn.'

He planned on making her pay dearly for her mistrust, although deep down, he knew she was in the right. No woman in the world, even one with only a few functioning brain cells, would have welcomed an unknown man into her house at night.

Still, the woman had hurt his pride. Darn it all! He didn't look like a criminal. Yes, he'd walked for a few hours and he'd been dusty.

He'd intended to be there late in the morning, but the dang car broke down and he couldn't do anything about it. The battery had finally given out and nothing he tried revived it. No cars had passed by and he had waited there close to two hours. So, no help from that corner.

A film of dust and sweat covered him when he finally arrived on her doorstep. He'd marched a long way from the other end of the forest to that God forsaken place.

'I even wore my best pair of jeans and my favorite shirt in her honor. And she looked at me like I was a piece of shit,' he thought and scowled, not caring if the woman was wary of his appearance on her steps.

While he was washing his neck and strong muscular arms at the pump, she watched him from behind the curtains. Her eyes swept over the expanse of his muscular back and a tinge of attraction fluttered in her belly.

She'd known immediately when he woke up. Maybe the screech of the barn door had woken her. Or maybe she'd heard his steps in the yard or the water flowing at the pump.

Anyway, she'd gone to the window at once and now she was watching him with something close to fascination.

She refused to analyze her reasons. Her mouth had never watered seeing a handsome body before. *'There's always a first time for everything,'* she mused.

His strong arms showed sculpted muscles and his broad chest, covered with dark coarse hair, glistened with water drops.

She fisted her hands because her fingers ached to brush through that thick hair and she bit her bottom lip. Then, she shook her head, *'Damn it! What are you thinking, woman? Get a grip!'*

She left the window, and headed to the bathroom to take a long shower to wash away her desire for the man she'd locked outside the night before.

Cold water whipped her body and punished her for a few minutes. She welcomed the grueling punishment because she needed her sanity back and fast.

Afterwards, she chose a modest t-shirt and a pair of jeans, which had seen better times. A brief glance in the mirror assured her she was decent enough. She didn't want to raise his eyebrows over her choice of attire. Satisfied, she headed downstairs and unlocked the front door.

He was already there, in front of the door, rubbing his skin with a rough towel he'd taken from the backpack he'd had with him the night before.

She tried hard to take her eyes from his chest. *'Damn! Why am I so obsessed with that damn chest?'*

"If you want breakfast, you may come in," she abruptly said and then, turned her back to him, as if he'd been of no consequence.

She sauntered to the kitchen, apparently uninterested whether he followed her or not.

His eyes zeroed in on her behind snuggled in tight frayed jeans and grinned. He imagined she'd chosen them to stop him looking, but the result was the opposite. His desire ran deep and strong now.

Those might have been some old pants, but they looked perfect on her. They fit her like a second skin. When she moved, they hugged her hips tight and he needed all his ragged control not to jump her.

He laughed at himself and finished drying his body with the towel. He pulled on a clean t-shirt and went into the house looking for the kitchen.

The smell of freshly cooked food had already filled the room, and his hunger clawed at his stomach.

"People usually say *'good morning'* or at least *'hi'* when they see each other in the morning," he said in a conversational voice, leaning on the jamb of the door, his legs crossed at the ankles.

"Maybe they do, but I don't have time for niceties, especially with the likes of you," she threw over her shoulder with disdain, keeping busy at the stove.

"Oh, really? The likes of me? And what's so important that you can't pay the slightest courtesy to a guest?"

She made a grimace and thanked God he couldn't see her face. *'Courtesy, indeed! To a guest! As if I had invited him!'* Yet she didn't find an appropriate reply.

She should have worked for her next exhibit, but inspiration evaded her for the moment. She actually didn't have anything special to do. She'd already finished cleaning the ranch house.

Now, she thought of listening to some music, reading a book or simply admiring the nature. She'd find herself something to do and she didn't need him around.

"Things," she replied unfriendly, to close the subject.

"What kind of things?" he insisted, which prompted her to roll her eyes with exasperation.

He was like a terrier with a bone in his teeth. His jaw was stubbornly set and it was obvious he wouldn't let very well go.

"Various," she replied without showing any particular interest in him. "Not that it's your business, by the way."

She worried that if he hadn't left soon he would have driven her mad. Turning to him with the pan in her hand, she laid the omelet on his plate and snapped at him angrily, "Now, eat and leave!"

"Nice manners, really," he drawled his words without backing down.

Her rude treatment didn't seem to affect him. He looked as if he had the time of his life and she couldn't understand why.

"What's wrong with you?" she gave up and asked, watching the man with astonishment. "Don't you feel when you're not wanted somewhere?"

"Oh, yeah, I do, don't worry," he waved his hand. "It's not like you haven't gone out of your way to let me know you didn't want me here, sugar," he replied matter-of-factly. "Now, whether I want to or not, I have to stay here," he said, sitting down and forking some of the eggs she had prepared for him.

"What on Earth do you mean?" she asked him completely stunned.

She crossed her arms under her breasts and threw him a dark glance. She couldn't believe her ears. He had simply stated he had to stay there as if her wishes hadn't mattered at all.

"It's simple, sweetie pie. I have to stay here. Didn't your attorney read your aunt's will to you?"

His words left her speechless for a few seconds. She was just staring at him as if he'd suddenly sprung a new head.

"I didn't listen very attentively," she admitted in a mutter. "But I am pretty sure that I am the only one who inherited this house," she waved her hand around.

"Yeah, you are. But there's something else in there. She asked that you share the house with me for at least two years. That's the condition attached to your ownership. I'll take care of the property for two years, until you decide whether you really want to live here or not."

Her eyes grew so round that he was afraid they'd burst. The next moment, she rushed out of the kitchen and went noisily into the next room. A drawer was opened with nervous gestures.

A satisfied smile flourished on his lips at the sound of papers shuffled around. He knew he'd just stated the truth and wondered how she hadn't seen that condition before.

His reasons for being there were a bit more complicated than that, though. He couldn't care less about the state of the house or of the property.

He was there for her protection and to uncover some dark truths. Some people were long overdue a payback. The late old woman had just made it easier for him to find satisfaction when she wrote her will.

Those thoughts turned his smile into a sneer. There were things he couldn't forget or forgive. Payback was a given.

Her loud outraged shout and the sound of a drawer slamming in the other room prompted him to school his features into a mask of indifference. He resumed his eating with measured gestures.

She came back, mad as a hornet's nest, and leaned over him, "What the hell is this? Why is she doing this to me?"

"Doing? Sweetie pie, she's already done it," he replied quietly and continued eating his breakfast, unconcerned.

"You know what I mean," she stomped her foot. "Damn it, I'm too furious to think," she snapped and started to pace the length of the kitchen.

"Are you? Then, sit down and eat," he said, pushing the plate with eggs in front of her. "Maybe that will help your thinking process."

"I'm not in the mood to eat anymore," she snapped back. "Do you think I can eat when I know that a stranger is going to share the house with me? And not any stranger, but you...," she sputtered.

"Why not?" he raised an eyebrow. "You can't do anything about it, can you? The will is extremely clear, if I'm not wrong. It's ironclad. You can't change a thing. And what's wrong with me? Is there another man more suited for this than me?"

She didn't bother to reply to him. She looked for a way out, but she knew very well that there wasn't any. The will was clear and it wasn't as if she could have changed it.

She glanced at him with a frown between her eyebrows. She found herself literally at his mercy.

That realization made another thought pop into her head. She tilted her head and watched him through her lashes.

"What would it take to make you leave here for good and leave me alone, hmm?"

"I won't leave, so sit down and eat," he said, always calm, without emotion.

"Why not?"

She had almost shouted at him like a banshee, losing the thin shreds of control she had over her temper.

"Why can't you be a reasonable boy?" she asked meanly, and her eyes narrowed into thin slits.

He raised his eyebrows when he heard the appellative and his features turned sterner.

"Okay, a reasonable man, then," she said quickly, trying to appease him. She imagined he didn't care for her choice of words.

Yet, she knew she needed his consent after all, so perhaps it wouldn't do to alienate him.

"I'm reasonable. I'm reasonable because I don't intend to let the judge know of your pathetic attempt to make me leave. It sounded like a bribe, didn't it?"

"You are the worst -" she started but he stopped her with a brief gesture.

"I wouldn't continue if I were you. I've already finished eating. I'm going to wash my plate, so that you didn't have any reasons to complain that you are the only one doing any work around here," he mocked her, taking his plate to the sink.

She huffed behind him and because her temper was pricked again, she threw her fork to him, nailing him straight in the middle of his back. She'd already realized her childishness when he turned his head to her, his eyes as icy as a cold winter day.

Now, he turned completely to her and watched her for a long moment, as if he couldn't believe his eyes. He braced his hands on his hips and stared her down.

He'd thought she was just a pretty little thing. He hadn't imagined she'd have it in her to really get angry. Now, he realized how wrong he'd been and promised himself not to be so rush in his assumptions in the future.

He sighed and then, he asked quietly, tilting his head, "What the hell is wrong with you?"

"There's nothing wrong with me, beside you, of course," she replied and she crossed her arms over her chest. "I didn't ask for a housemate, did I, now?"

'*You've got a point there, sweetie pie,*' he thought. He reckoned she felt cheated and with her back to a wall, but he wasn't stupid to say it out loud. She'd have taken advantage of his understanding and he couldn't have any of that.

"Okay, sweetheart, let's settle this," he said and walked toward her with measured steps.

Her eyes sparkled with anger. She clearly didn't like to be called '*sweetheart*'. She bristled every time he used an endearment. He merely grinned at her and that fed her anger more.

"There's nothing to settle. You just have to leave. That's all!" she snapped and stomped her foot on the floor, at the same time.

'*Way to go, girl. You're just regressing more and more,*' she chided herself with derision.

"Now, you know I can't do that, don't you? I'd like to respect the old woman's last wishes. You should too. After all, she was your aunt, not mine," he replied with false sadness.

'*As if you cared,*' she tightened her teeth and scowled at him.

He knew she'd have liked to throw him as far away as possible, but unfortunately for her, he was there to stay.

He had some unfinished business to deal with and he didn't have any intention to let a pretty face get in his way. Yet, he commiserated with her because he understood how it was to feel powerless at the whims of fate.

"So, how do you see this situation?" she asked after a few moments of silence.

She pinned him with her narrowed eyes, while she was tapping her foot impatiently.

"As it is. I will live here for the next two years, whether you like it or not. You choose what bedroom I'll use. I'm not pretentious so I can sleep in any of them. Keep in mind, the barn is out of question." He put his hand up to forestall any replies. "My mother raised a gentleman, not a farm boy."

She snorted at his words and stared at him coldly. At first, she didn't make any effort to reply. Then, she couldn't keep her mouth shut anymore and said, "I doubt it."

"What?" he asked with a frown, although he had a good guess what she was talking about.

"I doubt the part where you're a gentleman," she said and headed to the kitchen door.

"Hey, you, where are you going?" he hurried after her, afraid she might think of running away.

That would have put a serious hitch in his carefully laid plans. He needed her there.

"Hey, you?" she turned back to him with visible irritation. Suddenly, she felt so sick of his manner of talking to her that she felt like slapping him over the head.

"Till we make the introductions, sweetie pie, I'll call you that," he said coldly.

He felt a twinge of guilt because he had to trample all over her to reach his own goals, but he smothered it at once. The final goal mattered. What happened in the process of reaching it wasn't relevant at all.

Only then, she realized she didn't even know his name or where he came from. She knew nothing at all. She'd scanned over the words in the will and his name hadn't registered in her mind.

He was a stranger and she was supposed to share the house, and implicitly her life, with him. She doubted she'd be able to have a completely separate life with someone else in the house.

"Yes, we skipped that," she admitted morosely. "Our conversation was so titillating that we didn't find the time for introductions," she continued, sarcasm dripping off her tongue. Her eyes shone with scorn and something else, he couldn't put his finger on.

A grin claimed his lips. He was relieved that, at least, she had a sense of humor. Living with her might prove less boring than he'd expected.

"So, sweetheart, what's your name, then?" he asked leaning with his hip on the table. His arms were crossed on his chest, as if he'd wanted to keep her at bay.

"Diane and not sweetheart, so don't call me that anymore," she retorted with a scowl.

"Okay, not a problem for me, baby," he said, and his smile reached his eyes this time.

His lips twitched with pleasure when she clenched her fists at his new term of endearment.

"Damn it, man, I'm not your baby, is that clear?" she scolded him.

"Crystal clear, don't worry. I will try not to say it again," he replied, laughing now. "It's Adam to you," he said and bowed his head with ridicule.

"To me? Does that mean you have several names you use?" Diane asked him befuddled.

"It depends on the situation," he admitted. "Anyway, you have the honor to use the real one. Isn't that something?" he asked mockingly and a playful light danced in his dark pupils.

"Oh, stop doing me any favors. I can live without them," she snapped, stomping out of the room, her back straight as an arrow.

"I'm sure you can," he mumbled to himself as she was leaving the room.

CHAPTER 3

Adam decided to let Diane cool down for about half an hour and take care of his own problems. She'd been pretty riled up and he doubted she'd listen to reason.

He washed the dishes stacked in the sink, his mind mulling over the plans he'd already made and ticking the security measures, he had to take, off a mental checklist, one by one.

When he finished with the dishes, he brought his things from the barn into the house and left them in the kitchen until he had somewhere else to store them.

Adam intended to keep his part of the bargain and let Diane decide which bedroom he could take. She wasn't the enemy and he didn't want her to become one, even though he enjoyed nettling her all the time.

He knew that choosing a bedroom for him wouldn't have been a difficult decision to make. There were only three bedrooms in the house and she'd already moved into one. She had to decide if he'd take the one on the right or the one on the left.

The thought made him smile. Adam imagined that Diane regretted that she hadn't listened to that lawyer more carefully, now. If she had, she'd have known that company was about to come and she'd have chosen one of the other bedrooms, not the one in the middle.

He'd seen her in the window earlier when she was watching him and he'd guessed which room was hers. Her aunt had given him a tour of the house when they met a few months before her demise and he'd committed everything to memory.

Old habits always died hard. He'd been conditioned for several years to plot and memorize the layouts of the buildings where he had to live even for only a few hours. He doubted that would ever change. Caution was too ingrained in him.

He'd liked the old lady. Martha was the salt of the earth and he'd felt comfortable in her presence. She liked him as well, not like her niece, who seemed to abhor the ground he walked on.

He'd spent several weeks with her but he'd had to leave for a short while and put his affairs in order. When she died, he was far away. The lawyer informed him after the will was read and he felt as if he'd lost another family member.

Martha Elgin was another one to avenge. Her death had been ruled an accident, but he knew better. The timing of her death was telling.

Adam shook his head to get rid of his bleak thoughts. He needed to look forward not backward. He couldn't bring Martha back to life, but he could keep his word and take care of her niece.

Adam glanced at his watch and lifted an eyebrow. Diane had taken a lot of time to get over her anger and he didn't intend to give her a minute longer.

He went out into the hallway and yelled, "Diane, come downstairs. We have to talk things over. I don't have all day to wait for you."

His voice sounded harsh, but a smile appeared on his lips when a door slammed upstairs and Diane stomped down the stairs.

She stopped a few steps from the bottom and with one hand braced on her hip, she scowled at him.

"Who died and made you my boss?" she asked with fire in her voice.

He just arched his eyebrow again and refused to answer. Yet, a blush powdered Diane's high cheekbones when she realized the insensitivity of her words.

"All right, forget that. What do you want now?" she scolded him.

Diane disliked herself because she behaved like a teenager. Her maturity seemed a matter of the past. The man brought out the worst in her. She lost any measure of control when Adam spoke to her.

"First, a bedroom to leave my things and second, your car," he answered curtly and, without waiting for a response, he headed back into the kitchen to pick up his backpack and the cowboy hat, he'd left on a chair.

"My car?" Diane came after him in a rush. "Why would I give you my car?" she asked with befuddlement.

He ignored her question and picked up his things with lazy gestures. Only after he had everything secured in his hands, did he glance her way and deigned to answer to her.

"Because I need to go back to my car and take what I left in the trunk. I won't walk all those miles again," he replied mildly.

The distance didn't daunt him. In his former life, he'd marched longer than that and had even run over longer distances. Yet, he didn't feel like spending the day walking over five miles one way, then back again to bring the rest of his luggage.

He didn't have a lot of stuff but carrying a suitcase through the woods was far from his idea of having fun. Besides, he didn't want to be away from the ranch for too long.

Leaving Diane alone for longer stretches of time was out of question. He'd cursed himself enough when he found out she'd been alone there for the funeral. His worry and self-loathing had increased when he couldn't make it there immediately after she moved in.

"I'll drive you," she said and went to take the car keys from her bag.

"No need," he refused sternly. "I can drive myself there and back without problems. I've been driving since I was fourteen."

"Fourteen? That's-"

"Precocious, I know," Adam interrupted her with mirth.

He knew she'd wanted to say something else and smiled. His charming smile wormed its way right into her heart.

'*No, not my heart. What the heck am I thinking? I don't find him anything but overbearing,*' Diane thought.

She gave herself a mental shake, and said, "It doesn't matter. I won't let you drive my car. Either I drive or you can walk. You choose." She ended in a voice that didn't leave room to bargain.

'*I thought she was an airy butterfly, but she seems to be a barracuda,*' Adam reflected with puzzlement.

He didn't like it when he was wrong. Some mistakes didn't leave room for new ones.

Martha had told him Diane was an artist. Artists lived with their minds in the clouds, didn't they? They weren't supposed to be belligerent.

"All right, your *Stubbornness*," he said and bowed mockingly. "Lead the way," he continued with a large gesture, and left his things in the kitchen. "At least this way, we can try to start my car. I have some jumper cables in my trunk."

Diane looked at him with suspicion and Adam found that amusing. The woman proved to have no gullible bone in her body.

That put a stitch in his plans but, in the long run, he preferred it that way. At least, he wouldn't be bored to tears in no time at all.

Those last few years had made him indifferent to women. Probably because he'd met a certain type of woman all the time. He rarely turned them down, but one encounter was more than enough.

"I can show you to the car," she replied, "but you'll have to show me where your car broke down," Diane turned her back to him and headed out of the house.

CHAPTER 4

Adam watched Diane drive and admired her competence. She took every bend with precision, even though her speed was just a notch higher than people would normally try on those meandering mountain roads.

"What?" she asked, slightly turning her head to him for a second. "You're staring. Have I grown horns all of a sudden or what?" she snapped when she noticed Adam's annoying smile.

She was irritated all right. The man knew how to smile. Every time he turned that grin toward her, the butterflies in her belly started a hoopla dance and that was disconcerting. She couldn't wrap her head around that reaction at all. It was both new and unsettling.

Adam muddled her mind and she needed her wits to stand up to him. She had the feeling the man would trample all over her otherwise and that wasn't something she would abide.

"Just enjoying the view, pumpkin," he replied with a grin.

"Diane, not pumpkin, remember?" she barked at him again.

She had to set him straight. Every time he uttered one of those silly endearments, her silly heart forgot that it was just for show and beat faster.

'I suppose it's the accent or because he drawls his words,' she reflected. Yet, she knew that she was well over the age when such things should make her reason melt into a puddle.

Adam just shrugged with indifference and replied, "You know that old habits die hard, Diane.

You're fresh and sweet enough, and that makes me call you pumpkin or sweetie pie."

Her eyes widened and bewildered, she looked at him for a moment, forgetting to watch the road. The car turned slightly to the right, where the mountain slope tilted toward a deep valley.

"Watch the dang road, woman," Adam shouted and immediately, she snapped out of her trance and righted the car.

"If you promise to watch the road, I'll promise not to call you pumpkin anymore, all right?" he said with obvious relief.

For a brief moment, he'd visualized the car flying into the abyss below and it unsettled his stomach. He hadn't survived bullets and bombs just to end up a statistic in a car accident.

"Or, if you prefer, I can drive myself, as I proposed from the beginning," he continued to mutter, although loud enough to be heard. "That way, I might get to my car alive."

"I can drive," she protested. "It was just a moment of distraction, that was all," she said defensively and a blush crept all over her cheekbones, neck and ears.

Diane hated it whenever she blundered something. In her book, there wasn't any room for mistakes. Her mother had drilled that into her head time and time again.

Her fingers clutched the steering wheel and she clenched her teeth. She'd have screeched in frustration, but didn't want to give him the satisfaction that he'd rattled her enough for that.

"One moment's more than enough," he replied heatedly. "Who the heck had the bright idea that women should drive? Who the heck decided to give them a driver's license?" he asked rhetorically, rolling his eyes and gesticulating widely.

"You're a chauvinistic pig," she observed, forgetting about her earlier mistake. "Women drive very well, even better than men, if you must know," she replied and increased the speed just to show him how wrong he was.

She'd never backed down from a dare and his words dared her big time. Diane knew her behavior was childish, yet, she couldn't control her reactions around him. She had to ponder about that.

"Hey, Diane, let's say I believe you. There's no need to kill me just trying to prove a point," he said in a conciliatory voice and patted her on the knee, which startled her.

His gesture shocked her and the car took another nose dive toward the edge of the road.

"Oh, God, woman," he groaned and tried to grab the steering wheel with his left hand.

She growled at him and steered the car back on the road, after she slapped his hand away. She pushed the gas pedal down some more.

His eyebrows shot up and not only because of her growl. He stared at her, speechless. Diane kept surprising him.

Once the road widened for a fraction, she brusquely pulled over on the shoulder of the road and turned off the engine. Her hands trembled on the wheel but not because of fear.

Diane was so angry that she barely controlled herself. She felt like hitting him over the head with a blunt object and she didn't like it.

She'd never thought of herself that way. She wasn't a violent person, but since his arrival in her back yard the night before, she'd gone through the wringer.

"Get out of my car, now," she said in a low and menacing voice.

Or what, pumpkin? Adam replied mutely, but decided to try a different path. He turned to her and watched her steadily.

The wisps of coppery hair framing her face tantalized him. His fingers itched with the need to push them away and touch her skin.

"What now?" he asked as if he hadn't understood what was going on.

"You've picked on me since the moment you arrived," she bellowed, forgetting everything about her own lecture about control and self-restraint. "I'm sick of your macho behavior and your misogynistic views. I'm sick of you, period. Now, out," she practically roared and her small hands clenched into fists and pounded the steering wheel.

She'd have preferred to pound his face, but she refused to lower herself to a physical attack. Plus, she didn't know how he would react and she was smart enough to guess that she wouldn't win in a contest of brute force.

"Yeah, as if…" he smirked at her. "Just because I pointed out your driving shortcomings," he shook his head. "Diane, Diane, it seems to me you don't take criticism too well, sweetheart, even when it's warranted. You can't say you weren't about to drive us down there twice." He pointed his thumb toward the slope of the mountain.

He glanced at the valley stretching at the bottom of the abyss and shuddered mentally.

"And it's not a gentle slope, you know," he thought to mention and glanced again toward the side of the mountain. *'Dang, it's a long way to the bottom of that valley,'* he noticed.

"Because of you, not because I can't drive, stupid," she replied hotly, and this time, she did slap his arm.

"Because of ol' me?" he asked with innocence, pointing his thumb to himself and beating his lashes with exaggeration.

"You know very well what you did," she replied with tiredness in her voice.

She braced herself and breathed deeply. She tapped her impatient foot on the floor of the car and, then, she repeated with calm, "Now, get out. You should be close to your car. I'll be home. Don't expect a warm meal when you come back," she continued and looked straight ahead. She refused to acknowledge what he might thought of her.

Adam noticed that she avoided looking at him and felt a perverse joy knowing he rattled her. That joy disappeared fast enough when he realized she was serious.

'*The dang woman does expect me to walk to my broken car and back to the ranch,*' he thought and decided to pay more attention to her from that moment on. Diane proved more difficult than he'd expected. He thought he'd handle her with ease.

"You can dream on, little girl," he snorted. "I'm not beyond grabbing you and throwing you in the back of the car, Diane," he said, his icy eyes trained on her.

Diane looked up sharply and shuddered when she met his look. Her eyes searched his face and she cringed. *'He's serious. He'll do it. Oh, Lord, what now?'*

"You're threatening me?" she chose to attack, even though her voice shook a little.

"If necessary, yeah. You should know something about me, pumpkin-"

"Ah!" she interrupted with another growl. "First of all, I told you not to call me pumpkin anymore," she started in force, but he put up his hand and stopped her.

"I said I wouldn't if you watched the road. Should I remind you, *pumpkin*, you didn't?" he observed, just to needle her some more.

Adam didn't understand his need to pick on her and drive her mad. *'Maybe because she drives me mad just because she breathes,'* he had a brief moment of honesty with himself, but buried it immediately.

He couldn't take that road. His priorities laid somewhere else. Besides, he didn't do steady relationships and Diane definitely didn't fall under the one-night-stand type.

"You touched my leg," she accused and her green eyes flashed at him.

"So what?" he replied nonplussed. "Has no man ever touched you?" he shrugged with nonchalance, as if his gesture hadn't been out of the ordinary.

And it wasn't, Diane admitted, but with him, it seemed different and she didn't like that different. She preferred relationships that didn't make her think too much. She liked polite men who understood to leave her alone when she wanted to be alone and didn't dare to take the initiative and order her around.

"Only when I said they could," she retorted with disdain. "I didn't give you permission to touch me," she specified in a haughty voice.

"Don't tell me you went out only with guys who asked nicely if they could touch your hand or kiss you," he exclaimed and looked at her in shock.

"Not that it's any of your business, but, as I said, I prefer polite men," she said and nodded with emphasis.

"I think you confuse polite with milquetoast, Diane. A considerate man would back off if you said no, but there's no way, no way in hell, a red-blooded man would ask permission for every touch," he shook his head.

"Whatever, get lost," she gave up. "Walk straight ahead and you'll find your car," she continued, waving to the road.

"You said *first of all*," Adam said as if she hadn't asked him to leave.

"So what?" She looked at him befuddled.

"That means you also have a *second of all*. Let's hear it," he proposed.

Adam had no intention of getting out of the car or losing sight of her. He planned to stay as close to her as possible for the following two years. If his plans needed two years to be completed.

Even if his constant presence nettled her, he had a job to do. Her wishes came second or even last, depending on the circumstances.

"I forgot what I wanted to say." She threw her hands into the air. "So, there you have it. Now, get out," she repeated meanly.

"I haven't," he replied. "I remember perfectly." He decided to enlighten her. "I said *'You should know something about me, pumpkin'* and you replied, *'First of all, I told you not to call me pumpkin anymore.'* So, you do have a *second of all*," he ended with glee.

"Now I remember, thank you so much for reminding me," she replied sarcastically.

She crossed her arms under her breasts, which pushed them higher, and his eyes zeroed in on them in a nanosecond flat.

"I intended to tell you that what I know about you is enough. I don't need to hear anything else," she nodded with determination.

"Well, that's where you're wrong," Adam replied with a false compassionate voice, looking up at her face.

"What do you mean?" she asked, with a feeling of dread invading her body.

"You'll have enough time to find a lot out about me," he replied. "Well, not everything," he admitted. "I'm not an open book after all. And the first thing you'll find out is that I'm not a doormat, Diane," he specified, his eyes boring into hers. "You can't trample all over me and bring me to attention with a few choice words, pumpkin. I'm the boss, not like the men you've led on a leash so far," he said with authority and put his hand up again when he saw she wanted to interrupt him. "Don't bother. You can do whatever you want as long as it doesn't clash with what I want," he explained very matter-of-factly.

"You're out of your mind," she concluded and her eyes widened again. "Do you really believe you can order me around?"

"No," he shook his head, "I'm not thinking of ordering you around. I'm just stating how things are. What I say comes first," he said in a serious voice.

"In your dreams, big boy," Diane waved him off and rolled her eyes.

Suddenly, his demeanor changed. His eyes turned hard and he leaned toward her.

"I'll let that slide," Adam responded in a low voice, "because I know you don't know what I know. But listen well, Diane, and I'm darn serious about this, girl. You do what I say, for your own good."

"You threatened me again," she observed with amazement and shook her head. She couldn't believe his boldness.

"It's not a threat," he said and grabbed her arm, which startled her again.

A trace of fear appeared in her pupils and he didn't miss it. His heart cringed at the thought she believed that he'd hurt her.

"I don't want to scare you," he said in an even voice. "You needn't be afraid of me. I won't hurt you, Diane, but you need to listen to me from now on and listen well. Your aunt didn't put me in your proximity just to play a prank on you," he explained further. "She had a serious reason. You're a smart woman, from what I could gather. Think before doing anything unreasonable."

Diane just stared at him. His fingers burned her skin and his words shocked her.

"What do you mean?" she asked in a small voice.

He might not have wanted to frighten, her but he did that all the same.

"It's not the moment now. We'll rehash all that later." He shook his head. "You only need to know that my presence here is necessary and your cooperation is imperative," he decided to tell her.

"Oh, no, you don't," she snatched her arm away from him. "Either you tell me what's what or I do what I think I should do, what I please, and the heck with everything else," she said.

Stubbornness was written all over her face. Her green eyes sparkled with rebellion.

Adam sighed deeply and prayed for patience. He decided to end the stalemate and offer her an olive branch.

"Okay, you drive for the moment. Go on, I think we're close to the place where I left my car."

Diane wanted to insist, but noticed his weariness and that stopped her. She turned the key in the ignition and drove away, paying attention to the road so he wouldn't find yet another reason to cut her to ribbons with his words.

CHAPTER 5

Adam found his car exactly where he'd left it. With satisfaction, he noticed that no one had touched it.

He'd left telling signs and they hadn't been disturbed, with one exception. An animal had probably climbed onto the hood and fooled around with the windshield wiper, because, otherwise, if someone of the human variety had checked his car, the other signs he'd set up would have been disturbed as well.

Diane's eyes followed Adam's every move. After what he'd said in the car earlier, she decided to keep her eyes wide open. Something was going on and it was definitely something fishy.

She didn't know whether she could trust Adam or not. Her aunt had trusted him, though, and Diane knew Martha hadn't been anyone's sucker. She could sniffle a bad man better than any hound.

Curiosity lit the green of her pupils and her teeth bit into her lower lip in concentration. She rubbed her hands warily, while watching Adam's telling movements around the car.

Adam glanced at her. She amused him and at the same time, she touched his heart. He could read everything on her face and a smile fluttered on his lips.

"What are you doing?" she asked with impatience. She couldn't keep her curiosity in check anymore.

"Just making sure no one tempered with the car," Adam shrugged her question away.

After he answered to her, he crouched and checked underneath the car. Satisfied that no devices had been attached anywhere, he stood and said, "I have some battery cables in the trunk, as I said. Do you think we could try to jumpstart my car?"

"Yes, of course. That way, you may leave me and my car alone," Diane replied maliciously. "It's not like we have to be joined at the hip all the time."

"Don't count on that," Adam replied in a quieter voice and opened his trunk.

He needn't look at her to know that his answer angered her. Her tension was palpable and enveloped him from everywhere. *As if I'd cared,* he thought.

He returned to the front of the car with a pair of jumper cables and found her in the same spot she was before. She hadn't moved from where he'd left her. A scowl etched on her features and she clenched her fists so hard her knuckles turned white.

"Why don't you lift your hood?" he inquired mildly.

Adam didn't want to alienate her completely because he needed her cooperation in the long run. Diane just speared him with her glare for a few more moments and then, she turned stiffly and headed to her car to lift the hood.

They worked in tandem for the following few minutes and their work was soon rewarded. Both Adam and Diane cheered when his engine started to purr.

They high-fived each other and laughed merrily together, for the first time, not at odds. Still on a peaceful ground, they started their trip back home, their differences put aside for the brief period they shared that small triumph. Neither of them lied to themselves. They knew their truce was temporary.

Diane parked behind his car and stopped the engine. She grabbed the keys and got out of the car, only to freeze with her hand on the car door.

Adam had already unloaded a suitcase from his trunk, but now he took out two rifles.

'What the heck does he do with a rifle? No, make that two. Is he a wacko with a penchant for guns?'

Adam glanced at her and grinned. He guessed what bothered her. As always, her face reflected her thoughts.

"It's close to hunting season," he explained the presence of the rifles with nonchalance.

'As if I knew what season it is. Huh! Although, I'm here for a hunt, so...'

"I don't know anything about any hunting season," Diane replied in a shaky voice, "but do you really need two rifles? And don't tell me you want to kill Bugs Bunny or Bambi," she shouted at him, regaining her gumption.

Adam rolled his eyes. *'Bugs Bunny? Bambi? What are you? Two years old?'*

"Hadn't thought you'd still watch cartoons at your age. I'd have thought you were out of kindergarten." He shook his head. "I'd have brought you a Barbie if I'd known differently," he continued with biting sarcasm.

Diane bared her teeth at his words, which prompted him to laugh heartily. He did enjoy egging her on.

"Don't worry, I won't shoot Bugs Bunny, Daffy Duck or Bambi. I am trained for bigger game," he winked at her.

"I don't care what you're trained for," Diane snapped his head off. "You're a killer," she accused him with a frown.

"That, you got it right," Adam replied in a serious voice, and the light in his eyes died, which chilled her to the core.

He turned away and carried the suitcase and the guns into the house. Diane, riveted in place, looked after him, a dreary feeling creeping in her mind. The way he'd said those words didn't leave room to interpretation.

'I'm sharing my house and life with a killer,' she reflected and her hands shook. *'What were you thinking, Auntie?'*

Diane forced her feet to move and anxiously, she stopped next to Adam's open trunk. She glanced inside the trunk and her eyes bulged out.

CHAPTER 6

"What do you hunt with grenades?" she asked in a shaky voice.

Diane leaned on the jamb of the door to keep standing. When she'd seen the case with grenades aligned in their little holes like soldiers, she almost fainted. She'd seen grenades only in movies and that was some time ago, as she wasn't too fond of war films.

Adam slowly turned to her, his eyes two dark, unreadable pools. He tilted his head and his eyes swept over her body from the top of her head to the tip of her boots.

Adam's stance frightened her. The man looked like a panther ready to jump at her throat and sink his teeth in her jugular.

His latent strength and his secrets played havoc on her nerves and put forbidden thoughts in her head.

'*You need to pull yourself together, girl,*' she scolded herself. '*This is the type of man from which you have to steer far away. Forget about those biceps that made your mouth water in the morning.*'

Diane shook her head to get rid of her crazy thoughts and headed for the kitchen table where she let herself fall into a chair. She didn't think she could stand for another second.

The day hadn't spared her for one moment. She felt light-headed and she shook all over.

"That's for big game," Adam answered with nonchalance.

A grin appeared in the corner of his mouth, making him look like a rascal. Yet, his eyes were hard.

Diane was afraid to ask what he meant, but she needed to understand what was going on. He clearly hadn't come there just to annoy her.

"You have a freaking arsenal with you, Adam," she said and waved to the rifles he'd set on the kitchen table. "What, with two rifles and a case of grenades..." she continued.

"And to think you haven't seen it all," Adam replied softly and flexed his shoulders to work out some kinks in his muscles.

The last few days hadn't been easy on him. Sleeping in the barn the previous night didn't help him much, either.

"What do you mean?" she perked up.

She was sure he would get to the interesting stuff now.

"I mean I'm prepared for everything. What you saw is just the tip of the iceberg, Diane," he replied with a shrug.

"You mean to say that you have other weapons in your car?" she asked wide-eyed.

He nodded briefly and waited to see what else she was going to say or do. He didn't dare to guess her reactions any more. The woman had proved unpredictable enough.

"I see," she whispered and stared at him. "But why?" she asked. "Rarely wild animals come over here, you know. If you steer out of their path, they leave you alone. You don't need a... rifle or grenade for them," she explained patiently.

Adam laughed out loud. His laughter sounded ugly and hurt her ears. She winced visibly.

"What's so funny?" she asked, her shackles up.

"You, Diane, you're funny," he said and came to her.

Under her cautious eyes, he nudged the side of her jaw with his thumb. It felt rather like a caress and something jolted in her belly.

"Why?" she whispered, unable to speak.

"Because you make all these assumptions," he shrugged, and his thumb trailed the line of her jaw absently.

Then, he turned away and went back out to his car. Wide-eyed, Diane watched him leave.

She wanted to insist on getting real answers from him, but she felt rattled. She decided to wait for him there.

He returned with two duffel bags, one on each shoulder, and then picked up the suitcase he'd left near the table. He headed upstairs to the bedroom she'd assigned him.

Diane noticed he'd left the rifles behind. She eyed the guns with mistrust.

She'd always been a pacifist and she abhorred guns. She hated what people could do to other people using a weapon.

His jogging steps on the stairs pulled her back from her reveries. She glanced at the kitchen door. Adam came in and picked up one of the rifles, he'd left behind, and under her incredulous look, he stuffed it under the sink.

"What are you doing?" she shouted. She couldn't have stopped her words even if she'd wanted to.

"Prepping," he answered curtly to her, and grabbing the second rifle, he went into the hallway.

This time, Diane followed closely, just in time to see him conceal the rifle in the umbrella holder.

"Prepping for what?" she shouted exasperated, throwing her arms in the air. "Look, I'm sick of your ambiguous answers," she said. "I want the truth and I want it now," she continued and slapped the wall on her right.

Adam turned to her and pierced her with his look. He looked at her for something that felt like a long time and Diane started fidgeting under his unnerving gaze.

"You want the truth," he said softly. "All right, I'll give you the truth," he decided. "We can very well have some coffee with that, what do you think?" he said and strode back to the kitchen.

Adam didn't glance behind him. He knew she would follow him. He'd seen her curiosity. Her eyes had widened and her pupils had dilated.

"Have a seat," he invited her, but didn't turn to check if she followed his invitation.

Adam went to the coffee maker and filled the pot with water. He rummaged through a couple of cupboards until he found coffee and filters.

He prepared everything with measured gestures and didn't flinch once under Diane's sharp scrutiny, even though her eyes drilled holes into his back.

"Where's the sugar?" he asked her. "I suppose you take sugar in your coffee," he glanced at her, an eyebrow raised inquiringly.

"Not really," she shook her head. I prefer my coffee black and unsweetened."

"Good, me too," he said and finally, turned away from her. "You're almost out of coffee. We'll need to buy some," he observed and then, he opened the fridge.

Adam looked inside the fridge and visibly winced. He closed the door and turned to her.

"There are no eggs left, no bacon, just some weeds and a tomato," he accused. "What did you intend to do? Starve?"

Diane shrugged daintily and pretended she had some lint to pick up off her clothes.

Silence stretched for a few moments and then, she replied quietly, "I didn't count on you showing up."

Suddenly, she looked up at him with a deep frown. "Those aren't weeds. It's salad," she defended her food choices.

He scowled and braced his hands on his hips.

"Food for rabbits or ducks maybe, but definitely not for me. I can take a weed or two in my sandwich if everything else obliterates the taste, but otherwise...." he shook his head.

Diane smiled and observed with amusement, "I suppose you're a steak-type of guy."

"You got that right," he agreed with her assessment. "We'll have to go shopping," he decided on spot. He didn't feel like fasting until the following day.

"I won't go anywhere today," Diane refused, shaking her head. "I've had enough excitement for one day and I don't feel like going down to the town right now."

"I can't leave you here alone," he discounted her words in a hard voice that didn't broach any argument.

"I've been alone so far," she stubbornly said, unimpressed with the authority of his voice.

"Well, not anymore," Adam reiterated very matter-of-factly.

"No, I won't go shopping this afternoon," she replied in a stronger voice. "We're not joined at the hip, Adam. I might have to accept you in the house, but that doesn't mean that I will turn my life upside-down because of your dictates," she shook her head with vehemence, and her hair bounced full of life and stole his breath away.

Adam shook himself mentally and then, he took in her stubborn demeanor. As a reflex, he flexed his fingers, praying for patience.

"I see that I have to tell you the truth now," he concluded and rubbed the bridge of his nose.

Tiredness had crept on him unnoticed. He felt weary after the last few days, which he had spent crossing the country by car, with only three or four hours of sleep at night.

He had also been worried about what might have happened to Diane if he hadn't got there on time. Yet, he couldn't take a plane, not with the arsenal he needed with him. Leaving it behind would have amounted to the same result in the end.

On top of that, he had spent the previous night in Diane's barn after a five-mile march and a few-hour-long stake-out.

Sparring with Diane hadn't been an easy feat either, although that had spiced his day somewhat. The woman kept him on his toes all the time. Not that he really minded that.

"The truth would be good," Diane replied quietly when she noticed he had started woolgathering.

She had already waited for a couple of minutes, but Adam seemed lost in his own world, which didn't seem to be like him or, at least, like what she knew about him.

"What?" he asked absent-mindedly, rubbing his face with the tips of his fingers.

"The truth," Diane pointed out. "You said something about telling me the truth," she reminded him about the topic of discussion.

"Yes, I did," he nodded. "Just a sec, the coffee is ready," he put her off when the steam of the coffee maker penetrated his haze.

Adam filled two mugs to the rim and brought them to the table. He left one on the table before Diane and sat down in a chair across from her so he could have her under observation. He could observe her emotions from there.

"I'm here on a mission," he confessed to her, looking straight into her eyes. He wrapped his fingers around the mug and let the heat of the coffee sip into his skin. "Your aunt had been threatened a few times when she didn't agree to sell her land," he brusquely revealed.

Diane's eyes widened and her mouth opened in a mute *wow*.

"Close your mouth, sweetie pie," Adam said out of habit. "You wanted to know the truth, so that's what you get. But I don't want any hysterics or anything," he warned her in a hard voice, his eyes trained on her unnervingly.

"I'm not given to hysterics," she replied heatedly, her voice one note higher than normally, which belied her words.

'*As if! My mother would have had my hide for a simple tantrum,*' she scoffed.

"Good, then. Let me continue. A few of those threats materialized, but Martha still didn't agree to sell. She didn't like what those people wanted to do on her land and besides, I understand this ranch had been in her family for about five or six generations," he shrugged and sipped from his mug.

Diane nodded and she also took a mouthful of her coffee. She was parched and needed the strength of the coffee to hold her through his story.

Indeed, the ranch had been in their family for a long time. Her grandmother didn't want to have anything to do with it. She felt smothered there and wanted to make a life for herself in the city. She had hated the work on the ranch.

Aunt Martha had been the last one there. She had taken care of the cattle until she couldn't anymore.

As she had never married, she didn't have children to help her and a couple decades back, she stopped working the ranch. She sold the livestock and everything related to cattle breeding, and lived frugally from the benefits and her own vegetable garden. She rounded her income by renting land to her neighbors, but she had never accepted to sell.

"The last threat Martha received was a threat to her life. She knew that they would keep their word. However, she wanted to make sure you got the ranch and you were well taken care of. Then, she started looking for help and found me," he said pensively. "Or better said, we found each other," he almost whispered, musingly.

"How come?" she inquired in a nonplussed voice.

"There's no need to go into my personal life," he brushed her off, "but let's say that your aunt's enemies were mine as well. She knew I was determined to... take care of them and she needed someone like me to take care of you," he said in a no-nonsense voice and flipped his hand.

"You mean to say you're here for me?" she asked, and her cynicism showed not only in her voice. Her eyes lit with mistrust.

"Partly, yes. Mostly, I'm here because I have some payback to shovel and because I promised to Martha," he replied with a shrug, unconcerned with her mistrust, and then, he picked up his mug and drained his coffee.

He put the cup on the table, drummed his fingers on the tabletop for a few seconds and then asked, "How much time do you need to get ready to go into town?"

"I won't go into town," she replied and shook her head stubbornly. "I've told you I had enough today."

"You can't stay here alone," he retorted.

"The heck I can't. Just watch me," she said and, pushing her cup aside, she headed to the door.

"I can't leave you here by yourself," Adam stood up.

"Should I remind you that I was here by myself before you came?" Diane asked, turning to him. "Nothing will happen to me until you come back from town," she refused to back down. "I'm taking a nap," she announced him and left.

Adam felt uncomfortable leaving her alone. They needed food and coffee, but he needed much more to know she was safe.

"Will you promise to stay in your room?" he shouted, going after her.

"I'm not a child," she turned to him, a hand on the handrail.

"No, you're not," he muttered for his own ears. Of course, he'd noticed she was far from a child and that was the ban of his life. "It would be easier if you were," he replied loudly. "I could just ground you in your room. Diane, keep safe and stay inside. Don't go out until I come back. It's not a joke," his hard eyes held hers.

Diane just looked at him and then nodded. She turned around and jogged up the stairs, feeling his eyes glued on her back all the way up.

CHAPTER 7

Diane did try to sleep. She was exhausted, but her mind was restless and scattered all over the place. Adam's appearance and everything that followed had taken their toll on her.

She punched the pillow to make it more comfortable. It didn't work, though.

Diane willed her muscles to relax, using a relaxation technique, she'd learnt in one of her yoga classes.

Her eyes drifted to sleep and, with a soft sigh, she surrendered. Her muscles relaxed completely, yet her mind worked a double shift, filled with unsettling dreams.

After about an hour and a half, Diane woke up with a startle. Some noise had reached her ears, disturbing her fretful slumber. She slowly sat up and listened intently.

'*Yep, here we go again. Probably, the wind whipped the barn door,*' she thought and got out of bed, intending to go out and secure the screeching door.

Diane pulled her boots on and stood up. Only then, she hesitated. Adam had told her to stay put and not leave the house and she felt somewhat guilty for not listening to him.

'*He might have a point,*' she conceded and reflected some more. '*Nah, he just wants to scare me so that I didn't ask questions about him being here and his... personal things,*' she decided to dismiss his warnings and went out of the door.

Half way down the stairs, she stopped. '*What if he didn't lie?*'

She drummed her fingers on the bannister, reflecting on what he had said earlier.

'No, his story was too outlandish. Too much cloak and dagger and all sorts of plots,' she shook her head and started down again.

Diane went out of the house and paused on the veranda. Feet wide apart, her hands braced on her hips, she surveyed the yard.

The wind had picked up, indeed, and leaves danced all over the place. Fall came earlier in the mountains.

The barn door had been slammed against the wall and the wind kept swinging it. The hinge screeched every time the door moved and Diane cringed. She had to do something about that hinge. She couldn't stand it anymore,

'Well, not right now,' she thought. *'I'm not even sure what to use,'* she grimaced. *'Well, I'll see. For now, I'll just secure it and the wind won't move it anymore,'* she decided and headed to

the barn with long strides. '*There must be some rope or something inside that barn,*' she decided.

Diane got to the barn and headed directly inside to look for a rope. She barely got inside the barn that she felt something move on her left and goose bumps broke on her skin. She dreaded what lurked in the shadow.

She turned to see what was there, but she didn't move fast enough. Something hit her over the head and she fell face down on the grimy floor of the barn.

'*Adam was right after all,*' she thought before she passed out.

When she came, her hands were already tide behind her back and someone was coiling a rope around her ankles. Her mind froze, any defensive thought flying out of the window.

She felt someone standing up over her and she kept her eyes shut, playing possum.

'*Maybe they just leave me alone if they think I can't see or identify them,*' she reasoned, yet her heart had already sunk into her boots. She had never been in such a dire situation and she didn't know what to do or how to react.

She couldn't see who was inside the barn with her, but she could feel their movement. There were at least two if not three people shuffling around. Their steps told her they had finally turned around and gotten out of the barn.

"My idea paid off," one of them said on their way out.

"Yeah, yeah, yeah," another replied bitterly. "We know, you've already said it twice," he chided.

The barn door shut after them with a bang. The sound of a latch falling into place reached Diane's ears and her eyes opened wide. Horror marred her features. It didn't sound too good for her.

The men were still talking outside and their voices still reached her.

"So what," the first one puffed. "I was right when I said we should wait down the road and see which one of them would leave. And now, we're finishing her off and have a convenient scapegoat. They'll think that guy did it. We got rid of both of them in one single move and that thanks to me," he gloated.

Diane had the wrenching feeling they were talking about Adam. '*They want him to be the scapegoat, but for what?*' she wondered at a loss of ideas.

But then the answer came unexpectedly. Her nostrils flared at the gasoline smell. She heard the gasoline splashing against the wooden walls of the barn.

Scared, out of her mind, she desperately looked around for some means to escape.

The barn was mostly dark. A sliver of light came through between two panels of wood where time and the elements had eroded the wood. Not that it helped much.

Nothing could help her, short of a miracle. She shook and the rope coiled around her wrists and ankles bit into her flesh. She was so terrified that her belly churned with a wrenching feeling. Tears ran down her cheeks, washing off the dirt, and stinging her skin with their salt.

Diane made an effort to keep her wits about her, not to give in to her terror. She needed something to cut through her binds and fast because she was almost out of time.

Then, time ran out and she cried out. The crackling of flames engulfed the barn. Her heart skipped a beat or two and she bit her bottom lip, frantically looking around for anything she could use.

The tongues of the raising flames helped her see more of the interior of the barn.

'Not that flames are a good thing, Diane. Oh, God, I'm losing my mind. I have to do something, and now,' she thought, eyeing the flames licking the ground her way.

Tears flooded her eyes and helplessness strangled her. Her fingers shook and she bit her lower lip again.

CHAPTER 8

Adam saw the flames through the trees lining the road and roared his anguish. His foot floored the gas pedal.

He didn't care about the sharp bends of the road anymore. Losing Diane meant a new failure and probably, one he couldn't live with.

Handling the steering wheel with his left hand, he rummaged through the glove compartment and took a revolver out. He laid it on the passenger seat without taking his eyes from the road or the flames painting the sky reddish. He leaned forward, and also took out the gun he had stuffed at the small of his back.

He left it on his thigh, handy if necessary.

In less than three minutes, Adam reached the ranch yard and slammed his brakes hard, at a distance from the barn. He remembered he still had the grenades in his trunk and he was confident that they didn't need a bigger bonfire.

Adam didn't bother to turn the engine off. He just jumped out of the car, both guns in his hands, and ran toward the barn.

The flames had already engulfed the entire wooden building. The sound of wooden boards falling inside the barn brought a hideous scowl on his face.

With one second to think, he threw himself through the burning door and landed on the dirty floor, next to Diane. Flames licked at her, and her pants had caught fire.

Adam left the guns next to her and indifferent to the flames reaching for him, he patted down the flames on her pants with his palms.

The air smelt of burnt hair and he noticed the fire had singed a few of Diane's locks. The burning bite of a flame on his back jarred him into action.

Adam stuffed his guns into his waistband and gathered Diane up in his arms.

By now, both of them had been coughing in earnest. Their eyes had teared up because of the smoke and they could barely see around.

He crouched with her cradled in his arms and surveyed their surroundings.

'We get singed no matter what way I choose,' he thought. *'I'll have to move fast, at least to help her survive.'*

Adam stood, always bent over the woman in his arms, and then made a run to where the barn door had been. Flames licked at his shoulders and hair and kissed his pants, but he didn't pay attention to the pain. He pushed ahead.

Once he cleared the building, his lungs burning, he ran to the pump. A blanket would have worked better, but he didn't think he could take the time and go inside for one.

He gently settled Diane down near the pump and quickly filled the bucket with water from down the old well and pulled it up.

'*I could have put her under the pump directly,*' he thought and shook his head. The idea had already come too late.

He threw the water from the bucket over her head and upper side of her body and she jerked.

A cry of indignation followed. Staggering, she tried to stand up, and pushed hard with one hand on the stone wall of the well.

"Calm down, Diane, don't move, just take your time," Adam said softly, and gently pushed her back down.

Diane looked up at him with red eyes and he winced seeing the traces of her ordeal on her face.

"Everything will be fine, sweetie pie," he whispered, "don't worry now."

He gently brushed his fingers over her stricken cheek.

Diane tried to focus her eyes on him and suddenly, her eyes bulged out and she shouted, "You're on fire, you… stupid."

She tried to stand up again while he took stock of the flames biting their way through his pants.

Adam pushed her back down and she started patting his legs, to smother the flames.

He looked at her as if she'd lost it, and then lowered the bucket back into the well.

'*Good going, man,* he thought. '*You've lost your fucking mind for a broad and forgot about your well-being,*' he shook his head with disdain.

'Who'd take care of her if you went up in flames? Luckily these pants won't let the flames go through.'

He pulled the bucket out of the well and splashed it over his head. Then, he stretched his legs, one after another, under the pump and let the cold mountain water take care of the remnant flames.

He knew he had a few burns on his back, arms and legs. It hurt badly, but at least, they both were alive.

"Thank God, you came back when you did," Diane whispered barely audible.

She'd prayed for a miracle when she couldn't untie herself and her efforts to crawl to safety didn't have any results. Adam turned out to be her miracle.

Adam's eyes checked her all over. She seemed all right. Yet, he couldn't discount the effect the fire had had on her lungs and airways. He knew he had to have her checked out in a hospital.

He pulled her up and said, "I'll take you to the hospital in a few minutes. On the way there, you can explain to me why I found you in the barn when I asked you not to leave the house."

At his hardened expression, her eyes widened and her hand shook. Diane hadn't recovered completely and she wasn't sure she could withstand him.

"Now, where can I find a hose to douse this fire down? We can't risk having the entire forest go up in flames," he explained.

With a shaky finger, she showed to Adam where Martha had kept the hose for fighting fires. Her great aunt had also had a hydrant installed so a fire wouldn't extend to the neighboring areas. With so much wooden area around, fires weren't taken lightly.

CHAPTER 9

Adam put her in his car and strapped her in with the safety belt. He flexed his shoulders to work the kinks out of them. He had a new respect for firemen. It wasn't such an easy job to douse a fire. He felt scorched to the bones. Sweat dripped on his face and along his spine. He wiped off his face with a forearm, not paying any attention to the black streaks which marred his skin.

He went around the hood to get into the car when he remembered the food he had left inside the trunk.

'Damn, some of it will spoil until we're back,' he thought.

"If I leave you here in the car for a few minutes, can I hope to find you in the same spot?" he asked her, leaning inside the car.

Diane nodded, even though she didn't like how he constantly reminded her that she'd left the house.

Adam stared at her for a few moments and then, he took one of his guns out of his waistband and pushed it to her.

"If you need it, point it to the threat and just press this here," he told her, his finger indicating the trigger.

"I... I can't shoot someone," she stammered.

"Of course, you can," he nodded confidently and pushed the gun on her. "When your life is at stake, you can, trust me. Now, I'm going to unload the trunk and put a couple of things in the fridge. Keep your eyes open and do what I said if you're in danger," he repeated and slammed the driver's door shut.

The drive down the mountain was quiet. The silence was weighing down on her and the frown between Adam's brows never left his face.

Diane had been watching him since he came into the car after he finished unloading the groceries. Adam rarely spared a look at her. She couldn't read what was going on in his mind and it bothered her.

He drove down the mountain as fast as he dared and the car jolted her whenever he took a sharp bend.

"Adam," she said, at the same time grabbing at the handle above her window.

Adam had negotiated another hairpin bend and thrown her into the door.

"I think you can slow down," she tried to speak again.

The first time, she'd bit her tongue and she still tasted the metallic flavor of her own blood against her tongue.

"No, Diane, I can't slow down," he growled, baring his teeth. "Smoke inhalation is no joke, and God knows how much you had inhaled before I came."

Despite his display of anger, he used the same tone someone would use to talk to a child and she gritted her teeth in frustration.

"Probably, not so much," she said through her clenched teeth. "I'd have been burnt alive if you'd been five minutes late."

He shook his head in denial, although her account seemed accurate. Yet, he didn't want her to go down that road right then.

"But no car came out of the ranch. I don't believe they'd come on foot," he bit out.

"Probably, they took the trail behind the house. It leads somewhere down the road," she said and waved her hand in that direction. "Yeah, right there, do you see it?" she pointed to an opening masked by two big trees.

He glanced at the trail and swore a bleak streak. His fist hit the steering wheel repeatedly and made Diane wince.

When he visited Martha, he hadn't thought of verifying the trails. He'd imagined he'd have enough time to do it later.

Diane looked at him with wide eyes. Her fingers trembled on the handle she was holding with all her might.

Adam's face had darkened, his eyes threw spears and the diversity of his curse vocabulary surpassed anything she'd ever heard before.

She'd never witnessed anything remotely close to Adam's fury. She just hoped he wouldn't remember about her leaving the house again. She could live just fine without having that raw anger directed to her.

After a few minutes of raging against himself, Adam quieted. He glanced at her and took in the fear and fascination in her eyes.

'I frightened her,' he noticed with self-disgust and grimaced. Her fingers shook on the handle and his guilt deepened.

Adam slowed the car down a notch and took her other hand in his. Lifting it to his mouth, he pressed a tender kiss on her shaky fingers and squeezed them.

"Diane, I might get angry at times and I might bellow and swear... Never, but never, fear I'd hurt you in anger," he stressed out and looked directly into her eyes. "I might lash out verbally, now and then, but nothing more. You're in no danger with me, okay?"

She faintly blushed and nodded. His lips on her fingers had done strange things to those butterflies who had taken permanent residence in her belly since his arrival.

"Now that I'm calm, can you explain to me why I found you in the barn, in the middle of that inferno, when I specifically told you to wait inside?"

He squeezed her fingers again to encourage her to talk and then freed her hand.

"Was it to goad me?" Adam asked again.

"Of course, not," Diane rushed to explain. "I just heard a noise and…"

"And you said, '*What the heck, let me go investigate. That Adam's so stupid he can't find his ass with both his hands so what if he said not to go out? What he says doesn't matter*,'" he snapped at her.

"If you continue to talk to me like that, I won't say another word," she threatened and frowned at him.

"Oh, yeah, you will," he said and sped up a little more.

The road had widened now and he could see the top of the rooftops in the valley.

"No, I won't. I won't be the subject of your ridicule," she tapped her foot on the car floor with determination.

"No, of course not," Adam said mockingly with a wide gesture. "As if it hadn't been ridiculous enough to go out to investigate a noise after someone had already explained the danger to you. Just like in a bad horror movie, Diane," he said and glanced at her with a frown. "You know what I'm talking about. The girl knows the guy with the axe is out there and she'd be safe inside but, no, she has to go out and get herself killed," he finished in a roar. "How smart is that? Now tell me, how smart is that?"

Adam glanced at her again and saw the tears running down her face. Guilt squeezed his heart again and he shook his head.

"All right, I'm sorry," he apologized.

'Why the heck I have to apologize is beyond me but I can't have her crying.'

Diane wiped her tears off with a nervous gesture and looked away from him.

"Diane," he called her softly but she didn't turn to him.

Adam chose to make her react otherwise and put his hand on her thigh. She practically jumped up.

"What are you doing?" she asked breathlessly, her eyes riveted on the big dark hand resting on her thigh.

"Just begging for your attention," he replied softly and grinned at her ruthlessly.

He squeezed her thigh and she flinched under his fingers.

"Are you afraid of me or does my touch disgust you?" he asked, his voices mildly curious, although his thoughts were far from mild. He waited her answer with dread.

"None of the above," Diane swallowed hard and replied in a small voice. "I was just… startled. I… didn't expect that and… Anyway, it's all right," she tried to put an end to her stammering, sick with her weakness whenever he touched her.

"Now, can you tell me what happened?" Adam asked again. "Right after you tell me where the hospital might be because I really don't know," he winked at her.

Diane felt a laughter erupting from her throat and she felt better than she'd felt all day.

Adam was unbelievable. He was outrageous and cynical and protective.

She had moments when she wanted to smother him in his sleep. Yet, there were moments like this that made her feel terribly alive.

CHAPTER 10

The visit at the hospital wasn't very funny. Adam hovered all over her and refused any kind of medical assistance for himself.

Diane made him accept to be checked out by the doctor when she informed him she would follow suit and wouldn't let the doctor examine her either.

Adam begrudgingly submitted himself to the doctor's checkup, although he knew he hadn't been severely hurt. Yet, he had promised her he would, and he didn't take a promise lightly.

He wanted her lungs checked out and all her scrapes tended to, so he relented. He demanded a CAT scan as well when he found out that she'd been hit from behind.

Right after he laid his eyes on them, the doctor insisted on calling the police. Adam didn't care one way or another, so he just shrugged.

The sheriff came and left, shaking his head in disbelief. As there was nothing left of the barn and the thugs had used gasoline, he didn't think a trip to the ranch would help, but he had to check the fire though.

He didn't believe he'd find any traces leading to the guilty party, but he had a job to do. Not doing his job meant to lose in the next election.

Adam shared the sheriff's opinion and promised to take care of Diane himself.

The sheriff had suspected him in the beginning. Diane had clarified everything when she divulged the discussion those men had after they tied her up. She might have suspected Adam as well if she hadn't witnessed their exchange of words.

The trip back to the ranch was mostly silent because both were exhausted. Dusk reminded them of the full day they had gone through and they felt tired to the bones.

Adam drove steadily now. He didn't rush. He knew the ranch wouldn't go anywhere and he still had to make a tour of the property when they arrived there. He needed to make sure no surprises waited for them. He took his time and cruised at forty miles an hour.

Besides, he wanted to give the sheriff enough time to finish his investigation, not that he expected any results out of that.

Suddenly, the ringing of a phone pierced the silence and Diane practically jumped out of her seat. The silence had been so deep before that she didn't expect it. Adam just glanced at her and smiled.

He leaned over her and took the phone out of the glove compartment. He checked the display first and then answered, putting the phone on speaker to keep his hands free for driving.

"Hey, Ryan. You're on speaker. What's up?"

"Just checking in. Everything okay?"

"Hmm. Why do you ask?" Adam replied and a frown formed between his brows.

"You know Kate," Ryan said apologetically. "She kept badgering me that something was wrong with you and... Kate, don't you dare hit me with that spoon again," he bellowed.

Adam laughed. "Spoon, Ryan?"

"Yes, she's making spaghetti and hit me with a big wooden spoon, so don't laugh. It's not funny."

"Poor, little baby," Adam crooned and Ryan swore.

"If he can ridicule me, he's fine," Adam heard him telling Kate. "You're fine, right?" Ryan asked again.

"Now, yes, I am," Adam confirmed. It felt good to hear his friend's voice.

"What do you mean, now?" Ryan's hard voice reached Diane's ears.

"We've had... let's say, a lot of lively moments around here today," Adam disclosed.

"Here being where?"

"Told you I was heading out to Montana," Adam reminded him. "Showed you on the map..."

"Right, you did. What happened? I can't believe Kate was right. Yeah, yeah, yeah, you were right, don't hit me again."

Adam laughed again. "I didn't know Kate had premonitions or visions or whatever they call that."

"No, she doesn't," a melodic low voice came through the phone, and Diane imagined it was that Kate they were talking about. "I just felt something was wrong with you and you needed help."

"Thanks, sweetheart," Adam replied. "I managed."

"But do you need help?" Ryan inquired. "Fess up, mate. Once a team, always a team. We always help each other, Adam," Ryan stated seriously.

Adam knew Ryan would react like that but he had been determined to solve that matter by himself. He glanced at Diane and her huge green eyes tugged at his heart.

"I might, mate," he replied without too much conviction.

"All right then. Nick will be there before me," Ryan told him. "He's in Montana after all, even though on the other side of Montana. I have to come from Montreal so it might take me twenty-four or forty-eight hours. I don't know yet," Ryan explained.

"I'll go with you," Kate said.

"No, you won't," Ryan replied in a hard voice.

"See that I will," Kate repeated very matter-of-factly.

Her stubbornness brought a grin on Adam's lips. He knew Kate well enough and he also knew that Ryan didn't stand a chance. Adam shook his head with amusement.

"We'll talk about that later," Ryan tried to detour the conversation.

"There's nothing to talk about. I'm coming with you and that's it," Kate didn't concede to his opinion.

"Damn woman," Ryan started to say and then, Adam and Diane heard, "Ouch! What the heck, Kate, you hit me over the head with that freaking spoon again!"

Adam burst out into laughter.

"Oh, man, you're done," he told Ryan.

"Yeah, yeah, yeah," Ryan replied. "Your turn will come, no worries. See you soon, buddy," he said and rang off, stealing Adam's chance to reply.

Adam shook his head with amusement and handed his phone to Diane.

"Could you put it back in the glove compartment?"

Diane took the phone and asked, "Who are Ryan and Kate?"

"A married couple," Adam chuckled and mischief shone in his eyes.

"And what's so funny about them being married?" she asked. Her voice showed she was cross.

"They're funny. They're perfect for each other," Adam specified and glanced at Diane. "Kate shovels a lot of things at him and Ryan is almost tame around her."

"Ryan's coming here to help you, isn't he?"

"Well, if I could have trusted someone to stay put when I said so, I wouldn't have needed him," Adam said and looked pointedly at her.

Diane blushed violently and waved her hand, "Are you going to hold that over my head for eternity?"

Adam seemed to think a few seconds about it and then said, "Yeah, I think so."

Diane's mouth opened in a perfect '*o*'.

"You're ridiculous," she said with bewilderment.

"No, I'm not. I'm not the one going out to the barn to check on an open door after I was told not to leave the house," he pointed out in a steely voice.

"For God's sake, it was windy. I thought the wind opened the door and I just wanted to close it. The hinges are rusty and the door screeches at every move," she replied with exasperation.

"Nope, not anymore," he observed in a pragmatic tone of voice. "At least we don't have to worry about those hinges anymore," he shook his head.

Diane clenched her fists. '*Self-righteous prick*,' she thought, and the urge to hit him made her boil.

"Who's Nick?" she asked to change the subject.

"A friend."

"I presumed that," she said with frustration. "As Ryan is a friend. But what kind of friends?" she insisted.

"The best kind," Adam answered.

"Argh…"

Adam just grinned and continued to drive. Diane tapped her foot on the floor nervously.

"Hold your horses, sweetie pie. I'll tell you everything at home tonight," he promised and patted her knee.

Surprisingly, she didn't flinch. *'Hmm, that opens new possibilities,'* Adam thought and his brows shot up.

"I remember I told you not to call me sweetie pie," Diane observed, still cross with him.

"And I remember to have asked you to stay in the house, which you didn't," he retorted, and she growled impotently.

On the other side of the mountain, a grey-haired man threw his cell phone on the coffee table next to him and roared.

Blind with fury, he threw the glass with bourbon he had in the other hand. The glass shattered against the grill protecting the fireplace.

Panting with frustration, he stood up and went limping to the window. He'd hurt his leg while riding the week before, and his slightly overweight figure didn't help the healing too much.

He looked out the window for a few moments, then returned and grabbed the phone. He punched a number with shaky fingers. His fury raged in force.

"Mr. Phelps, good evening," he was greeted.

"Monroe," he said curtly. "How did your little task go?"

"We got her good, sir," the man snickered. "We tied her up in the barn and started a fire. The guy who was living there with her will get the blame."

"Are you sure?" Phelps asked through tightened teeth.

"Yes, sir," Monroe answered, but with less conviction than before.

Phelps's tone didn't announce anything good. It wasn't as if he hadn't known his boss's tone of voice.

"Did you make sure she was dead?"

"She couldn't have survived, sir," Monroe replied. "You should have seen the blaze…"

"You idiot," Phelps bellowed. "She's fine and dandy."

"It isn't possible, sir," Monroe replied with apparent conviction, but fear still rang in his voice.

"It is possible," Phelps retorted. "My driver saw her in the hospital. She wasn't even seriously hurt, you, imbecile. If you're not able to finish the job, I'll find someone else. You have a week," he ordered and rang off.

'No, I won't give him a week. Not even a day.'

CHAPTER 11

Adam checked the perimeter and, despite his exhaustion, laid out warning alarms all over the yard and at each possible entrance in the house. He knew motion sensors would be useless out there, with all the wild animals on the loose.

His eyes swept over the yellow tape the sheriff had put around the area where the barn had stood, and shook his head. It was just dust in the eyes.

Confident enough that they would enjoy a good night of sleep, which they both needed, he came back to the kitchen. The aroma of homemade food watered his mouth.

Diane kept busy in front of the stove. She looked adorable barefoot, her hips moving slightly while she stirred something in a pan. As if she had felt his presence, she turned and smiled at him.

His eyes swept over her heated rosy face. A few wisps of hair flirted with her skin. She blew them away and with a wave of her hand, invited him to seat down.

"I'll bring out the food now," she told him and turned the heat off. "Have a seat."

Adam sat down and his eyes followed her every move. He couldn't look anywhere else. He was bewitched.

She grabbed a couple of plates from the cupboard, together with two forks and knives, and laid them on the kitchen table.

"Need help?" he asked, ready to stand and join her.

"No," she patted his shoulder. "Just sit there and I'll be just a moment," she reassured him.

She went back to take the bread she had warmed in the oven. She had stuffed it with garlic and olives, and peppered it with Parmesan.

On her way back, she also grabbed two bowls with salad and brought everything back to the table.

"It smells fantastic," Adam smiled at her.

Then his eyes fell on the salads and grimaced. Diane just laughed.

"You won't die if you eat some salad," she reassured him, patting his shoulder. "You'll also have meat, don't worry. You won't starve."

"I didn't think I would," he mumbled, but she heard him and smiled.

When she returned with the stir-fry, he breathed easier. For a moment there, he had been afraid she went overboard to punish him and make him feel bad, and she cooked only vegetables.

They shared the meal seasoned with small chit-chat. When they finished eating and she brought the mugs filled with hot chocolate to the table, a feeling of contentment filled him.

"So, about Ryan and Nick," she said.

Adam grimaced, not very comfortable with the subject. He had forgotten she wanted to know about them.

"Is it a secret?" she asked, noticing his discomfort.

"No, not really… Or not anymore," he shook his head. "We worked together. A sort of spec ops team, if you want," he replied and looked straight at her. "When you said I was a killer, you were dead on."

"I didn't mean it that way," she rushed to say. "I thought you wanted to kill some defenseless animals."

He shrugged but didn't point out that some of the animals out there were anything but defenseless. Even for a man with a rifle, some were lethal.

"Anyway, I did kill, when the mission asked for that. I didn't kill for fun but that doesn't make me less of a killer," he explained in a very matter-of-fact tone of voice.

"I understand the difference," she protested.

"I doubt it," Adam replied drily. "You're a pacifist, remember? You abhor guns."

"As a norm, yes. But I understand that a man has to protect himself in a war or in missions like the ones you're talking about," she counteracted.

"Well, sometimes the mission was to kill so..." he said with nonchalance and then, he studied her to see how she took that.

Diane paled and her non-violent nature warred with his words. Yet, she knew that nothing was white or black and grey existed more often than people thought.

She met his studying gaze and tilted her head. Something occurred to her then.

"You want to shock me," she concluded and nodded.

"Yep," he admitted without any qualms. "Does it work?"

"Why would you want to do that?" she wondered, nonplussed.

"I want you to understand the type of man I am and what I'm capable of," he said, then braced his elbows on the table and leaned his chin on his fists, his eyes always trained on her.

"I doubt that killing defines you entirely," Diane replied softly.

"No, it doesn't," he conceded. "But I'm more than capable of doing it, and you can be confident I'd kill anyone who'd touch you."

That shocked Diane more than anything he'd said before.

"I don't want to bear that responsibility," she shook her head. "I don't want anyone dead because of me."

"Not even the men who tied you in the barn and set you on fire?" he inquired with disbelief.

She shook her head again.

"Are you serious?" he asked. "I bet those men are the ones who killed your aunt, too, Diane," he pointed out.

"I want them punished," she admitted. "Locked away so they couldn't harm anyone anymore," she replied in a small voice. "I don't think I want them killed."

"Listen to me and listen good," Adam stood up and leaned over her. His voice was hard and unyielding. "You won't interfere and get yourself killed in the process. You'll let me do what I have to do. Is it clear?" he thundered and his eyes shone with ice.

Diane nodded. She wasn't stupid and she knew she could get *him* killed if she interfered. That was the last thing she wanted.

Adam was a continuous pain in the neck but that didn't mean she wanted his demise. Quite the opposite.

She had to be honest with herself. The rogue attracted her and a lot. She'd never felt such a pull from any other man before.

Adam stared at her, trying to make sure she didn't just try to placate him. Satisfied with what he read on her face and in her eyes, he sat down again and drank half of his hot chocolate in one go.

Diane opened her mouth to ask something else when his cell phone rang again.

Adam put up his hand to signal her to wait and took the cell phone out of his pocket. He checked the name on the display and answered.

"Hey, Nick, how's it going?"

"You sound well enough," Nick's voice boomed out of the phone. "I'm on speaker," Nick noticed.

"Yeah, it seems I touched the darn screen again," Adam muttered. "Anyway, what's up?" he asked and laid the phone on the table.

"I'm on my way there," Nick informed him. "I was lucky to find someone to take care of my horses starting with tonight. I've been on the road for over half an hour. I'll get there before midnight. Is that fine?"

"Yeah, perfect. Just let me know before you drive into the yard. I set up a few booby traps," Adam explained.

"Nothing less than I expected," Nick observed.

"All right, I'll wait up," Adam said and disconnected the call.

Diane looked at him and her big eyes reflected her befuddlement.

"You're not very polite."

Adam just shrugged and stood up. He flexed his shoulder muscles in a move that seemed to be an ingrained habit to him. Diane couldn't stop herself to admire his physique.

"You work out," she observed and then blushed deeply when she realized she spoke aloud.

Adam just grinned at her and nodded. "Yes, it came with the job and now it's a habit. You like the results, don't you?" he winked at her.

Diane stunned him when she nodded her agreement. He had expected another potshot at him.

"We can give Nick the third bedroom," she observed to change the subject. "What about Ryan and Kate?"

"I'll give them my room and sleep on the sofa," he replied and pointed his thumb to the living room.

"I can sleep on the sofa," she remarked. "I'm smaller and I'll fit better there."

"No," Adam said.

Diane waited for a moment but he didn't comment anymore.

"Just no?"

"Yes, just no. You want explanations, I see," he said with resignation and brushed his fingers through his hair.

"All right, then. I can't leave you here downstairs alone. You'd be the first in the line of fire. And anyway, one must be here on guard so it can be me," he pointed out.

"But you won't be able to rest," Diane observed and picked up the two mugs to bring them to the sink.

Adam shrugged again and left the kitchen to verify the windows one more time. Diane shook her head after him and decided to wash the dishes.

CHAPTER 12

Nick arrived half an hour before midnight. Adam directed him through his booby traps and Nick managed to go through them unscathed.

Behind Adam, Diane watched the men bumping fists, tapping one another on the shoulders and then sharing a manly hug, without shame.

A smile fluttered on her lips when she noticed how strong their connection was.

Nick's eyes stopped on her and Adam took her hand and pulled her near him.

"Diane, this is Nick. Nick – Diane," he made the introductions, but he didn't let go of her hand.

Nick noticed and smirked at him. Adam felt awkward, but didn't care too much. He preferred feeling awkward than having Diane falling head over heels with his friend.

Nick looked like a bear, but Adam knew women had always found him very sexy. He didn't want to test that theory with Diane.

He didn't like the taste of jealousy. *'I don't even know why I'd be jealous. It's not like she belongs to me.'*

"Come inside," Diane invited him. "Adam will show you to your room and I'll make something for you to eat."

"You don't have to trouble yourself," Nick waved her offer away. "I can have some biscuits or…"

"No trouble at all," she smiled at him.

"How come you never smile at me like that?" Adam asked without thinking.

'*I should sew my mouth, darn it,*' he thought. He had the intense urge to club himself over the head.

Nick burst out into laughter and Diane blushed.

"What do you mean?" she asked him.

"Doesn't matter," he said and passed by her in a hurry.

"I think it matters," she replied and grabbed his arm.

Adam looked at her small hand on his arm and then looked up into her eyes. Diane really seemed concerned.

"With pleasure. Carefree… I don't know. But I know you've never smiled at me like that," he answered. He didn't make any effort to pull his arm away either.

"Probably because you needle me all the time," Diane replied. "Yes, I think that's it. You make me so angry all the time that I can't smile at you that way," she nodded.

"Well, I have reasons, don't I? Imagine," he said turning slightly to Nick, "I tell her she's in danger and she has to keep out of sight until I come back and what does she do? She goes to check on the barn door. It was open, you see. And she had to close it."

"You're mean," she slapped him over his arm and took her hand away.

"Mean? I am mean, did you hear her?" he asked Nick.

"I think there's much more than that here," Nick intervened in the discussion. "Adam wouldn't have been so angry if it had been a mere barn door open," he told Diane.

Diane blushed violently and Adam's lips twitched with mirth.

"Of course, there's more. She was clubbed over the head, tied up and locked in the barn. They set the barn on fire afterward and if I hadn't come when I came she'd have been barbecue," Adam remarked insensitively. "You can see the results on her face. Her hair was singed as well…”

“You’re a pig, you know that,” Diane cried out and tears appeared in her eyes.

She rushed past them to the kitchen and discreetly wiped her eyes. Adam took note of her gesture and sighed.

“Women are so difficult, Nick,” he observed.

“Especially when you care about them,” Nick replied quietly.

“What the heck do you mean?” Adam asked quarrelsome.

“Come on, bro, it’s obvious. You’re crazy about her and she’s crazy about you. Yet, both of you go out of your way to hurt each other and keep one another to an arm’s length,” Nick replied and his voice sounded tired.

“I think you’re too tired to think straight,” Adam said. “Let me show you to your bedroom and then you can come to the kitchen, have a bite and turn in."

Adam started ahead of Nick and shook his head.

'Oh man, Nick's got barmy. Listen to him! I'm crazy about that contrary woman. And she's crazy about me.'

Suddenly, Adam stopped and tilted his head. 'Now, that's interesting. So many possibilities.'

He shook his head to clear it and turned to Nick.

"Did you have a fine trip?"

Nick burst into laughter, and laughed heartily. He bent and pressed a hand to his midriff.

'Adam was always a wacky one,' he thought.

***

Nick had already gone to sleep. Adam had taken a shower first in the bathroom he was going to share with Nick, and now lay on the sofa, on his back, his head on his crossed hands.

His legs hung over the end of the sofa. It wasn't very comfortable but he had slept in worse conditions in the past and didn't care.

Diane appeared in the doorway. The moon lit her slender figure.

"Are you all right there?" she asked him quietly.

He shrugged but then realized she couldn't see him as well as he saw her and answered, "I suppose."

She shuffled her feet. Uncertainty marred her features and Adam smiled.

Suddenly, he blurted out, "Nick says you like me. Do you?"

She froze and a blush crept all over her face and touched the tips of her ears.

"I... I... don't... know," she stammered and his grin widened.

"I see," he replied. "He said I like you too," he observed and she blinked.

After a few seconds a silence, she asked in a small voice, "Do you?"

He stared at her for a few moments and then shrugged, "I suppose."

Diane hugged herself and lowered her head. He couldn't see her face and didn't like it.

"Do you want to sleep with me?" Adam asked and her head came up with a jolt.

"What? I don't... I don't just sleep around," she managed to say.

"I didn't ask for you to sleep around. I was talking about sleeping. I know you're not like that," he chided her.

"Just sleeping?" she asked for confirmation.

Adam rolled his eyes and said, "Yes."

Diane took her time to think about it. Adam waited patiently but after a couple of minutes, he lost his patience and said in a hard voice, "Forget it."

"No," she replied. "I was just thinking we'd be more comfortable in my bedroom upstairs. You don't fit on this sofa by yourself. With me there…"

Adam stood up in a fluid move. He picked up his gun and phone off the coffee table and closed the distance between them.

"Lead the way," he said and laced his fingers through hers.

CHAPTER 13

Nick and Adam took turns to check around the ranch the entire morning. One of them always remained with Diane, although she had promised Adam not to go out if they weren't there. Adam didn't say whether he believed her or not but he didn't leave her by herself in the house either.

Nick knew where Adam had spent the night. He'd heard the two of them going upstairs the night before, and he had seen Adam coming out of Diane's room in the morning.

However, he didn't ask any personal questions. He was a very private person and he respected other people's privacy, as well.

The three of them shared a hearty lunch around one o'clock. Adam insisted on grilling some steaks and Diane gave in.

She prepared some salad, which Adam ate while grumbling. Nick enjoyed it and praised Diane for her cooking talents until Adam rolled his eyes and said, "Drop it, Nick. That's enough."

The men regaled Diane with stories from their past. Of course, they didn't go into any gory details and talked only about the funny moments they had shared together.

Diane knew they edited the stories to match with what they thought of her. She didn't mind. She actually preferred not to know the particulars.

While they were eating, Ryan sent a message to let them know they would arrive that afternoon. Adam read it and grinned.

"What's so funny?" Nick wanted to know.

"I was sure Kate wouldn't stay at home. Ryan's putty in her hands."

"Don't be so sure," Nick shook his head. "When it comes to her safety, he's anything but putty," Nick replied. "I'm sure you remember what happened before their wedding," he reminded Adam of the adventure they shared together.

"What happened?" Diane asked, her curiosity pricked.

Adam grimaced. Diane assumed he didn't want to tell her that specific story and wondered why.

Nick smiled when he noticed Adam's scowl. He leaned forward, took another slice of bread and broke it in two.

Then, he said, "I'll tell you what happened."

"Come on, man," Adam protested, but Nick waved his hand to shut him up.

"This smart guy here was lured into a trap," Nick started, pointing to Adam. "He accepted a mission on the side after we all had decided to get out of the business," Nick said with reproach, staring at Adam, who shrugged. "When we got to him, he'd already been in hiding for a while. The thing is, those guys were waiting for us. They wanted to take all of us out in an ambush. Adam got shot," Nick continued under Diane's widened eyes. "Three times, if I remember correctly," he said turning to Adam for confirmation.

"Does it matter?" Adam growled.

"Was it bad?" Diane asked in a small voice.

When Nick confirmed with a nod, she felt a twinge of pain in her heart. Unconsciously, she stroked Adam's arm.

'Maybe it's not so bad if Nick tells her the story. Oh, Gad, can I be more pathetic?' Adam mused. A moment later, he shook his head with derision

and that move drew Diane's inquiring eyes. He shrugged as if it hadn't been important.

"What happened afterward?" Diane turned her attention back to Nick.

Yet, her fingers didn't stop from stroking Adam's arm. He didn't feel the need to point that out to her and decided to enjoy her ministrations.

"We had to keep a very low profile for a few weeks... Make that a few months... Adam was badly hurt and for a while there, it was touch and go. We didn't know if he'd live," Nick remembered with a scowl on his face.

Diane's fingers shook on Adam's skin and he covered them with his. He squeezed her fingers in comfort, and then pulled her hand to him. After a light kiss on her knuckles, he drew her small hand between his two big palms.

Nick pretended not to see anything and went on with his story.

"Ryan looked on Internet and connected with Kate. We needed money since we couldn't use our cards and-"

Diane jumped off her chair and interrupted him, "You mean Ryan wanted Kate to get her money?"

Her eyes widened because of the unpleasant surprise.

"It wasn't like that, for God's sake," Adam interjected and pulled her down in her chair. "Ryan had already decided to find a woman on the Internet for a relationship. And we didn't ask for her money and then ran away. We intended to give her the money back, Diane. We're not like that," he protested, a frown etched on his face. He thundered her with his eyes, finding her reaction unpleasant.

"Kate reacted exactly like you, Diane," Nick intervened with a shake of his head. "Still, she came through. She brought the money to Ryan and that actually saved all of us. They both got smitten like crazy in a matter of hours," he smiled warmly.

"Yep," Adam said. "We weren't even on the plane and he'd already asked her to marry him," he shook his head as if he couldn't understand Ryan's behavior.

Nick nudged him with his fist.

"Come on, bro, it was Ryan's best decision. They have a good marriage, I'd say, even if it's been just a little over a year."

"Yeah, it was," Adam smiled. "They're never bored and they clicked like firecrackers," he laughed.

"I wonder how they could get here so fast," Diane mused. "I thought Ryan said they were living in Montreal."

"Yeah, they live in Montreal. That's where Kate's shop is and Ryan opened a business in that area," Adam said.

"It was a smart move," Nick intervened. "He didn't have anything steady somewhere else but Kate already had her business there."

"I didn't say otherwise," Adam remarked, lifting a brow.

"Didn't say you did," Nick replied mildly. "But, yes, Diane has a point. How come they can be here so soon?"

"He said details would follow," Adam shrugged. "How could I know?"

"So, what's the plan for the afternoon?" Diane inquired to put a stop to their bickering.

"A routine check of the perimeter every two hours, I suppose," Nick ventured to say.

Adam nodded. "Exactly. I'll take the first one in about an hour and you'll take the next, all right?"

Nick agreed and they finished their lunch in silence. Reality always found a way to intrude.

The men helped Diane to clean the table and offered to do the dishes, which she accepted wholeheartedly.

She felt a twinge of guilt knowing that they had their work anyway, but her guilt was short lived. It didn't last for more than a second. She wasn't very fond of doing the dishes.

She left them by the sink, Adam with his hands in the suds, and headed to the hallway.

"Hey, where are you going?" he turned and asked her.

Diane turned and stared pointedly at the water and foam dripping on the floor. Adam didn't care. A frown between his brows, he stared her down.

"Oh, for Christ's sake, I'm not leaving the house," she threw her hands in the air, frustrated with his mistrust. "I might sit on the veranda for a short-"

"Why?"

"To draw, smart guy," she replied. "I have an exposition coming up, soon enough, and I haven't done much."

"Ah, all right. Be there where I can reach you quickly," he ordered and returned to the dishes.

He could hear the wheels in her head turning and felt the heat of her frustration. A grin plopped on his lips, he continued to do the dishes meticulously.

Diane stomped out of the kitchen and Nick shook his head.

"You like to needle her, Adam."

"So what?" he shrugged.

"You might lose her if you keep it up like that," Nick replied wisely.

Adam turned to him slowly. His eyes revealed his astonishment.

"What the heck are you talking about?"

"Come on, mate, it's me, Nick. You don't have to play possum with me. It's crystal clear the two of you have the hots for one another."

"So what?" Adam asked defensively. "It'll pass, you'll see," he affirmed with nonchalance.

"You try so hard not to care, it's laughable," Nick shook his head.

"Drop it, bro," Adam growled.

"If you say so," Nick replied and started drying the plates.

CHAPTER 14

At around four in the afternoon, Kate and Ryan drove into the ranch yard. Ryan drove slowly, following Adam's directions. The booby traps were still in place and he'd have preferred to get to the house in one piece.

Ryan didn't even turn off the engine that Kate got off the car and slammed the door behind her. She stomped to the stairs where Diane, Adam and Nick were waiting. Adam's eyebrows rose and Nick scowled.

Ryan followed her in long strides and caught up with her before she reached the stairs. He attempted to grab her arm, but she pulled away irately.

"Troubles in paradise?" Adam mused and Ryan sneered at him.

Nick elbowed Adam to keep his mouth shut. Adam had a talent to enrage Ryan, especially when it came to Kate.

"She lied to me," Ryan accused pointing to Kate, and his mouth tightened in a hard line.

She whirled around to him and pushed her sunglasses up so he couldn't miss the contempt in her eyes.

"I didn't lie to you, Ryan. I just didn't tell you before we left home. There's a difference," Kate replied.

"That's lying, Kate. Check the dictionary," he retorted.

"Do you have a dictionary?" Kate turned peevishly to Diane. "I want to prove this baboon that I'm right."

For a second, Diane looked like a deer caught in the headlights of a car tumbling down the freeway at full speed. She glanced at Adam and then at Nick, but they didn't help with any kind of suggestion. They just grinned.

Then, she turned back to Kate and said hesitantly, "I think there's one in the office," she pointed inside of the house. "If you want, we can check now," she proposed, unsure of what she should do.

Adam grinned. Diane's confusion showed on her face and amused him.

'*She's so damn sweet,*' he thought, and, for a moment, he forgot about his own hesitations. He gathered her on his side, an arm around her waist.

Diane turned her wide eyes to him and bit her lower lip. She'd thought he liked her somehow, but he was always careful to keep his distance. Last night, when he decided to sleep beside her in her bed, she thought it an aberration.

Adam squeezed her slightly. "First, I think we should find out what this discussion is about," he said and smiled at her.

"I'll tell you what's about," Ryan said heatedly. "She's pregnant," he continued in an accusatory voice, pointing his finger to Kate.

Kate just shrugged and kept a cool appearance. The others looked between Kate and Ryan, not really understanding what was going on.

Nick recovered first and asked with a discreet cough, "And that's a problem because…"

"I thought you wanted kids," Adam jumped in. "You kept blabbering about your age and wanting kids while you could keep up with them... It was downright nauseating. So, I don't see what the problem is now."

"The problem is that she didn't tell me until we were halfway here," Ryan bellowed.

Always calm as a cucumber, Kate contradicted him, "Actually, I told you after we rented the car."

"Exactly," Ryan shouted at her.

"That's not halfway, Ryan," she explained patiently and Ryan exploded.

"Argh."

He braced his hands on his hips and turned around. He took two steps back into the yard, then came back.

"The problem is we came here to help Adam with his situation," Ryan tried to reason with her.

"So?" Kate inquired, raising her brows. "And that's a problem how?" Kate mimicked Adam's words.

"You're pregnant, woman," Ryan stated the obvious again.

"And that troubles you why?" she asked for clarifications.

"I can't have you in the middle of a situation when you're pregnant. What's so difficult to understand?" he threw his hands in the air.

"I don't see why one thing would exclude the other," she shrugged. "Anyway, we're here and we should make the best of the situation," she concluded in an icy voice.

"Yes, we're here because of you. Because you lied to me," Ryan bellowed again.

Kate just rolled her eyes and extended her hand to Diane.

"I'm Kate, by the way. The one yelling like he's lost his marbles is my *sweet* husband, Ryan. I hope we're not imposing," she inquired, shaking Diane's hand.

"No... no..." Diane stammered. "I mean I'm glad you're here. Would you like to freshen up? I could show you to your room," she offered.

"That would be fantastic. I do need some freshening up after the drive with that shouting overbearing male," she threw over her shoulder to Ryan, and practically pulled Diane into the house.

Adam grinned and Nick patted Ryan on the shoulder.

"Everything will be fine," he told him. "You'll see. We won't let anything happen to her, bro," he reassured Ryan.

Ryan nodded and hugged them both. He took a deep breath and said, "Let's talk shop."

Adam and Nick nodded and showed him the way to the kitchen. The room had become the operational center because Adam had noticed Diane had a special fondness for it.

Following Nick and Ryan into the house, Adam thought of Kate and Diane. Their physique would have confused anyone. Diane seemed to be fiery and collected at the same time, while Kate seemed very calm and warm. Yet Kate could bite someone's head off without qualms, always using that cold and controlled voice of hers.

Adam liked Kate, but he preferred Diane. She was more open. She didn't hide what she felt and she didn't step back from a hot confrontation with him. She could give as well as he could.

'Yeah, I love how she looks and I love her reactions. I love... Oh, my God,' Adam froze. He brushed his fingers through his hair and tried to come to terms with what he was about to think.

"Are you coming, mate?" Ryan inquired.

Adam didn't hear him. He was still riveted in place, contemplating his revelation.

"How the mighty fall," Nick whispered to Ryan. "I think he's just realized he's fallen hard, hook, line and sinker," he smirked. "Let's give him some privacy. We have all the time in the world later to remind him about what he said at your wedding," he laughed.

CHAPTER 15

"Mr. Monroe and his people are here, Mr. Phelps," Vera, the housekeeper, said, stopping at the threshold.

"Very well, Vera, show them in. Then, take the day off. You work hard and you deserve it," he complimented her. "I instructed Jim to drive you to Florence. You can shop and unwind for a while," he said and leaning forward, he handed her an envelope with some bills.

Vera took the envelope and the pleasure brought color in her cheeks. She murmured her thanks, hardly believing her luck.

"I don't need you until tomorrow morning around 10, so you don't have to hurry back. And Jim will keep you company," Phelps said standing up behind his desk.

He knew the middle-aged housekeeper and his driver had a thing for one another. He made his business to know everything about the people he employed. One never knew when something would come handy. Like now.

"Please, before you leave, let Duffy know that I need him and his team in here in about ten minutes."

"Yes, sir, thank you, sir," Vera replied happily, her happiness making her accent heavier.

She left in a rush, practically skipping down the hall. Phelps looked after her with condescension.

He skirted around the desk and went to pour himself a bourbon from the bar concealed behind a panel with legal books.

Phelps fancied such an oxymoron. When he was in his twenties, he kept his condoms in a box with a plump baby painted on the lid.

A knock sounded on the door. At Phelps's invitation, Monroe entered followed by his two associates, Webb and Donald.

Phelps didn't bother to glance at any of them. He sat down in an armchair next to the brown settee laid in the sitting area of his study.

He sipped his bourbon leisurely, and only when he concluded he had let them stew enough, he glanced at the three men.

They appeared uncomfortable and insecure, which Phelps had intended all along.

An ugly smile on his lips, he asked, "So, how's it going with our little business, Monroe?"

"We're still planning, sir," he said, rubbing his hands.

Phelps made him uncomfortable every time they met.

"Is that so?" Phelps asked in a hard voice. "What are you planning?"

"How to get to the woman. It's a job of finesse, sir. We need to throw the blame on that guy who lives there with her," Monroe specified.

"And how do you think you're going to do that?"

"We're still thinking of possible scenarios, sir," Monroe said and the other two nodded.

"Well, your thinking's over," Phelps replied in the same hard voice. "Three other people moved into the ranch already. Your window of opportunity's gone, Monroe," he said standing up and waving to someone behind the three. "And so are you," he said in a flat voice.

Monroe registered the threat then, but it was too late. Someone grabbed his arms from behind and coiled a rope around his wrists. He tried to fight back, but the man who was holding him was bigger and stronger.

His two companions started shouting and explaining. They ended up begging, but didn't meet with success.

Phelps signaled the men to take the three out.

"Duff," he addressed the man in charge, "I want you to dispose of them in such a way so that no one could ever trace them back to this ranch or to me."

"I've been thinking," Duff said lazily.

He scratched his head for a few seconds and chewed his tobacco. He looked everywhere but at Phelps.

"The best way is to fly them over The Rockies and set them free somewhere. I don't think anyone can trace anything on a body that crashed from 5,000 feet. Huh? What do you think?" he asked and spit on the floor.

Phelps despised Duff, but he knew he'd get the job done. He nodded his assent and his three former employees were taken out.

"I want to go over your plan about that woman tomorrow morning," he said, and Duff turned his head and acknowledged the request. "Be here at eight," Phelps ordered.

Phelps continued hearing his former employees' shouts until they had been trussed and stuffed into a trunk. He congratulated himself for having given the afternoon and evening off to the only two employees that lived on the premises.

He had expected their laments and all that begging. In a way, they made his day.

CHAPTER 16

They'd discussed the perimeter and possible ways of attack the previous evening. Adam and Nick had showed the surrounding area to Ryan.

Now, they simply patrolled the area now and then. Sometimes they made the rounds after forty-five minutes, sometimes after an hour. They didn't want to become predictable. Predictability always led to defeat.

As Kate was in the house with Diane, Adam didn't worry so much that she would take off somewhere on her own. He knew Kate wouldn't allow it and Diane didn't want to upset her.

Adam grinned. Kate knew to milk her pregnancy for all its worth. She already had Ryan eating out of her tiny palm. Nothing seemed beneath her.

When she got sick that morning, Ryan went through living hell.

As if he'd been having morning sickness, Adam thought and shook his head.

Ryan's face had been green for over half an hour.

Kate also convinced Diane not to leave her alone. She had explained that she needed constant company because she had dizzy spells and she didn't want to endanger the baby if she fell.

Adam didn't buy it. Kate must have been well enough to make Ryan take her with him. She couldn't have suddenly gotten dizzy spells.

Yet, he didn't feel like pointing that out. Kate kept Diane with her and that was what mattered to him.

Adam patrolled his side of the forest and even though he paid attention to everything, his thoughts turned to Diane all the time.

He had had a shock the day before when his feelings for Diane asserted themselves out of the blue. He had realized what Diane meant to him, and that scared the hell out of him.

Adam had never been in a relationship before. Even as a teenager, he had avoided any kind of complications and a relationship was written down as a major complication in his book.

He had dated a lot but he had never dated the same woman more than three or four times. He had also enjoyed his share of one-night stands. He always took precautions, so it didn't seem like a big deal.

His brother, James, had qualified him a cavalier man. Adam frowned remembering their last conversation. They'd shared hard words, yet, even then, Adam had known his brother was right.

James attempted to mend bridges in the letter he left for Adam with his will. He had hoped Adam would never read that letter and he would be able to tell him everything, face to face, but fate deemed it otherwise.

James had advised Adam not to be afraid of making a life for himself. He knew that their parents' skewed perception of Adam had left him in doubt of his abilities to care for someone else and assume responsibility.

Adam never liked the chores assigned to him at the ranch and did his best not to be lassoed into any kind of project his parents would plan for the farm.

He dreamed of seeing the world. He wanted a broader horizon than that small dusty ranch offered to him.

When Adam had joined the army, they had berated him. They couldn't understand why he would give up the work at the ranch. They told him he behaved like a spoiled brat who refused to grow up.

James was convinced that Adam's unwillingness to get involved with a woman, beyond sharing her bed once or twice, was a consequence of the guilt and bad-mouthing their parents had doled his way over the years.

He wrote that much in his final letter and asked Adam to understand he was his own man. He had to leave the past behind, where it belonged, and build a future for himself.

Adam hadn't thought of James's letter very often. He'd often thought of avenging him and his family but nothing else.

Diane changed all that. Her presence made him willing to believe he could have what James had urged him to build.

Adam stopped in his tracks. A slight noise from the left alerted him of an intruder. He didn't know if it was an animal or a person and decided to wait and see.

He took cover behind a wide tree trunk, his right hand on the gun in his waistband.

A whisper reached his ears, "That way, Tom."

The threat identified now, Adam crouched down, his gun in his hand, ready for attack. He didn't have to wait long. Suddenly, he found himself in a crossfire from two sides.

'Oh, no, you don't,' he thought. He waited for another volley of bullets to pass by him so he could accurately determine where the threat lay. Then, he started to share his bullets and had the satisfaction to hear a shout.

'One down, two more to go,' he thought, when another volley of bullets came his way from another angle.

It took him three tries to take out another attacker and he started enjoying himself. He had missed the adrenaline rush in his veins, such ops brought his way.

Suddenly, the forest seemed alive with shots. Adam scowled. Nick and Ryan were under fire as well.

It didn't bode well. The women were alone at the house and they were pinned down there.

Guessing their game, Adam roared with rage. He jumped up and from the cover of the tree trunk started to rain bullets in a wide circle. He took out the other gun he kept at the small of his back and fired both of them.

'Not very smart for ammo conservation, but impossible to miss them,' he thought.

He had plenty ammunition boxes at home, so it didn't really matter.

Adam emptied both magazines in short order and reloaded the guns. It took half of each gun to quiet the place. No one shot at him anymore.

Carefully, he advanced towards the attackers' location. He counted five bullets in the first body he encountered.

Not far away from this one he found a second man. He had been shot in the head and probably, shot a second time through his arm when he fell.

After searching the area some more, he found a third man, who was still breathing. The man tried to grab his gun and fire at Adam, but a bullet had passed through the back of his palm and he couldn't curb the hand around the gun.

"How many more?" Adam asked him in a hard voice, after he kicked the gun away.

He had grabbed the man's shirt and pulled him in a seating position. The man wheezed. Blood ran down his chin and added new splashes on his white shirt.

"How many?" Adam growled again through his teeth.

"Enough," the man said with difficulty, and then, he passed out.

Adam stood up and kicked him for good measure. He knew the man wasn't going to survive as at least one of his lungs had been perforated.

Suddenly, Adam realized the silence stretching around. No shots came from Ryan's or Nick's position. With a scowl on his face, he took out his cell phone and speed dialed Ryan.

"I'm fine," Ryan said before Adam could ask anything. "Just spoke to Nick. He's fine too."

"We have to go back to the ranch," Adam groused out. "The women are alone. I'm afraid we've fallen into a trap," Adam continued and then started cursing himself.

"I know," Ryan replied. "Calmed down. We need to keep calm now. We meet at the ranch," he said and hung off.

***

They met in the front yard of the ranch. Their faces darkened with

491

worry when they advanced to the house. The door had been broken in and Adam's heart skipped a beat. He started running up the stairs.

Nick shook his head over his action. Adam had thrown any caution to the wind. He knew better. It could have been a trap.

Both Nick and Ryan took out their guns. Nick signaled Ryan that he should go in the back and Ryan nodded.

Nick took only a few steps when Adam's chilling roar came from inside, followed by his shout to Ryan.

"Ryan, come here, now."

Ryan's blood froze, but he forced himself to run up the stairs. His legs shook like overcooked spaghetti.

Nick forgot about caution too and followed him. Adam was alive after all, so there wasn't a trap.

They found Adam leaning over Kate in the living room. She lay on the carpet, her body coiled in a ball.

She looked small, much smaller than she was.

Ryan rushed to her side and touched her face, where the blood trickled down. Anguish washed over him and his fingers shook.

Ryan felt a fist squeezing his heart. Coagulated blood had stained Kate's hair, and one of her eyes already swelled.

A second later, he noticed the blood under her nails and the shadow of a smile shook on his lips. His ferocious little kitten had taken a layer of skin off someone.

"Is she...?" Nick started to ask, but couldn't finish his question.

Ryan nodded. "Yes, she's alive. I'll still have to see the extent of her wounds, but she's breathing," he said, watching Kate's chest rise and fall rhythmically.

"That's good," Nick nodded and said with relief.

He turned around to speak to Adam, but Adam wasn't there anymore.

"Adam, where the heck did you go?" he yelled.

A door slammed upstairs and gave him the answer. Ryan and Adam looked up toward the ceiling, as if they could see through it. Another door slammed into a wall and then Adam's steps boomed down the stairs.

White-faced and disheveled, Adam appeared in the door. His eyes burnt with rage.

"They've taken her," he announced in a bleak voice.

He pushed his shaky fingers through his hair and closed his eyes. His mouth was tight and his entire body was rigid. He had failed to protect Diane and the guilt ate at his core.

Suddenly, Adam roared and hit the wall with his fist, leaving a hole behind. His knuckles bled, but he didn't notice.

"I'm going after her," he decided and with determination, he started to the door.

Nick stepped in front of him and Adam growled. "Step aside, Nick. I don't care if it's you. I'll plant my fist into your mug."

"No need for that, Adam. We will all go after Diane," he said and touched Adam's shoulder.

Adam brushed his hand off and replied, "She's my responsibility. I let her down. I have to make amends."

"How did you let her down?" Kate's weak voice came from behind him.

Adam turned to her and the light in his eyes showed that he was glad that she was conscious again.

"I'm glad you're all right, Kate," he said. "Ryan will stay with you. I have to go and get Diane."

"Where?" Ryan asked, helping Kate to sit up.

"I have my suspicions. James, my brother, told me who wanted his land. James and his family ended dead because he refused to sell. I suppose the same guy is after Diane," Adam explained.

"A Mr. Phelps?" Kate asked and all eyes turned to her with astonishment.

"How did you know?" Adam asked.

She shrugged and snuggled better in Ryan's arms. When she was comfortable enough, she continued, "They thought I was out already, so they didn't care what they said. I remained conscious enough to hear something like *'Mr. Phelps will be satisfied now. He'll get the little bitch.'* I'm sorry, Adam, that's what they said."

Adam waved her concerns away. He didn't care what those two-time pricks had said.

"What do you know about this guy?" Nick asked Adam.

"Very wealthy. Very respected and feared. I understand he has the sheriffs in about five counties in his pocket," Adam explained, rubbing his neck.

The tension had knotted his muscles and he needed to be able to move fast.

"That means very well protected," Ryan observed.

Adam just nodded and then, he shrugged.

"It doesn't matter, Ryan. I'll get to him," Adam said and turned to leave.

"Adam," Kate called him back. "I heard their thoughts. You need to be able to go in and take her. If you don't have a serious plan and die trying, she's dead as well," Kate said quietly.

Nick didn't believe Adam could get paler than he was, but he did.

"What do you mean?" he asked.

"They want to make her sign some papers. I understand they've been given a lot of leeway in that considering the methods. Their only purpose is to make her sign the ranch over to them. I read their minds. They'll kill her anyway. It doesn't matter if she signs or not," Kate explained in a sad voice.

"Okay, people, we have to think strategy here," Ryan said.

He took Kate in his arms and carried her to the sofa. He sat on the sofa and held her in his lap with care.

"Why does this man want her ranch?" he asked Adam.

"I can guess only," he replied. "James wrote that there were rumors. Phelps wanted to own this entire side of Montana. He made a lot of money being ruthless. He holds two types of hunts on his lands, and both are very expensive to attend. He's got clients who hunt exotic game and clients who hunt people."

"What are you saying?" Kate asked, her face so pale that the blood which had spotted her skin stood out.

"Real man hunt. They free one of the people they have under lock and key, usually illegal immigrants or refugees, and they hunt them with dogs and everything. Like a fox hunt if you want," Adam explained.

"Oh, my God, Ryan, you've got to do something!" Kate shouted, shocked to hear that such things were real.

"We'll do, don't worry Kate. We'll end this enterprise right now. Did they say they'd take Diane at this Phelps's house?" he asked her and smoothed her hair over the head.

"Yes, that's what they said," she nodded.

"I understand. All right," Ryan addressed Adam and Nick, "I think we'd better call Mark."

"I don't have time to wait for Mark, man," Adam replied furiously. "Diane will be dead by the time he comes."

"We won't wait for him, but we'll need him in the end, Adam. We're going to attack a very wealthy man. And we'll definitely take him down and end his illegal activities. We need back up for that, Adam," Ryan tried to reason with his friend.

"All right, then," he accepted. "But make it fast. I want to leave now," Adam replied in a steely voice. He barely held himself in check. He just wanted to go and hunt the man responsible for Diane's kidnapping.

Ryan nodded. He understood Adam's state of mind and tension. He admitted that he would have been in the same state if those goons had taken Kate.

"Adam, while I talk to Mark, will you help Kate go upstairs and clean all this blood? I'd like to see the extent of your wounds, baby," he told her and stroked her arm with tenderness.

Ryan also hoped that giving Adam something to do might forestall his impatience. He counted on Adam's protective side. Adam wasn't aware that he had one, but Ryan had seen it time and time again.

"Don't worry, Ryan, I'm fine. I just got punched in the face when I didn't sit still to tie me down. That's when I got this cut here above my eye," she said and touched the spot gingerly.

She grimaced at the touch. The spot was sore and still hurt.

"Only one guy attacked me, and believe me, he regretted it. The entire left side of his face is slashed to ribbons. You see, these nails are good for something after all," she waved her fingers before Ryan's eyes and smiled.

Ryan squeezed her fingers and kissed them. He nodded to Adam who helped Kate up and led her upstairs.

Ryan looked after them for a few seconds, and then dialed Mark's number. He explained the situation to Mark and told him what he intended to do.

CHAPTER 17

Diane was tied to a chair in the middle of one of Phelps's barns. Her upper lip had split and blood had left a trail down her chin.

She knew a bruise of a man's fist will appear on her right cheekbone later. It hurt badly, but the ache was one of many and didn't matter so much.

Phelps sprawled in a chair brought from the house. He indulged in a glass of bourbon and a satisfied smile fluttered on his lips when he looked at her.

Four other men were standing around her. They all looked at Phelps, waiting for his orders.

"So, Ms. MacLean, we finally meet. You caused me a lot of problems and I'm afraid you'll have to pay for that," he said in a hard voice.

He sipped from his glass again, thinking to let her squirm for a little while. People dreaded the unknown.

Early in his career, he had learnt not to show his cards too soon in the game and he had never strayed from that principle.

Diane just watched him and tried to steady her breathing. One of her ribs was probably cracked because it hurt every time she breathed in deeply.

"This business would have been concluded some time ago if you only had the decency to answer to my letter," Phelps observed.

Befuddled, Diane stared at him.

"Letter? What letter?"

"Don't play dumb with me, missy," his voice whipped. "You know very well I sent you a letter and offered to buy the ranch. I even offered you a reasonable price," he mentioned.

"I haven't received any letter," Diane shook her head and regretted it immediately.

She hadn't recovered completely from the blow she had received at the back of her skull the previous day. To make things worse, one of the thugs had snapped her head to the floor when they came after her. Her head hurt and every sudden move made her dizzy.

"Don't lie to me," the man bellowed and stood up in a huff.

"I'm not lying," Diane said quietly.

Phelps, already annoyed with her stubbornness, stomped toward her and slapped her face, cracking her bottom lip, as well.

Diane whimpered but then she bravely looked at him and repeated mulishly, "I'm not lying. You can hit me again if you like, but that won't change the facts."

His small eyes narrowed even more. He assessed her for a few moments, and then, he waved his hand.

"It doesn't really matter. What matters is that you sign this paper here," he showed her a piece of paper.

Her eyebrows went up interrogatively. When he didn't elaborate, she asked, "What paper's that?"

"Why, it's the paper through which you sell me the ranch and all the land," he replied, an ugly grin on his thin lips.

"I don't think so," she retorted.

"Oh, you will, don't worry. Duff, she's yours. You can stop when she signs," Phelps nodded toward Duff and left the paper on the chair.

He left the barn without looking back at her.

The fine hairs at her neck stood up. Fear trekked the length of her spine and she felt her insides shaking.

Duff cracked his knuckles and the noise attracted her eyes. The savage satisfaction in his eyes chilled her, and her eyes widened with terror.

Duff smiled at her and crossing the space between them, backhanded her and she fell backward and of course, as she was tied to the chair, she took it with her. She yelped and, for a moment, she saw red spots before her eyes.

Two of the men approached and straightened the chair. One of them pulled her hair hard and her head fell back. A groan flew off her lips, but that wasn't the end. Duff backhanded her again and she lost consciousness.

***

With the help of the night goggles, Adam had packed when he

came to Montana, they assessed the number of guards around Phelps's property. Nick indicated two on the right side of the yard and Adam found four in the back.

Ryan found it interesting when he noticed two guys smoking and talking in front of a barn. The barn was lit, which was strange at that time of the night.

He elbowed Adam and showed the barn to him. Adam checked it out and nodded. He was sure Diane was kept in there.

"You take the barn, Adam," Ryan whispered. "Nick, you take care of the guards, one after another. I don't want to hear a sound until the perimeter is secured. I'll go into the house, all right?" he asked.

Adam and Nick nodded.

"You're sure Kate will be fine?" Adam asked Ryan.

He didn't want to sacrifice Kate for Diane. He knew that Diane wouldn't have ever forgiven him if he had let that happen.

"She'll be fine. She's got two guns with her and she's very well hidden," Ryan reassured him. "You know I wouldn't let anything to happen to her and she's already been hurt once today."

Adam nodded and crawled away. He would have loved to run to the barn and free Diane at once, but he knew he needed to be patient. One wrong move, and he could lose her forever.

It took him some time until he reached the side of the barn. It felt like an eternity and it strained his patience.

He advanced slowly and tried to block out the words that came from the barn and especially, Diane's cries. Every time he heard her cries, something acid burnt in his stomach. His lips were tight and his back teeth locked because of the fury which ate at him.

Adam reached the side of the building and listened carefully. Only one man paced outside the barn and the smell of smoke from a cigarette itched at his nostrils.

'There's one more inside now,' he thought.

Adam patiently waited until the man got closer. When the sound of the man's steps let him know that he was just a foot away, Adam slipped behind him.

He covered the man's mouth and nose with one hand and the back of his head with the other. The man froze, and Adam just twisted his head in a practiced move. The man's neck snapped like a twig. Adam dragged him quietly on the side of the barn and laid him there in a shadow.

'One out, God knows how many more to go,' he thought.

With silent steps, he advanced to the door. Light filtered through a crack and he looked inside.

His blood boiled instantly when his eyes fell on Diane's bloody face. A sturdy man punched her in her midriff and she whimpered again.

Adam fought hard to regain his calm. He had to take Diane out of there and he needed all his focus on that. He could take care of her afterward.

He counted four men inside. He took out his gun and installed a silencer on the muzzle. He had one shot for each and in fast succession. If he was one second too slow, Diane could end up dead.

He tightened his mouth and pulled the door open. The second the door opened and the first man turned to him, he fired. He didn't stop firing until the last one was down.

The man behind Diane tried to pull her head back and probably, snap her neck. He was Adam's second target. It was a clean shot. The bullet crossed his skull and lodged into one of the boards behind him.

When he fell, he pulled Diane down too, by her hair. Adam ignored that until he finished off the other two men, as well.

Then, he rushed to Diane, untied her and smoothed her hair away. Her teary big green eyes stared at him in wonder.

Adam cradled her in his arms and whispered, "Don't look at me like that, sweetie pie. I don't deserve it. I didn't protect you, as I should have."

Her mouth opened and for a few seconds she couldn't say anything. Then, with her last strength, she punched him in his arm and said, "Are you out of your mind? You saved my life, you lunatic. They'd have killed me if you hadn't come," she said.

He just shook his head and stood up with her in his arms.

"We'll have to get out of here first, Diane. I will check you out once we're in the clear, all right?"

She nodded and closed her eyes. A satisfied sigh flew off her lips when she nuzzled him, and his scent enveloped her.

CHAPTER 18

That night and the following morning were full of frantic activity. Ryan had restrained Phelps, who started threatening and throwing important names left and right. Ryan didn't bother to listen to him.

By the time Adam came out with Diane, Nick had already annihilated all the guards, and beside the men Adam had killed, everyone else was alive and secured to be sent to prison.

Ryan verified every prisoner, intent on finding the one who had hurt Kate. He wanted him so badly that he could taste revenge. Yet, his wish remained unfulfilled. Adam had already taken care of him.

They knew the sheriff was on Phelps's payroll, so they didn't bother to call him. They just waited for Mark's people.

They arrived just ten minutes after everything ended. Mark had sent a team from Bozeman by plane. They had landed in Missoula and driven to Phelps's property at full speed.

They were armed with search warrants, based on Kate's and Diane's accounts. Apparently, they had had their eyes on Phelps for some time but nothing had ever stuck to him and they couldn't make a move.

They checked every crack and niche in the house, and found enough evidence to burry Phelps and his associates in prison for life.

Adam, Nick and Ryan left them do their job and they drove the women to the hospital. There, they requested to have both women checked and patched out.

Kate bristled when she heard the term *patched out* in relation to her, but she relented and was satisfied to hear that her baby was still in good shape, untouched by the goon that had attacked her.

Diane hadn't been so lucky, and the doctor decided to keep her in the hospital for observation, at least for one night. She had two cracked ribs, several lacerations at the level of the face and she was bruised almost everywhere.

Adam had been terrified when he became aware of the extent of her wounds and bruises. At Diane's request, the doctor allowed him in the examination room and every time he learned about a new bruise or wound, he died a little inside.

Diane didn't want to stay there, but she accepted when Adam promised to spend the night by her side.

***

"I want to go home, Adam," Diane squeezed his hand and pleaded with her green eyes.

Adam was aware she made good use of her charms in order to bend him to her will, but he couldn't have denied her anyway.

"All right, Diane, I will talk to the doctor. If everything is fine, I'm sure he'll let you come home," he promised and kissed her forehead.

Diane's eyes flared with anger. "I'm not a child, Adam, to placate me. I'm telling you I'm fine and I want to go home. If you don't want to help, just say so and I will take care of that," she said mulishly.

"Sweetie pie, of course I want to help. And I definitely want you home," he whispered and touched her bottom lip with the tip of his finger. "But I won't do anything to jeopardize your health," he said in an implacable voice and his hard eyes held hers with determination.

"But-"

"No buts, Diane," he shushed her. "I died a thousand times knowing you were in danger. I won't go through that again," he replied stubbornly.

Diane's heart sang when she understood the meaning of his words. She only hoped he would remember them when everything had quieted down.

***

Luckily, the doctor signed her papers and she was able to check out the hospital. Adam drove her home, with a slight detour to buy some coffee and pastries for both of them. Hospital food hadn't been very appetizing and both were famished.

When he stopped the car in the yard, everybody came out to hug

517

them and rejoice that everything had ended well.

Ryan and Nick had already disarmed Adam's booby traps because they couldn't spend all their time giving indications to the agents coming by.

"Good to have you both home," Ryan said with a smile in his voice.

He hugged Diane carefully with one arm, so he wouldn't hurt her ribs. Then he kissed the top of her head, while hugging Adam with his other arm.

"Payback is a bitch, Ryan," Adam observed. "I should do to you what you did to Nick and me when we met Kate for the first time," he joked and elbowed his friend.

Ryan laughed, but his eyes promised all sorts of punishments to Adam. He didn't like to be reminded about his jealous behavior at that time. In retrospect, he realized he had been way over the line and he felt ashamed of how he had reacted.

They went inside and gathered around the kitchen table. Kate and Nick brought mugs with hot coffee at the table while Ryan brought Adam up to speed.

The agents had already found one camp with locked people and one with exotic animals. Phelps wouldn't ever see the light of day out of a prison cell.

Ryan doubted he would see it inside a cell for long either. Apparently, many important people were involved in Phelps's scheme. Some of them would certainly try to get rid of the most important witness against them, so Phelps's days were counted.

Phelps had liked to show his power and muscles when he dealt from a strong position. Now, that he was under arrest without the possibility for bail, he sang like a canary. He didn't like the idea of going down by himself but seemed determined to bring down with him as many people as possible.

After discussing the case, they began talking about mundane things. The men shared funny memories to entertain the ladies and mocked one another. Diane and Kate enjoyed their antics and the strong bond between them.

"I'm thinking of going back home," Nick said. "I don't really like having other people taking care of my horses," he confessed.

"Stay at least until tomorrow," Diane begged him. "We'll have a nice barbecue, exactly the way Adam likes it," she winked at him, although it wasn't easy. Her right eye had swelled badly and the left one was just a little better.

"She's right," Adam agreed. "I'm sure you'll survive if you stay one more day."

Nick pondered their invitation but in the end, he accepted, although his heart cringed at the thought that someone else looked after his horses.

"What are you going to do now, Adam?" Kate asked.

He shrugged.

"I'm not very sure. I was thinking of teaching some survival courses. I understand they work fine."

"Not a bad idea," Ryan said, thumping him over the shoulder. "You're good at survival, so I can see you being a success."

"That's what I thought," Adam nodded. "And I was also thinking of marrying Diane," he blurted out and everyone was rendered speechless.

Diane's eyes widened and shone with unshed tears. She stared at him, unable to utter one word.

Kate punched him in the arm, "You scamp, is that how you ask a woman to marry you? You're one brick short of a full load, Adam," she shook her head with reproach. "I'd club him over the head if I were you," she told Diane.

Adam frowned for a few seconds, not understanding what came over her. He didn't find anything amiss in what he had said. Then, the truth dawned over him.

'Oh, right," Adam said and slapped his forehead. "Women want romance. Do you want romance, Diane?" he asked her, an eyebrow hitched up on his forehead.

Diane didn't answer. Poleaxed, she just kept looking at him.

Ryan put his head in his hands and Nick shook his head. Adam looked from one to the other and another truth dawned on him.

"I blew it, didn't I?" he asked Diane. "Sweetie pie, I don't have any experience with this romance stuff. Never been romantic before. If I go and buy you some flowers and a box of chocolates and come back and kneel before you, will you say yes?"

Wide-eyed, Diane still stared at him and said nothing.

"Oh, for God's sake, give a guy a break. I love you, isn't it enough?" he shouted and threw his hands in the air.

Kate and the guys burst into laughter.

"You're pathetic, man," Ryan said, shaking his head. "Not even I could have made more of a mess of a marriage proposal than you."

Adam didn't pay any attention to any of them. He kept looking at Diane.

She finally nodded and said, "Yes, Adam, it's enough. I don't need the flowers and chocolates."

That's what he expected to hear.

"Hurrah!" he shouted and jumping off the chair, he pulled Diane up into his arms and started spinning her around.

Despite her aching ribs, she burst into laughter. Her happiness filled the room and fed the others' joy.

Diane and Adam married on Christmas Day. Diane had always dreamed to have a white wedding: white dress, white flowers, snow on the road and on the roof.

Kate and Ryan came for the wedding from Montreal even though Ryan grumbled about Kate's exhaustion. Luckily for him, Kate had already stopped paying attention to his excessive care because of her pregnancy.

Nick asked someone to take care of his horses and came together with Mark, their former boss.

When the bride walked along the aisle, holding Nick's arm, Adam's eyes shone with tears and the sight made everyone smile. They remembered well what he had declared at Ryan's wedding and couldn't stop making fun of him whenever they had a chance.

The bride wore a simple coronet of weaved white flowers and her dress had turned her into a princess. She sauntered toward Adam with elegant and graceful steps.

'*My princess,*' Adam thought, when he took her hand in his and kissed her palm.

After they said the '*I dos*', he impatiently waited until the pastor declared them husband and wife. Then, he kissed her hard, leaving her breathless.

After his lips left hers, he stared into her eyes and whispered '*Hurrah!*' Her eyes danced with joy and satisfaction.

When he lifted her in his arms and strode out of the church to the car with huge strides, her laughter joined the others'.

The snow had covered the road and the smell of pines filled the air. Adam kissed her hard again, opened the car door and sat her inside.

Without a single look at their guests, he drove her away, up the road to their ranch, under the stunned eyes of the people who came out of the church.

They knew a wedding feast was waiting for them at the ranch, but they had believed that the bride and the groom would wait for them.

Laughing, Ryan slapped Nick on the back and said with enthusiasm, "Your turn now, mate."

Nick shook his head and shuddered with apprehension. *'Not in this lifetime if I can help it'.*

EXCERPT BECKA'S

AWAKENING

(BOOK ONE IN THE WINSTONS SERIES)

PROLOGUE

"Come on, man, this is so not right!" Josh exploded.

He threw his fork back onto the plate and made his aunt, Marjorie, frown. She loved that set of dishes and feared that the young man's frustrations would sooner or later put a crack in them.

"You're complaining, huh?" Maggie waved her fork at him in mockery and rolled her eyes. "You're still fairly young compared to some of us and you have enough time ahead of you, so you shouldn't be the one complaining!" she retorted angrily.

"He has the right to complain, Maggie, as well as any one of us!" Becka replied in support of her cousin. "So what if we are younger? We're all in the same boat!" she punched the table with her little fist. "Auntie, can't we do something about this?"

"I know you want to, pumpkin, but there's nothing you can do about it," Aunt Marjorie stroked her arm in an attempt to soothe her. "What must be done, must be done!"

"So, we have to pay for something that happened a hundred years before we were even born? How does that make any sense at all?" Alex snapped and joined the others in voicing his outrage, though it didn't stop him from scarfing down another piece of pie.

"It's less than a hundred, you nitwit!" Lily replied with disdain and punched his arm.

"Who the hell cares?" Alex retorted with his mouth full.

He never did learn not to talk with his mouth full, try as his parents might. Anyway, he wouldn't have given a rat's ass on such things, anyway, especially at home.

"One hundred, two hundred, same shit, pardon my French. You know what? I don't feel like paying for some jackass's mistakes!" he ended his heated speech, his finger still pointed at Lily.

"So, what do you propose to do, then?" Matt, who had kept his mouth shut until then, asked with nonchalance.

He had been sipping from his glass of whiskey quietly, with a detached expression on his face that suggested that nothing they discussed could affect him.

"Don't tell me you're okay with this!" Alex answered back in disbelief. "Come on, Matt! You're the oldest, man, and you've only got one year left. You've got to be as angry as I am, if not more! Don't pretend it doesn't bother you because that's not possible!"

Matt took a few moments of silence, sipped a little more from his glass, then looked at Alex and shook his head.

"Angry? Maybe. Can I do something about it? I don't think so," he replied to his cousin with his usual coolness, his eyes gazing steadily at him. "So why should I bother?"

No one had anything to say to that. They were all aware there was one stipulation they had to fulfill and only then they could get their trust funds and also reach their full potential.

The worst part was they had to do so before turning thirty-five, because once one of them turned thirty-five without fulfilling that condition, their share of the fund would be divided among the remaining younger ones who still had time to succeed or fail.

"You know what? I don't really care about unlocking my powers," Ariel said pensively, without addressing anyone in particular, "although, it would be nice to see what you can do if you use your full potential..." she continued, lost in her thoughts as always.

Her cousins gave her time to get to the point. They knew she had the bad habit of rambling on and on or getting lost in her own thoughts only to leave everyone hanging. Yet, sometimes, if not most of the time, she could come up with some very interesting solutions if they had the patience to listen to her.

"But I do care about doing something for myself. I'd like to open a little business..." Ariel finally said longingly.

"Keep dreaming, girl," Maggie snapped, already bored with the way Ariel always liked to drag things out. She wasn't one for patience and, unfortunately, that trait had had some unpleasant results in her daily life. "Till you take care of your part of business, Ariel, girl, you won't be able to open a shed."

"Why are you always so mean to her?" Alex snapped at Maggie. "If she wants to dream, let her dream away. What else can she do? What else is there for any of us?" he asked, his infuriated gaze scanning each one of them to see their reactions.

"Beat the curse?" Marjorie asked softly, trying to defuse a potentially explosive situation.

"Not so easy, auntie," Ariel said sorrowfully. "I tried, you know... Do you remember? I thought that guy, Eric, the one I met two years ago, would be the one. It wasn't meant to be, you know… It's not so easy, and you know it very well. You see how things are. There's no real romance left in this world, I'm afraid. If there's no romance left, where can one find true love?"

Marjorie nodded. She did know it. Finding true love wasn't easy-peasy. She'd been in the same situation when it was her turn and she'd almost lost everything because of her own stubbornness and her family's meddling.

"It's never easy, my dear, I know," she answered and stroked the young woman's arm with love again. "But, Ariel, sweetheart, you have to keep trying. You can't simply give up. Think about it! You will be able to use your powers and get your money, but only once you find your true love and commit to it. You'll be truly happy then!"

Ariel turned her eyes to her plate on the table. She knew her eyes would show everyone she'd already resigned herself and she was sick of hearing platitudes and encouragements whenever her family got wind of something like that.

Everybody around the table remained silent for a few moments. Jay helped himself to some more of his mother's amazing pie.

Marjorie was the best cook in their family, which was why they always chose to meet at her house. Everything was easier to swallow if there was a good pie or cake on the table. At least, in Jay's opinion.

"I think we should see if there's any legal way to get out of this situation, guys. We need the money now, don't we? It's not like we can wait around forever!" Alex broke the silence, when the idea came to him suddenly. His eyes analyzed them carefully and saw them nod their assent. "Look," he continued, "I'm already thirty-two. I don't have time for stupid things and games and all sorts of idiotic attempts at love! I want to do something for myself like Ariel said. Now, while I still can."

Although almost everybody found themselves in agreement with him, they still looked at Matt. He was known to be the smartest guy in the family and they knew that any kind of solution should have come from him. Matt's eyes shifted around the table, feeling their expecting gazes on him and finally shook his head.

"There's no way out, buddy," Matt put his glass on the wooden table at the same time and stood from the bench. "If you called us here just for this discussion, then I'm out of here. I've got real things to do, places to see…"

"You don't even want to try," Becka cried out, jumping out of her seat. "You've just given up because you have so little time left and you don't care anymore."

"I tried, sweetie," Matt told her with a sad smile on his lips.

Becka was his favorite cousin. Maybe because she was the youngest or maybe because she was unspoiled and funny and had a very big heart. His fingers stroked her cheek in a loving, yet sad caress, and he kissed her forehead.

"Becka, I tried hard to find any kind of loophole in the wording of the trust funds papers. Believe me, there's none. If I couldn't find one, sweetie, then no one can, and you know it. There's a reason I'm one of the best attorneys in the country, and all of you know this isn't just my vanity talking. Anyway, honey, these days, I content myself with making my own money the hard way and enjoying as much as possible the little spare time I have left. I've stopped chasing such dreams. It's not in the cards for me and that's it."

All of his cousins looked at him in shock. Only his sister, Maggie, understood him very well. She didn't have any patience, especially with fools, but Matt was something special.

She'd always looked up to him and she knew he wasn't the kind of guy to give up on anything without a fight. Hearing him say he'd resigned himself made her understand the depth of his anger, even though he hid it from them.

She felt like taking him into her arms and never letting go but she knew he wouldn't like that. He wasn't very big on displays of affection, her brother, so she just lightly petted his hand and left it at that.

"Matt, you should try to use that time you have left to find a girl," his mother said reproachfully and everyone's attention turned to Marjorie, who continued, "You still have a chance, son, and I'm not talking about the money here, you know it. I know that sad affair with Velma's left you afraid to commit again and I don't like that in the least.

That's not the Matty I know. That wasn't love, son, and you know it. Had it been true love, you'd have had your full powers by now even if you hadn't gotten the money."

"Mother, Velma's been out of the picture for a decade already. She's in the past. What's the point in bringing her back into the conversation?" Matt retorted curtly, shaking his head. He couldn't understand his mother's reasons for bringing up bitter memories.

"Because she was the reason you stopped looking at women with hope," Marjorie pointed out, shaking a scolding finger at her first born. "You think all women are like her and that's why you just take everything you can from them and move on. Another woman on the list! It's like you're keeping a score: how many women can Matt score?" she reproached acidly, which wasn't something that they'd witnessed before. Everyone's eyes were riveted on her. "It's not good for you, Matt! Even if you've already given up on the trust fund, which is stupid, by the way, you're still alive and you still need a reliable woman in your life, like I've already said over and over again. You'll grow old and alone and bitter!" Marjorie ended her unusual tirade by punching her son's chest with her finger.

"Thanks for the heads up, mom. It's always good to know what your future will look like!" Matt replied sarcastically and removed himself from the path of her pointy finger. Yet, he didn't leave. He seemed undecided and glance back at his cousins.

Marjorie shook her head bitterly, but chose not to continue that line of discussion. She knew her son quite well and she knew there was no way to make him change his mind when he was like that. It was like talking to a rock.

The silence stretched for a few minutes. Everyone was busy either eating their pie or playing with their drinks, pretending nothing out of ordinary had happened between Marjorie and her eldest son. But mostly, they were busy avoiding each other's eyes for fear someone might say something hurtful again.

In the end, Alex, the most outspoken of all, couldn't stand the awkward silence anymore and looked around the table, gauging everyone's mood. Uncertain whether it was even worth it, he shrugged and decided to try a new line of conversation.

"You know, you are the old lady's favorite great-grandson, Matt. Can't you persuade her to end this foolishness? She can change the papers if she wants to. It's not like the words are carved in stone!" Alex anxiously waited for his answer.

"Tried that too, Alex." Matt sighed, shaking his head. "She said she did it for our own good, whatever she means by that. So… I can say I've tried everything and it's time to limit my losses."

Again, no one said anything for a few moments and, again, they couldn't bring themselves to look each other in the eye and the silence stretched on.

Encouraged by the unusual silence, since such get-togethers were normally a very chatty and loud affair, Matt took his leave with a simple wave of his hand and started down the path to the kitchen door, whistling softly to himself.

Ariel, pensive as always, looked after him until he was out of earshot, and said dolefully, "It's sad… It's really sad. He's the oldest and he's already given up."

For a few moments, everyone stared at her absolutely speechless. It was like she'd grown a second head during the last hour.

"Well, we're close to that too, Ariel," her brother Alex retorted angrily after a moment of disbelief. "It's not like we have too much time left, is it? Just about three years, you dimwit! Once we turn thirty-five, everything will be gone: the money, the powers, everything. And we can't do a single thing to stop this!"

"We can't even cheat," Jay intervened bitterly for the first time and the others burst into laughter.

"Oh, yeah, I remember," Lily said. "You tried to pose as a fool in love and came with that simpleton. Camilla, I think her name was?"

Jay nodded smiling. He had already forgotten the ridicule he'd suffered at the time. His easy-going nature didn't allow him to keep a grudge for long.

"Yeah, but it didn't work, did it?" Josh said very matter-of-factly. "Those two fossils sniffed you out."

"Well, they can read minds, so it was a piece of cake to sniff him out,"

Aunt Marjorie pointed out with an enigmatic smile on her lips. "That's why they've been appointed trustees, you know. No one can fool them. You shouldn't have tried to cheat, Jay. The old lady hasn't forgiven you for that yet."

Jay shrugged. He knew very well where he stood with his grandma those days. He didn't think she would ever forgive him.

The old bat was a real piece of work. She was resentful and bitter.

Just a few of them could steal a smile from her and lately he hadn't been part of that group. After the stunt he had pulled with that woman, grandma didn't even acknowledge him at the family dinners anymore. She pretended he didn't even exist.

He looked around and noticed all the others had gone quiet, each of them thinking about the implications of what had happened to him.

He truly hoped he wouldn't go through a new period of veiled mean jokes or even innocent teasing. At which Becka was a master. He even flinched when she started speaking, expecting the worst.

"So, we only have to wait for them to die..." Becka tentatively began to say, her gaze passing from one to the other.

"Not so fast," Marjorie interrupted her hastily. "The rule says that if they pass away, two others will take their place. Same type of power, pumpkin, so no way to fool them either. You have to understand there is no way around this. You have to play by the rules."

"Damn it!" Alex swore. "All this drama only because great-grandpa had the nerve to abandon great-grandma for another woman and then another idiot left aunt Evelyn at the altar and she killed herself!" he shook his head as if everything was inconceivable for him. "So, now, generation after generation has to pay for those two idiots! Where the hell is the justice in that?"

"Well, I think it was a radical conclusion from my grandmother, as well," Marjorie replied conciliatorily, "but there's never been a way to change grandma's mind, unfortunately. I know my father tried hard at the time, but she wouldn't listen to him. He tried again when my happiness was at stake and still nothing. He didn't have any success. She wouldn't give in. Not even a bit. Since the money was still hers, she had the right to decide what she wanted to do with it."

"But why the curse on our powers? I really don't understand that," Becka wondered.

"Same reason. Grandpa was a witch himself and he used those powers to entice a very young woman and leave grandma. And the man who left Evelyn at the altar was also enticed by a witch. She didn't want any other witch to misuse their powers."

"I wouldn't!" Becka cried out.

"I know you wouldn't, pumpkin," Marjorie patted her hand tenderly. "Not all apples are rotten, I know that much. But grandma didn't want to hear a thing, so… Here we are: now, everyone in my generation paid for that and yours has to pay, as well. However, if you succeed in finding your true love and get your trust funds, then at least the money problem will end and the next generations will have only the curse to defeat," Marjorie tried to lift their moods, but with little success.

"Oh, just that," Lily sighed and put her chin in her hand, fixing her dreamy gaze somewhere in the distance.

"I really wanted to open that nursery," Ariel whispered inconsolably and her brother stroked her fingers, his eyes shining with deep concern for his sister's dreams.

"Nothing is lost, sweetheart," Marjorie said and stroked Ariel's hand at her turn. "You'll see. You'll find your soul mate, Ariel. Everything will be fine."

"Where? Where could I find my soul mate, auntie? The people I deal with every day are not even lover material, believe me. I wouldn't let them touch me with a ten-foot pole, so finding a soul mate is quite out of question. There's no chance for me out there! I've looked around for years and nothing!" she said, this time with tears in her eyes.

"Wait and see, Ariel. These things have a way of working out," Marjorie whispered to her, then started picking up their plates to show them that the conversation ended.

There was no point in debating something they couldn't fix. There wasn't anything more to add and whining wouldn't help. The older woman knew it well. Whining never helped. You had to roll up your sleeves and do something.

Although the others jumped out of their seats to help her, they were all still thinking about the conversation and a none-too-rosy future, which looked pretty hopeless for them at that very moment.

CHAPTER ONE

Becka left the coffee shop in a hurry. She was holding a hot coffee cup in one hand, while, at the same time, she was trying to stick a muffin and a toasted bagel in her handbag with the other.

She'd forgotten to ask for a hot sleeve for the cup and on top of that, she'd also forgotten to take a napkin. Her head was deep in the clouds that morning, and now, the searing heat burned her fingers through the paper cup.

She couldn't go back to the coffee shop. She was already late for her morning classes and the last thing she wanted was to miss the entire lecture on her favorite subject.

Becka kept struggling. She tried to make the muffin and bagel fit in her handbag, at which point she wondered why she'd left the house with such a tiny purse.

The people and things around her became a blur the more she wrestled with the bag and the more she rushed toward the bus stop.

No more than a moment later, just as she turned around the corner, her eyes still on the tiny handbag that wouldn't cooperate with her, she ran into a tall man and as luck would have it, the lid of the coffee cup came loose and all the hot liquid spilled all over the giant's pristine, white shirt.

Of course, Becka thought, things couldn't get any worse! Not only did she scald him but the damn shirt had to be white! Why not black? No one would notice a coffee stain on a black shirt!

"Oh, my God, I'm so sorry! Really, really, sorry!" she blabbered and tried to clean his shirt with her bare hands, forgetting about the cup lying on the pavement, discarded like yesterday's news, all but empty. She'd also forgotten about her coveted breakfast, which was leaning precariously on one side of the handbag, ready to fall out as well.

Her hands shook the man's shirt as fast as she possibly could. Her meager attempts hoped to limit the burns at the very least.

Becka knew the hot coffee must have already penetrated his shirt and she didn't even want to think of what had happened to the skin beneath it, badly burnt by the freshly boiled brew.

"I think you'd better take your shirt off!" she cried out, without taking her gaze off the task at hand.

Remorse drove her actions. Images of the emergency room flashed at the back of her mind. Focused to a frenzy on her nearly catastrophic mistake, Becka never noticed the rest of the man to whom the chest belonged, much less the eyebrow which shot up as soon as she ordered him to strip.

"May I ask what exactly you're trying to do?" he finally asked in a deceptively mild tone.

Until then, he'd simply looked at the top of her head, completely shocked by the actions of the little woman before him.

Hearing his voice, she finally looked up and blinked. Not once or twice, but three times. The man she had in front of her wasn't the regular polished and polite man she'd encountered in her life before. He was a far, far cry from that.

This man's rugged face was set off by a long, pale scar on his left cheek that began somewhere close to the corner of his eye and continued to nearly the corner of his mouth, giving him a dangerous allure. He looked like one of the mercenaries she had seen in one of the documentaries about the civil war in former Yugoslavia. It wasn't reassuring.

His eyebrow was still raised scornfully and for a moment there, she asked herself how he did it. It wasn't easy to pull off that move for so long, she imagined. The young woman just about forgot her curiosity when she met his eyes, colder than the Arctic Ocean. She almost shivered.

She blinked again, swallowed hard and tried to find her voice. She forced herself to be brave, refusing to even consider the thought of being a scaredy-cat. She'd always tried to face any danger, not run away from it, and that wasn't the moment to change her ways.

"Hmm…. I was thinking… you know… your shirt…"

"I heard that bit about my shirt, don't you worry, but I really don't know what difference you think it would make if I took it off now. With or without the shirt, my skin is still scalded, my morning's still ruined and I'm still pissed off…" he said in a level tone, which didn't show the slightest hint of anger and that made her even more fearful.

While it was true he didn't sound mad, the complete clash between his words and his tone made her nervous. Becka couldn't even begin to think of how to talk to him.

She swallowed again and bravely said, "Yes, I know that, but the coffee is mostly on the shirt, so if you take it off…"

"Now?" he mused, when he saw she stopped without finishing her sentence.

"Well, yes," she nodded and stressed her words, in an effort to lend them more confidence than she had.

She pretended she knew what she was doing, although her face was burning in absolute embarrassment and shame.

It was the first time she'd ever asked a man to take his clothes off, even though it was only the shirt. On top of all that, his tone and attitude made her terribly uncomfortable and she was afraid that everything showed on her face.

She couldn't say she had a poker face worth a damn. Every time she played cards with Jay, he would laugh at her best, yet failed efforts to bluff.

The man looked at her for a few seconds, but then, with a bold move, he took his shirt off.

"Do your worst!" he said and handed her the all but ruined piece of clothing.

However, Becka didn't take it. She didn't even notice he was holding anything for her to take. She couldn't even find her voice to answer back. Her eyes were too busy taking in the expanse of a chiseled chest peppered with curly coarse hair, still wet from her coffee. She'd forgotten what she wanted or was supposed to do entirely.

"Earth to the moon?" he mocked her in his grave voice and waved his hand before her eyes.

Finally, his gestures pulled her out of her reverie and Becka's eyes shot up to meet his in an instant.

"Sorry, just lost in thought for a moment there," she mumbled more than a little disappointed with her silly admiration of the male figure. She'd thought herself above such trivial endeavours.

Finally, she took the shirt from his waiting hand and used it to dry his chest more vigorously than it was necessary.

The coffee was already a dry sticky stain, but that wasn't on her mind and neither was the fact that she might take off a layer of vulnerable, burned skin, too.

None of those things dawned on her because, to be truthful, Becka was brimming with embarrassment, upset with herself for her carelessness and every reaction that followed.

Not only had she poured her coffee all over a stranger but she'd been caught staring at the man's chest like a lustful, simple-minded woman.

"Yeah, I noticed," he replied amused, watching her expression while she cleaned his chest.

The man enjoyed her train of thought. He could read it on her face with no effort whatsoever.

It was refreshing to see someone so unspoiled like the woman before his eyes. He was tired of all the games played in society and wanted something new.

After a few moments, he decided to ask, "Does any man's chest have this effect on you or just mine?"

There was a little malice in his voice and that made her straighten up and look directly into his eyes. Then, she replied sulkily, "I'm just trying to help, you know! Why are you acting like a jerk?"

When she snapped at him, his eyes became colder than they had been before and he yanked the shirt out of her hands.

"Yeah, with such help I wouldn't be surprised if I'm dead tomorrow!"

She tapped her foot in frustration, raised her voice a notch, and replied to him with her usual self-confidence, "You're just pissed off because I ruined your shirt."

Her voice mustered all the determination she could and she added a nod, for good measure, in the hopes it would give her more of a knowledgeable air.

"But it was just an accident, you have to understand. It wasn't like I wanted to spill my coffee all over you! I'd have preferred to drink it, you know," she scoffed and shrugged her shoulders.

She was standing tall before him, matching his confident, dominant attitude with her own, but spoiled everything when she continued in the tone of a stubborn and willful child, "I really could have used that coffee!"

Fascinated with the sudden change in her attitude, he looked at her more attentively. Only now, he noticed her chocolate eyes and especially her little mouth, arched like a bow, with rosy lips. A part of him was almost begging and pushed him to grab her already and just have a taste of her sweet, sensual mouth.

The longer she talked, his interest in her lips only grew more and he got to the point of an agonizing need urging him to lean in and claim what he wanted. He found them more tempting when the tip of her tongue came out and nervously licked her upper lip. Something stirred inside him and, suddenly, his interest changed completely.

"You owe me," he said so abruptly that it charged the atmosphere in an instant.

Becka opened her mouth in shock to reply. Yet, she couldn't make a sound for a few moments. She was too stunned by his sudden outburst.

The man didn't clarify his statement or expand on it. He just waited for her to process his words and get back to him with a bold retort. From what he'd seen so far, he was sure to get one. He didn't have to wait for too long.

"What are you talking about?" she finally managed to say, with a touch of thinly veiled indignation, and her wide eyes held his own intently.

"What you heard," he brushed off her harmless furor and continued, "You owe me."

"For this shirt?" she asked incredulously, showing him the shirt she held in her hand.

"Among other things."

His wolfish smile ran shivers down her spine, as her mind started dreading the worst and conjured unsettling scenarios.

"What other things?" Becka asked, although more than a little hesitation and uncertainty delayed her question.

Her eyes seemed to grow wider still and the tip of her tongue again touched her upper lip nervously, to torment him and make him more aware of his increasing desire for her.

He couldn't understand that irrational, unlikely desire for a clumsy woman he'd just laid eyes on, but something in him wanted her. He actually needed to have her, just like that.

She looked a bit young, maybe too young, that was true enough, but he knew that looks were sometimes deceptive. He still made a mental note to ask her about her age. He didn't want to fool around with jailbait even though he was agonizingly drawn to her.

He had a strict policy about going to jail. His policy was simple enough. Jail wasn't a place he ever yearned to see on the inside. He did once and even once in a lifetime was more than enough.

"You scalded me, ruined my shirt, and obviously, I can't go to my appointment half-naked. And, please, note, it's an important appointment, and I'm already late because of you," he explained patiently, as if he'd been talking to a small child.

Of course, it was all just a ruse. He was only trying to see what kind of reaction he could draw from her.

She felt the blood rush to her face and she cursed her pale complexion that revealed too much and in the most inappropriate of moments.

No matter how much she tried to appear sophisticated or cool-tempered, she always failed because her skin betrayed her. It was the curse of her life. Maybe not the only curse she had to contend with but it made the top three.

Becka thought of going a different way with him, to get herself out of the trouble that seemed to be brewing, and, very politely, said, "I'm very sorry for scalding you and for ruining your shirt. Of course, I'm sorry about your appointment as well, but I don't see how I could..."

She never finished her sentence because she saw a naughty smile flourish on his lips. That made her lose her train of thought again. This time she was afraid of what he'd say.

"I think you owe me something and you can set it right by going on a date with me," he finally specified his conditions in a tone implying too many things that would better remain unsaid.

"A date with you." she repeated automatically as if she weren't able to grasp the concept.

EXCERPT MATT'S DILEMMA

(BOOK TWO IN THE WINSTONS SERIES)

PROLOGUE

"Becka, move your butt upstairs, now," Bryan's voice boomed and made Matt smile.

Matt knew Becka's policy of not locking the front door. He also knew Bryan didn't have much success in making her heed his advice.

That was why Matt didn't even bother knocking. He just came inside. After all, he felt there like at home. Becka and Bryan were some of the kindest in the family, although their couple was strange by far.

"I thought you liked my butt," Becka shouted from the study, and then stormed out of the room.

She missed Matt by an inch. She didn't even notice him and started taking the stairs two at a time.

"I love your butt, and you know it. But right now, bring it up here. She levitates, damn it, and she won't listen to me," Bryan's harangued voice came from somewhere above, and Matt burst into laughter.

Matt's imagination wasn't very strong, but at least, he guessed how stressed Bryan felt, having two gifted children.

As an outsider in the Winston family, Bryan had to put up with a lot of things. However, no one could say he shrunk his responsibilities.

Even if he didn't have a clue what to do in some circumstances, he dug his feet in the ground, and took everything in stride. Now, though, he seemed overwhelmed with his one-and-a-half-month daughter, who inherited her mother's family's heritage.

Only whispers came from upstairs, so Matt decided to go there, and visit with his niece and nephew. He knew his apparition would make Bryan roll his eyes. He'd understand Becka had failed to lock the door again, and he'd probably give her hell after Matt left.

He wouldn't say a thing in front of Matt. No matter how upset he was, Bryan never said anything to Becka in front of others. He thought they had judged her enough for marrying a man twelve years older, and she didn't need to hear any *'I told you'*.

Matt knocked on the nursery door, and Bryan looked up, concern edged on his face. When his eyes fell on Matt, his tension eased away, and he smiled, shaking his head.

"You haven't locked the front door again," he said in a resigned voice, glancing at Becka.

"I forgot," she shrugged, and patted his hand. "Don't worry, no one will come in, but Matt. Hi, Matt, what's up?"

Matt couldn't hide his amusement. His younger cousin was always a delight, and he enjoyed seeing Bryan struggle both with his concern for her, and his ineffectiveness in making her understand the dangers of the city.

"Just passing by. I've got an hour to kill and thought of coming and seeing you two. And the munchkins."

Matt came inside and went to Becka, who was holding Lea in her arms. He kissed Becka's cheek, and then, stroked the baby's head and put a kiss on the top of her head.

"She's already causing problems, I hear," he turned to Bryan, who raised an eyebrow inquiringly. "I heard you when I came in," Matt confessed, and a naughty smile appeared on his lips.

Becka blushed. She remembered what Bryan had shouted to make her come upstairs. She speared him with a pointed look, and Bryan just grinned.

Matt chuckled. He loved both of them and his heart burst with joy whenever he thought how good they were together. Yet, he was jealous of them sometimes, because he couldn't have the same thing.

"So, the problems started, I understand," he said, nodding to the little bundle in Becka's arms.

'Yep, and it scares me shitless, to tell you the truth. Thank God, Sean hasn't manifested any kind of powers yet," Bryan replied.

"He will... In time," Matt told him, putting a reassuring hand on his shoulder. "You'll manage, don't worry. You've never struck me as a man who can't handle everything."

Bryan scowled, but didn't reply. He glanced at Becka, ready to say something, but she shushed him, putting her finger to her mouth.

"She's asleep again," she whispered, and Bryan came to her to take his daughter and replace her in her crib.

Becka and Matt started to the door, expecting Bryan to follow. When Matt looked back, Bryan was still watching his daughter sleep, and his expression was priceless.

Matt had liked Bryan since the moment they met. Yet, once he got to know him, his respect and feelings for the man evolved.

Bryan was a devoted husband and father, and it crushed Matt to see that hulk of a man so deeply in love with his family.

Matt went downstairs after Becka and found her in her study. She was typing something at her computer, checking a pile of papers at her elbow.

"What are you doing?" he asked her.

"I have to finish an essay. Just two more lines, and I'm done," she replied, but didn't look at him.

Matt leaned on the doorjamb, crossing his ankles, and kept silent so she could finish her work. A minute later, Bryan came downstairs, as well, and waved Matt to come to the kitchen with him.

Even before stepping into the kitchen, the aroma of a beef stew reached his nostrils, and he inhaled with pleasure. His stomach growled and Bryan, who was close to him, chuckled.

"Ready for lunch?" he teased Matt.

"I suppose you cooked," Matt inquired in a dry voice.

"You suppose well," Bryan replied. "I wouldn't let Becka into the kitchen. She's a walking disaster," he shrugged, and, going to the stove, picked up a wooden spoon to stir the stew.

"Am I?" Becka bristled from behind Matt, and Bryan winced.

"Come on, sweetie, you know you can't boil an egg," Bryan replied, yet, there was no reproach in his voice. "And we're fine, aren't we? It's no need for you to cook when I can do it very well," he added.

He came to her, took her head in the cradle of his palms, and kissed her lips tenderly. Matt turned to look out of the window. The tender display touched a yarning in his heart, he thought he'd squashed long ago.

"Hungry everyone?" Bryan asked, turning off the stove and taking bowls out of a cupboard.

"I'll set the table," Becka intervened.

"What's there to set, baby?" Bryan wondered. "Just take a seat and I'll bring everything to the table."

"But I want to help," Becka retorted with annoyance.

Matt knew she didn't want him to think she wasn't doing anything around, but he knew better. Bryan didn't allow her to do much.

"You've had enough to do today, Becka," Bryan stroked the side of her face and kissed the tip of her nose. "You had to go to school – and forgot to lock the door, in the process," he thought to add, "and you worked on your paper for the last couple of hours…"

"Yes, and you cooked, cleaned and took care of the babies," she replied. "And in a couple of hours, you'll have to go to the dojo for your afternoon and evening classes, so…"

"I can do it, don't worry," Bryan waved her concern away, at the same time, leading her to the table and helping her to sit. "You're a new mom, and must rest as much as possible," he pointed out.

"I was a new mom a month and a half ago, Bryan. I'm perfectly fine now," she replied stubbornly.

"And that's how you have to remain," he pushed on her shoulder when she tried to stand up. "Come on, Becka, just sit. I can carry three bowls to the table myself," he said in a frustrated tone.

Becka just shrugged, but didn't try to stand up again. Matt, who always enjoyed their sparring immensely, watched her. She was biting her lower lip, annoyed with something.

"What's the problem, pumpkin?" he asked quietly.

"He won't let me do anything," she snapped. "As if I'm fragile."

"I never said you're fragile," Bryan's voice came from a few feet away.

Becka and Matt turned to him, and Matt immediately stood up to help Bryan to put the heavy tray on the table. He'd filled three bowls to the rim and sliced warm homemade bread.

"I can tell you, you cook as well as my mom," Matt sniffed the stew, and grumbled in satisfaction.

Becka smiled, proud of Bryan. Aunt Marjorie was the best cook she'd ever met, and Matt's praise meant something.

She dipped her spoon in the stew, and fidgeted a little in her seat, before carrying to her mouth.

"Out with it," Bryan said. "Something's bothering you," he asked, looking at her sideways.

Matt knew Becka couldn't even sneeze without Bryan getting concerned.

"Well, if you want to know," she started saying hesitantly, "I don't think it is right for you to do everything. It's already been a month and a half since I gave birth, so I am perfectly able to…"

Bryan stopped her, touching her hand.

"Don't worry about, Becka. You do more than enough. You have to wake up at night and breastfeed, and…"

"Huh!" she snorted inelegantly, and Matt had to hide his smile.

"Huh?" Bryan asked. "What does that mean?"

"Whenever I wake up, you wake up too, so don't try to sell me on that stuff," Becka shrugged.

"I might wake up, but I don't breastfeed," he retorted, miffed.

Matt couldn't hold it anymore and burst into laughter.

"You two are comical. The first couple I've seen quarrelling because the other is doing more," he shook his head.

"You eat and shut up," Becka snapped at him. "I'm serious, here. Yes, I breastfeed, and yes, I go to school. That's the sum of my accomplishments," she sulked.

"I wouldn't say that," Bryan murmured. "You keep me happy, Becka," he said, taking her hand, and squeezing it with tenderness. "And don't worry so much. Your mom will send Rosa's daughter here tomorrow. She'll clean and do the laundry, so I won't have much to do."

"Finally," Becka said relieved. "At least, you won't do those anymore."

Matt grinned. He knew Becka wouldn't accept Bryan's hard work for long. Now, at least, she knew there was someone else to take up the brunt of the housework, because Bryan would have never accepted her help.

It wasn't easy to hire help in their houses though. They needed to keep the family's secret and they couldn't hire just anyone.

Luckily, their hired help worked for them generation after generation. Rosa was Becka's parents' housekeeper and Uncle Michael's housekeeper's daughter.

"So, she'll start tomorrow?" Becka asked.

Bryan just nodded and spooned more stew. Matt knew he must have been exhausted. He'd started doing everything long before the birth of his children, and also kept his training schedule.

They savored the beef stew in silence for a few minutes, and then Becka looked at him inquiringly.

"What?" he asked.

"I was wondering if you had any news," she shrugged, and took another slice of bread.

"What kind of news are you expecting?" Matt asked and following her example, helped himself to another slice of bread.

Bryan did know what to do in the kitchen. He imagined Bryan knew what to do in almost every situation. His cousin by marriage was one of the most resourceful and talented men in the family.

"You know, Matt," Becka insisted. "It's May 19th already."

"And?" Matt asked with dismay.

He knew where the conversation was going and didn't like it. Only Bryan looked from one to the other with curiosity.

"In July, it's your birthday," Becka doggedly continued. "On 27th," she thought to specify.

"So?" Matt asked, feigning disinterest. "Are you planning a party for me or what?"

"Don't try to play games with me, Matt Winston," Becka snapped, and her small fist hit the table. Bryan's eyebrows shot up. "You know very well what I'm talking about."

Matt shook his head, scooped more stew and chewed.

"Not really," he replied. "I was thinking of taking a cruise or something, that's true. I haven't made my mind yet, though," he shrugged.

Becka stared at him with disbelief. Then, she took a breath, ready to launch herself in a lecture. Bryan touched her arm and calmed her.

"Matt," he said. "I see there's something the matter here and I really don't want Becka riled up. So what is it?"

"Why don't you ask her?" Matt asked stubbornly. "I don't know what she wants from me," he answered with indifference, and continued eating.

He didn't really regret coming to their house. He liked watching them interact and loved the little ones. Moreover, he always ate well in Bryan's kitchen.

"Okay, sweetheart, what is it?" Bryan asked her. He understood Matt wouldn't give in.

"He'll be thirty-five on July 27th," Becka pointed out.

"And?" Bryan insisted. He knew there must have been much more than Matt's birthday.

"He'll lose everything then."

"What will he lose?" Bryan asked again, feeling like he was pulling teeth.

"His powers, his trust fund…"

"Oh, I see, now. So that thing has a deadline," Bryan nodded when the truth dawned on him.

He turned to Matt and expected he'd say something. Yet, Matt just continued eating. He wasn't interested in expanding on that story.

"Come on, Matt," Becka said. "You still have a little over a month and a half."

That made him freeze with the spoon half way to the mouth. His stunned eyes locked on Becka. After a few seconds of deafening silence, he put the spoon back in his bowl and asked, "Are you for real?"

"Now, what?" she asked, throwing her hands in the air.

Bryan mused. Becka had a real talent for drama sometimes.

Matt pushed the bowl away with regret. He did want to eat that stew. A frown appeared between his eyebrows and he stared Becka down.

"I couldn't find a woman to love until now and you seriously think I could find one in a month and a half," he noticed. "Bryan, your wife has lost her mind. I'm really sorry for you," he said, turning to Bryan.

"Nah," Bryan replied. "Becka's smart and you should listen to her. It doesn't always take years to fall in love. It took me a day and a half, maybe less. And you still have over forty-five days, I think," Bryan shook his head, chastising him.

"Okay, I see it now. You're nauseatingly happy, both of you, and see everything through pink glasses," Matt concluded, and started to stand up.

"Maybe yes and maybe no," Bryan replied. "That doesn't mean you can't finish your stew. Both Becka and I," he said, with a meaningful look at Becka, "will refrain from talking about this matter anymore. Right, sweetie?" he asked her and reluctantly, she nodded.

Undecided, Matt looked from one at the other, and, in the end, his hunger won. He sat back on his chair and pulled the bowl back in front of him.

AUTHOR'S BIO

Rowena Dawn writes romance, reads thrillers and watches comedies. She likes walking through the woods but insanely loves the sea.

She has a love - hate relationship with her writing and drives her dog crazy whenever she doesn't stop writing to take him out.

This series *Perfect Halves* will have four books and all of them will be about love, adventure and conspiracies. You have met all male characters in the first novel, *Double-Edged* and this second novel, *Eyes in the Dark*.

Look for Book Three in Rowena Dawn's *"Perfect Halves"* series: **PULLED IN.** Coming soon!

Also by Rowena Dawn:

Double-Edged – Book One in The Perfect Halves Series – eBook, paperback (soon audio book)

Leap of Faith – eBook, paperback (soon audio book)

Becka's Awakening (Book One in The Winstons Series) – eBook, paperback and audio book

Mr. (Almost) Right eBook, paperback and audio book

Matt's Dilemma (Book Two in The Winstons Series)

Forthcoming:

Pulled In (Book Three in the Perfect Halves Series).

Thank you for taking the time to read the box set **PERFECT HALVES**.

If you enjoyed it, please consider telling your friends or posting a short review.

Word of mouth is an author's best friend and much appreciated. Thank you,

Rowena Dawn

TABLE OF CONTENTS

children would love her. And the animal instinct in me knew I could trust Lucia, despite her murky background.

But even if I had the best of intentions when I hired Lucia, the only person truly responsible for the children's well-being is me.

I'm many things, with killer and utter prick at the top of the list.

But I've never been a liar. Particularly, I've never lied to myself.

The fear I heard in Mickey's voice isn't Lucia's fault for living under a false identity. Nor do I blame her for taking the children to the villa. Knowing how protective she is of both her own past and the children's safety, instinct tells me she would never risk either without good reason.

No. The only reason the children are currently shaken and unsure is because the one person on whom they are completely reliant failed to make them feel safe.

The fault here is mine.

If I had prioritized the children's needs over my own, Mickey would never have had cause to pick up that phone. He would have trusted me to act in his best interests. All three of the children would be certain that I would never place them at risk.

Instead, all three of them have just had their already fragile world shaken to the core. A teenage boy had to make a man's call that undoubtedly terrified him. After having been betrayed by every adult they should have been able to rely on to make them safe, my godchildren are now facing a heartbreaking confirmation of their experience thus far—that the world is a dangerous place, one devoid of love or safety of any kind.

Well, fuck that.

I pull the Maybach through the villa gates, nodding curtly at the guards.

I might have been slow to face my own culpability. But nobody can ever accuse me of failing to fix a problem when I find it.

Even if the problem is me.

I SEE MICKEY FIRST.

He's standing by the glass doors leading to the terrace, where he has clearly been waiting for me. Despite his pale face and rigid stance, his eyes behind the glasses are sharp and focused, oddly mature for a fourteen-year-old.

"Lucia said the man on the terrace is her father," he says quietly as I approach. "But he's bratva, Uncle Roman. I recognize his tattoos. I don't think my sisters should be around him."

His casual use of the term *bratva* gives me a severe jolt.

My chest tightens with an odd mixture of both guilt and, unexpectedly, pride.

When did nervous little Mickey become this grave-faced young man? I wonder how I missed that transition. I vow not to miss anything more.

"You did the right thing by calling me." I grip his shoulder. Holding his eyes, I smile, hoping that he reads in my face the reassurance I mean to convey. "I'm really proud of you, Mickey, for making that call. Your first instinct was to protect your sisters, and that says a lot about the person you are. The fault here is mine, for not explaining the situation properly."

His startled expression twists the knife of guilt in my side.

Have I really seemed so arrogant that they believe me to be incapable of admitting my mistakes?

Going by Mickey's face, the answer is a resounding *yes*.

"Come on." I turn him toward the terrace. "It will be easier to explain the situation to all of you at once."

I'm aware of Lucia watching me as I come onto the terrace. She's standing beside a long, lean figure in a wheelchair, who is just removing Masha gently from his lap. But I'm less concerned by either Lucia or the man in the chair than I am with the two small faces now watching me cautiously. Ofelia tugs Masha close, her arms crossed protectively over the little girl's chest. Her blue eyes are as hard and closed as I've ever seen them, and by the way her back is turned to Lucia, significant damage has already been done. Masha, on the other hand, seems as unconcerned as ever. She's waving some kind of tiny reptile in her hand.

"Potato," she says, holding a gecko up for my inspection.

"I'm happy to meet you, Mr. Potato." I squat down in front of her and gently remove the quivering creature from her hand. "Shall we put him in the garden for now, so he can play with his friends?"

Masha pouts. "I wanna play wiv him."

"I think he might be a little frightened, *myshka*. There's a lot of big people here." I place the poor creature into the terrace garden, where Mr. Potato makes an immediate and hasty getaway. "We can look for him later. Okay?"

"Okay." Masha nods, her wide blue eyes watching me with frank interest.

Taking her hand, I stand up and face Ofelia. "*Privet, umnyashka.*" *Hello, clever girl.*

Ofelia's eyes narrow, but she doesn't say anything.

"It's okay," I say quietly. "Everything's fine." Seeing her tension, I don't try to touch her.

"Mickey." I put out my arm, drawing him forward. "I'd like to talk to all three of you together, if that's okay?"

The look exchanged between Mickey and Ofelia stirs up the uncomfortable sensation of guilt once again. It isn't the first time I've watched this silent communication, by any means. I've just chosen to ignore it before now. I told myself it was the smartest thing for everyone. I'm hardly equipped to manage emotional teenagers.

But I wasn't ready to find myself homeless at ten, either. Or *pakhan* after Mikhail's death.

A man doesn't choose the challenges the world gives him. He just rises to meet them.

And equipped for it or not, this challenge is one I should have faced head-on long before now.

When they offer me slight nods, I take my chance and usher them inside. I still haven't spoken to either Lucia or the man in the wheelchair. They come second today.

I close the terrace door and wait until we're all seated on the U-shaped sofa. Masha, as ever, is cushioned between her siblings. I face them across the coffee table, hands clasped between my knees. "I'm sorry I didn't tell you about Lucia's identity," I say without preamble. "That was a mistake, and very wrong of me. I never meant for you to feel afraid."

"Who is she?" Ofelia asks the question with icy brevity. "Your girlfriend?"

Oh, fuck.

Of all the hard questions I was expecting, addressing the exact nature of my relationship with Lucia isn't one of them. I do a speedy calculation of what the kids might or might not have observed, while simultaneously being extremely aware of Ofelia's razor-sharp scrutiny.

In the end, I decide to go with as close to honesty as I can get.

"She wasn't my girlfriend when she came to stay with us." I meet her eyes steadily. "She was a friend who was in trouble and needed somewhere safe to stay. I like Lucia a lot, and I trust her. I thought you might like her too."

"I like her," offers Masha chirpily. "Like Poppins."

I smile at her. "I'm glad you like her, Masha."

"Yes," Ofelia interrupts impatiently, "but Lucia is just a fake